Praise

Also by Terry Spear

Heart of the Wolf

Destiny of the Wolf

To Tempt the Wolf

Legend of the White Wolf

Seduced by the Wolf

Wolf Fever

Heart of the Highland Wolf

Dreaming of the Wolf

A SEAL in Wolf's Clothing

SAVAGE HUNGER

TERRY SPEAR

sourcebooks
casablanca

Copyright © 2012 by Terry Spear
Cover and internal design © 2012 by Sourcebooks, Inc.
Cover design by Juliana Kolosova
Cover images © Dick Izui Photography
Models: Crystal McCahill and Todd Hansen/Agency Galatea

Sourcebooks and the colophon are registered trademarks of Source-books, Inc.

Published by Sourcebooks Casablanca, an imprint of Sourcebooks, Inc.
P.O. Box 4410, Naperville, Illinois 60567-4410
(630) 961-3900
FAX: (630) 961-2168
www.sourcebooks.com

Printed and bound in Canada
WC 10 9 8 7 6 5 4 3 2 1

To the men and women who fight the war on drugs, risking their lives daily. And to the exotic jaguars as much at risk at the hands of poachers, ranchers and hunters who would eliminate them from existence, if not for those who try to protect them.

Prologue

The Amazon Rain Forest

EVERYTHING APPEARED PERFECT. OR SO IT SEEMED. IN the Amazon, bliss could disintegrate into danger in the flash of a lightning strike.

After tangling with a caiman in the river as a jaguar and carrying the reptile back to the hut for his sister, Maya, to cook, Connor Anderson was half drowsing in a tree a couple of miles away, his tail swishing at flies, his eyes half-lidded as he focused on nothing much in particular. Just the way he liked it when they were on vacation here in the rain forest.

Since he had caught the caiman to eat, she had to prepare it. Often they ate as jaguars as nature intended, leaving the meat raw and without spicing it up, no fuss or muss.

But Maya was trying to talk him into searching for a shifter mate again, and this was one of the ways she presented her argument—by preparing a mcal fit for a king and giving him a list of all the reasons they needed to find mates, *pronto*.

He had heard it all before. If a female jaguar-shifter had crossed his path, and he and she had hit it off, he would have considered the possibility of a mating. But that hadn't happened.

Maya was insistent that they try harder to find more of their kind.

He was beginning to wonder if any others existed, other than their own parents and their grandparents before them.

In the distance, the sound of a woman's laughter and sweetly spoken English words without a hint of a Spanish accent caught his attention. The dense jungle foliage muffled the voices, male laughter, and boisterous talk—all in Spanish—following the woman's light chatter. His ears twitched as he listened intently to the sound of her voice as she spoke again, a breathy sugary voice that enthralled him. But then he thought she sounded—*drunk*.

That notion curdled the pineapple juice in the pit of his stomach. What was she doing out here with these men? And drunk?

"Gonzales will be grateful when he learns we have her. He'll like that we grabbed her even better than the hooker we got him last week."

Connor's hackles rose. If she wasn't a hooker, what would the drug dealer want with the woman who sounded American? Ransom came to mind.

"She will be worth a lot," another said.

Yeah, he had it figured right. A hostage, kidnap victim. Probably the men had spied her in a bar flashing a lot of money around. Most likely, they'd picked her up after plying her with alcohol, taken her hostage, and planned to hide her at a temporary camp in the jungle while they decided how best to get payment for her.

In the condition she was in, she most likely didn't know she was a victim—*yet*. She probably didn't speak Spanish and didn't know what the men were saying, or they wouldn't have been talking so plainly in front of her.

And these men worked for Gonzales, which was bad news any way they cut it. The man was a cutthroat with fingers in every pie that screamed corruption.

Without hesitation, Connor leaped from the tree in rescue mode and raced toward the sound of their voices. They were a long way off, but his jaguar hearing picked up their conversations just the same.

But how in the world was he to rescue her? The men would be armed to the teeth, and though *his* teeth could take out any number of them, he would never manage if there were many men.

"Take her and tie her up," one of the men said, "before her comrades come to get her. We will have a surprise waiting for them."

Her comrades? Either more hostages for the taking, or there was bound to be a lot of bloodshed.

Connor quickened his run, careful to ensure that no one else who might be in this part of the rain forest would see him as he ran in the direction of the encampment.

The woman was quiet now. Had she sobered up and was more aware of the danger she was in? Or had she passed out or been knocked out to make her easier to control?

Torn between feeling annoyance that the woman had gotten herself into such a predicament and concern that he couldn't save her in time, he pushed his big cat muscles to the limit.

"No!" she screamed, and the pain in her voice triggered another rush of adrenaline shooting into his blood, his heart pounding furiously.

Maya would never forgive him if he got himself killed in this venture and left her all alone. But he wouldn't be able to forgive himself if he didn't try to save the woman and she died.

"No!" the woman screamed again, and the men all laughed.

"You think you have fooled us, Captain Kathleen McKnight?" one of the men said in broken English.

Connor slowed his pace. *Captain? What the hell?*

"You wanted to see Carlos Gonzales, *sí*? You will see him, señorita, and you will be the last to die. He'll want you to watch the rest of your men die first."

All hell broke loose after that. Shooting, English commands shouted through the thick foliage, Spanish curses, screams of pain. Connor paused, his tail twitching, his nose tilted up, trying to smell gunpowder. But he was too far away from the fighting, and without a hint of a breeze in the dense jungle, he smelled nothing but the richness of the rain forest.

He wasn't stupid enough to go into the middle of a firefight. As long as the Americans were part of some kind of drug raid, which was what he assumed now, and were in on this with Captain McKnight, he had no business interceding.

Yet, he couldn't move from the spot of ground where he was rooted, listening for anything further from the woman—a word, a command, another cry of pain. He couldn't leave without knowing she and the Americans were successful, and that she had departed the jungle in one piece.

"No!" the woman cried out again.

More gunfire and swearing, then silence.

As if in the jungle anything could be silent. The bugs continued their raucous singing, the frogs croaked, birds chirped, and monkeys called out. But the sound of man had ceased to exist.

Then more shots were fired, followed by screams this time and sobbing from the woman.

Hell. Connor was certain the woman wouldn't be getting out of there alive.

He ran toward what he figured had to be a temporary encampment, intending to wing his attempt at rescuing the woman without any real plan.

He had come to the Amazon on his and Maya's semiannual visit to get away and commune with their jaguar half in their native environment—not to deal with members of the damned drug cartel. He avoided them unless the drug traffickers came too close to their hut. And then he and Maya dealt with them in the way they knew best—in their jaguar forms.

Maya would have fits if she knew what he was about to do.

Captain Kathleen McKnight struggled to breathe in the hot, humid air of the Colombian Amazon rain forest. She had managed to free herself long enough to wrest a gun away from a dead drug dealer and shoot two more of them dead. But then another man rushed into the tent and shot her in the thigh.

She gritted her teeth against the pain and shot back, aiming at a more lethal spot. One bullet to the head, and he went down. Then another bang, another sharp pain. This one to the fleshy part of her arm, effectively making her drop the weapon. *Damn it to hell*.

She dove for a rifle. The rush of boots pounded

the earth in her direction. Her fingers closed around
the weapon.

But something slammed into the back of her head. A
sharp, blinding pain shrieked through her skull. She fell
forward and landed on her hands, thinking for a flash of
a second that she was a dead woman before a black void
swallowed her whole.

When she came to minutes later, Kathleen hurt
everywhere—her arm, her leg, her head. Her hands were
tied with rope and bound to a metal pole that was holding up the top of the canvas tent. The stench of blood
surrounded her as her five Army teammates lay on the
dirt floor, limbs twisted, clothes bloodied, all dead.
Carlos Gonzales would keep her for last—the Trojan
horse that had brought the enemy to his camp. From
everything she'd read about the drug lord, she knew he
would not kill her quickly.

But he must have left the camp after she saw him running for cover, or she was certain he would be standing
over her, gloating over killing her team members while
she was at his mercy.

The mission to take down the bastard was a bust. It
was too late for the others in her team. Too late for her.

Her thigh and arm burned where the bullets had bitten
into them. Yet her skin chilled. She twisted her hands to
free herself from the ropes binding her. Blinding pain
shot through her leg, arm, and head. Her vision blurred
with the blood loss and from the excruciating pain, and
she knew if she didn't stop the bleeding, she wouldn't
make it. Three of Gonzales's men remained in the tent
with her, guarding her. One smiled with half-rotted
teeth, clearly amused at her futile attempt to free herself.

A shower of bullets popped again and again in the Amazon jungle, farther from the drug warlord's compound. *Rat-ta-tat-tat*. Men swore in Spanish, some screaming in pain, others shouting orders.

Her heart raced with renewed hope. A rescue attempt? For her? Well, for the team, but no one else was alive and whoever it was probably didn't know that. But… who were *they*?

"Captain McKnight?" someone shouted from somewhere far away, like he was on the other side of the planet.

"Here!" she croaked, her throat parched and hoarse.

Callahan? She thought. But the major hadn't been on this mission. He had been responsible for it, but she thought he had stayed behind the scenes.

Then silence. *Callahan?*

No one approached the tent, and the three men guarding her exited to see what was happening. "Jaguar!" one of the men shouted, terror in his voice.

Jaguar? No feral cat with any sense would come here in the middle of a shoot-out. Maybe she hadn't heard the man right.

She twisted to free her wrists from the rope. Not making any progress, she stretched out her uninjured leg so that the toe of her hiking boot could hook onto the hilt of a sheathed dagger of the dead man lying closest to her.

Weapons fired. She stopped and stared in the direction of the tent flap. Outside, screams and curses ensued. Fierce growling mixed with the men's terrified voices. Then silence.

Kathleen envisioned a vicious jaguar bounding into the tent and finishing her off, too. She struggled again to free herself. Then she heard movement outside, not sure what was happening.

With her skin perspiring and her wounds bleeding, the only thing keeping her conscious was the pain and the fear of what was coming next.

Footfalls hurried toward the tent. Kathleen braced for whoever it was—one of her captors or a rescuer—praying he was her rescuer.

His chest and feet bare, a man wearing a pair of jungle-green camouflage pants and carrying an assault rifle at the ready stopped in the entryway and stared at her, his mouth grim. His hair was short and blond but not cut in the military style. His face was angular and handsome, his torso bronzed and well sculpted. He didn't look like he could be one of Gonzales's men, yet he wasn't one of her men, either. His hair was too shaggy, and his face sported a shadow of blond stubble.

Even the pants he was wearing didn't fit. The waistband was slung low on his lean hips, the pant legs too short for his long legs, as though he had borrowed them in a hurry from a much shorter man. His gaze searched the tent, ensuring no one was a threat, then again fastened on hers, and for an instant his eyes reminded her of the golden eyes of a feral beast.

The female captain's eyes shut and Connor raced across the tent. He grabbed a knife from one of Gonzales's dead soldiers and cut a much cleaner shirt off a dead American soldier. Then Connor sliced through the rope tied around the captain's wrists. He quickly worked to bind her wounds to stem the bleeding. Her blue eyes opened briefly, but she was drifting off, her gaze attempting to focus on him, her lips parted as if to speak. He could tell she was having a devil of a time staying conscious.

Despite everything, she smelled like a bit of fairy heaven, a sweet flowery fragrance that forced him to take another deep breath, despite his attempt at staying neutral. Her sensual feminine smell assaulted his senses, irritating him at being cursed with his jaguar senses at this particular moment. His pheromones kicked up a notch, triggered by the firestorm of sensations he was experiencing.

"Stay awake," he ordered, trying to concentrate on keeping her alive until help could come for her and struggling to get his focus back on what was important and off his own primitive jaguar need to find a mate and procreate.

"American," she whispered, her eyes heavily lidded. She closed them.

He snapped, "*Captain*, stay… awake!"

"Easy for you to say," she said, sounding waspish, but as weak as she was, she didn't have the bite to her words.

He smiled darkly and continued to bind her wounds.

"Who are you? What… ah," she grimaced, reaching out to touch him, "are you doing here?"

"Connor Anderson's the name, and I'm vacationing in the area. Save your strength." As soon as he said his last name, he wondered why he had given her that much information.

"I'm… trying… to… stay… awake," she growled, but again the softly irritated tone didn't have the effect he imagined she was going for.

"Where is your rendezvous point?"

If he could take her to where her men would pick up the Army team, she might have a chance. The sound of men crashing through the trees made Connor rise quickly, grab a rifle, and slip out the back of the tent, intending to ambush Gonzales's men before they knew what had hit them.

"Connor," the captain whispered, and it killed him to have to leave her behind, even for just the moment.

But he couldn't protect her if armed men greatly outnumbered him. Hidden in the thick vegetation, Connor saw U.S. Army men scouring the campsite, and he assumed they were coming to rescue the captain. He tossed the rifle and borrowed camouflaged pants and shifted, then waited in the mesh of trees until he heard one of the men speaking: "Hell, Kathleen."

Kat.

The woman's rescue was now out of Connor's hands. So why the hell wasn't he relieved?

Chapter 1

A Year Later in the Colombian Amazon Rain Forest

THICK BLACK LINES, FORMING ROSETTES WITH BLACK spots dotting their centers, covered his golden body as Connor Anderson prowled through the Amazon as a jaguar, searching for his sister, Maya. He was certain the sound of her deep, throaty growl somewhere in the dark jungle had been a stern warning to something that had threatened her.

He knew that if he let her out of his sight for even a moment, she would be in trouble. As usual, she hadn't heeded his words about staying nearby while he went fishing.

Jaguars normally were solitary animals that only met up with one another when they were looking for a mate, or when a female was with her cubs until they were old enough to be on their own. But Connor and his sister stayed together. They needed to prowl the Amazon forest and swamps from time to time in their jaguar form to satisfy the urge to shift in their natural environment. But they didn't feel the necessity to run alone. In fact, quite the opposite.

Their human halves dictated that they stick together and watch out for each other. They were wary of hunters who sought to eliminate them, fearing they would kill a farmer's livestock, and those who would kill jaguars for their beautiful pelts. Wouldn't the hunters be surprised if they killed either Connor or his sister and then found the dead jaguar shifting into a human?

So much for retrieving a beautiful, salable pelt.

On the other hand, the hunters might think they could sell the jaguar-shifter for much more—although their genetics were purely human when human, and when they each were a jaguar, they were strictly a big cat. No scientist who examined the body would ever be the wiser. And the hunter who shot the shifter? He would be called a madman and a murderer. Not that Connor ever wanted that scenario to come to pass.

Stopping, he listened, his restless tail twitching. He lifted his head and smelled the aromatic fragrance of orchids and the ripe richness of the jungle—from rotting vegetation to the sweet smell of the giant lilies and the sap from a tree that cleared the sinuses in a hurry. He heard the sound of insects buzzing, toucans and macaws singing, a howler monkey howling, thunder in the distance that warned of an approaching rain shower, and water trickling nearby.

Feeling unsettled, not only about Maya, he couldn't return to their home in the jungle without thinking about Captain Kathleen McKnight and wondering what had become of her. Had she survived? Was she still traipsing around in the jungle, fighting the bad guys? He snorted. One little whiff of her scent a year ago had sent his testosterone into a raging battle of need. Even now as he explored the jungle, he thought he smelled her fragrance several times, but he knew how ridiculous that notion was. Even without that irrational spike of lust, he had been fascinated by her for some reason and had thought about her—even dreamed about her—many times in the past year.

He gave a low rumbling growl, attempting to get his sister's response so he could locate her.

The ancients revered jaguars as warriors, royalty, having strength and bravery in any kind of warfare. Connor wondered if any of the ancients had ever come across a jaguar-shifter. Maybe that's why they had revered them so much.

He suddenly heard a different kind of movement in the forest. Human movement, he thought. Jaguars moved silently through the jungle on quiet padded feet, so he knew it wasn't Maya. The hunter-gatherers in the area also were known to move soundlessly through the jungle, so he didn't think he was hearing any member of the local indigenous tribes.

Members of Gonzales's drug cartel hadn't returned here since the Americans hit so many of his men. But the rumor was that Gonzales had gotten away unscathed and was now living in Bolivia. As for the woman? Connor couldn't stop thinking about her, the way her blue eyes had tried to stay focused on him while he had bound her wounds, the way she had tried to reach out to touch him, and how he had wanted to feel her hand on his skin. But she had been too weak, unable to make contact.

A year had passed, and he couldn't believe how often he still thought of the woman. Annoyed with himself for being so distracted, he turned his attention back to the possible threat nearby.

Despite the noise of the surrounding jungle, the person was making a racket whacking through the bamboo, balsa wood, and tangles of vines, trying to clear a path and panting heavily.

Connor turned his head to determine which way the

person was moving. Away from him, or toward him? If toward him, Connor suspected the person had heard his jaguar growl and would be armed and ready to kill.

Fine. Connor would rather have the man head in his direction and stay away from his sister, wherever she was.

Then she growled again. Of all the damn times to alert Connor where she was!

The human turned and headed in his sister's direction, and Connor bounded after him—determined to change the man's mind.

Taking a deep breath in the heavily oxygen-laden and moisture-burdened air, Kathleen McKnight stopped in the Amazon jungle, unsure which way to go. She was hoping to find a waterway that she could follow and maybe come to a village or, better yet, the resort where she had a reservation. An almost invisible cloud of fog seemed to cloak the breezeless rain forest, every square inch filled with living, breathing organisms that belonged here. All except for her—an intruder in their world.

She thought she had headed away from the sounds of a wild cat roaring in the woods. At first she had wanted desperately to see the jaguar because he might lead her to Connor Anderson. She wasn't so sure now. Not after she had heard the cat roar. He sounded angry... and hungry. For some reason, she associated him with that long-ago jaguar roaming with Connor, but she couldn't give a rational explanation for the feeling. What if he wasn't Connor's jaguar companion? Yet, she just had this gut feeling that the two were together.

First, his cry came from one direction, then another. From everything she had read about jaguars and from the way this one had roared, he was one big cat. But she knew they lived alone, so two of them probably weren't roaming out here; the roars were just echoing off the jungle foliage or rocky cliffs or something. But she still was in big trouble.

Well, more so than she already had been. She surveyed the greenery surrounding her in every shade and hue of green imaginable to an artist and reminded herself that she was hopelessly lost.

As she maneuvered through the thick vegetation, the broad leaves and tangled vines brushing against and grasping at her, she hoped she was moving away from where the big cat had been roaring. She hadn't thought she would be all alone in the jungle, listening to a big cat growl while maybe next on his dinner menu. So much for seeing a jaguar up close and personal. This wasn't what she'd had in mind.

According to her research on jaguars, research she'd felt compelled to do though she couldn't say why, they normally slept during the day and hunted during dusk and dawn. If necessary, they would hunt during the day. This one sounded too hungry to wait until nightfall.

Heart pounding, she stopped moving, trying to recall what she had read. Stand still and make noise. Whatever you do, don't run. Jaguars rarely attacked humans. Unless maybe it was a very old jaguar and he needed something really easy to catch and eat. It could be old. She couldn't tell. Its roar was deep and low and, well, grouchy, like an *old* jaguar, she thought. They didn't roar like lions or tigers, but more of a deep, throaty cough repeated five or six times that sounded like, "Uh, uh, uh, uh, uh."

She was afraid that if she ran, she would be just too tempting for a jaguar of any age to ignore.

She heard something moving toward her from behind. The hair at the nape of her neck instantly stood at attention. Her heart was already tripping. She was afraid it was *him*—the cat with the deep, angry, growly voice. She knew the big cats moved silently through the jungle. She imagined the cat would appear before she would even be prepared to face him. And then what?

Turning slowly, she looked to see who or what it was. An armed man? Or a toothy jaguar?

She saw the most beautiful creature she had ever chanced to see up close—*way* too close. A *huge* jaguar. No fence or moat to keep him from her, like at a zoo. Her skin chilled, and her heart thumped erratically.

As much as she'd wanted to see one, she hadn't quite thought to observe one like *this*. If he did belong to Connor, she didn't see any sign of the man. Which meant this one could be a real danger.

In the back of her mind, she wanted to pull her camera out of her bag and take a picture, *take a hundred pictures*. That was just plain crazy. She stayed porcelain-statue still, afraid any sudden movement would trigger him to pounce. She had envisioned watching one swimming in a river or maybe drinking water at a riverbank. She'd thought she might catch sight of one lounging in a tree while she watched from a nice, safe distance, but not on the prowl like this while she was standing in its path.

Her heart still pounding out-of-bounds, she stared at the jaguar, which had the most beautiful golden eyes and matching golden body covered in large black rosettes. His belly was white and covered with more rosettes. His long whiskers bristled. He lifted his nose and sniffed the air, taking a whiff of her scent, she was certain, although there wasn't a whisper of a breeze with all the vegetation surrounding them. Was he trying to smell just how tasty she might be? Despite the muggy heat, a chill raced down her spine.

His eyes were round, fully watching her as he stood frozen in place. His tail twitched, jerking back and forth in a tight motion, just like her cat's would when she watched a bird on a tree branch near the living room window. Her cat's eyes would be just as huge as the jaguar's and her body just as tense, ready to pounce on her prey if she could have gotten beyond the glass windowpane.

Don't move, Kathleen screamed silently to herself. He is curious. Just curious. You are *not* dinner.

Who was she kidding? All she could think of was the Indian word for jaguar, *yaguar*, meaning "he who kills at one leap." Looking at the way he was standing so still, she wondered if he was thinking about it. He wasn't in pouncing form, crouched, ready to leap, but maybe he was waiting for her to run, offering more sport that way.

They would eat deer and tapirs. Why not a tasty woman?

Then to her shock, she heard another growl. This one came from behind her. Yet the jaguar was still standing in front of her, and he hadn't made a sound. Her skin grew a fresh rash of goose bumps.

Maybe he wasn't a he, but a she, and her nearly full-grown cub was behind Kathleen, coming for dinner. Or maybe this one was a he—he looked awfully big not to be, around six feet in length and weighing, she guessed, around two hundred and fifty pounds—and the other was his mate. How big was the other, then?

If they were mating, maybe Kathleen was needed to keep them well fed for another bout of tying it on. That didn't improve her outlook on the situation in the least. The only thing she could hope for was that they had the hots for each other, and one human wouldn't distract them that thoroughly. Maybe that's why they had been roaring. As a love call. Or maybe he would think Kathleen was a threat to his mate.

She hoped both cats had recently eaten and that she wasn't about to be on the menu.

He slowly walked toward her. She had to tell herself that was because the other jaguar was somewhere behind her with Kathleen inconveniently in between the two of them.

She wanted desperately to dash off. But she couldn't outrun a big cat that could take her down with one leap. Not to mention that if she turned and bolted, she would probably run straight into the other jaguar.

She meant to glance behind her for a tree that she could reach and quickly climb, but when she looked over her shoulder, she saw the other cat. And her heart nearly stopped. Her breathing definitely did.

Smaller, though not by much, the second jaguar observed her with the same golden eyes and had the same golden coat with black rosettes and the same *hungry* look. This was so not good.

She angled herself away from the cat behind her, returned her attention to the bigger cat in front of her, and backed toward the tree she'd spotted. If she didn't move, the big guy in front of her was going to walk right into her. She planned to climb the tree and stay up there until the cats went away, certain they had come to see each other and weren't interested in her.

If she just got out of their way, everything would be fine. That was what she hoped, anyway. She even had the dumb notion that she could take some great shots of the two cats once she was safely in the tree and they were still on the ground in perfect view for picture taking. What if she could even capture the jaguars mating on video?

She bumped into something and nearly had a seizure—thinking she had run into the other cat. She turned to find it was the massive tree instead, its roots sprawling all over the ground and nearly tripping her. Vines wrapped around the trunk, coiling upward while plants nestled in its embrace. But she didn't have time to enjoy the bit of relief she felt that she'd only bumped into the tree and not the cat.

She grabbed a vine and with a lot more difficulty than she thought she would have—the heat, the lack of sleep, her wet, slippery hands, the panic flooding her bloodstream—she finally managed to scramble up the tree into one of the lower branches. She was glad the vine hadn't ripped loose because of her weight. Then she tried to climb a little higher to put more distance between her and the jaguars. Thank God, the Army had taught her how to rappel off brick buildings and wooden towers and to climb mountains, although swinging from trees was something that might come in handy now. Come to think of it, she had swung on a rope across a very deep trench on the officers' obstacle course.

If her luck was anything like it had been running recently, she could just imagine grabbing a vine here as she tried to swing from tree to tree like one of the spider monkeys she had seen doing so, and accidentally getting hold of a nice meaty snake instead.

She hadn't made it very far up the tree's massive trunk, which was so tall that it shot up toward the sun like a skyscraper, when a huge golden body went sailing past her shoulder and landed on a sturdy branch to the left of her head. His sudden action startled her so that she let out a strangled scream, her skin heating with a sudden prickle of fear, and she nearly fell out of the tree.

As evidenced by his large male package, she noticed right away that he was a *he*.

She glanced down to see if the other jaguar planned to join him. But all she did was stretch her body up toward Kathleen, her claws fully extended like long, curved miniature daggers, and then she raked the tree trunk.

Marking the territory. *Her* territory. And one human who wasn't supposed to be here.

Now what was Kathleen to do?

—∿∿—

His pheromones were kicking up a firestorm again as Connor stared down at the drenched woman dressed in sturdy hiking books, wide-brimmed hat, long-sleeved tan shirt, and lightweight trousers, a field pack strapped to her back. She was pretty, petite, and petrified—as evidenced by the smell of fear on her. But even so, he could smell a hint of the sweet fragrance she wore and a sweet feminine scent that he swore was Kathleen McKnight's.

The captain he'd saved in the jungle a year ago. But this woman had the biggest sage-green eyes he had ever seen—green, not blue like the captain's had been. And her hair had been blond and cut ultrashort, not long, dark brown, and in curls, like this woman's.

Was she a botanist or wildlife biologist? Even if she was, what in the world was she doing in the rain forest without a guide or protection? Sure, he had witnessed an American biologist doing research in the Amazon on his own, but a woman normally worked with either a husband or a team of researchers. Women didn't usually venture into the jungle alone.

That made him believe she had become separated from her party and was lost. Despite the difficulties this would cause for him and his sister, he had to get the woman to safety. He wished in the worst way he could convince her she had nothing to fear from them, but as a jaguar, even if he kept his mouth shut and didn't expose his wicked canines, he was a predator to fear.

Loose tendrils of dark, damp hair framed her small face. The bridge of her nose was sprinkled with freckles, her cheeks rosy—maybe from heat and exertion in the jungle, or maybe from a little too much sun. Her wet clothes clung to every curve just up to her breastbone, but the very top part of her shirt and her hat were still dry.

He hoped she had drinking water in her backpack and wasn't dehydrated. That was all they would need. A sick woman on their hands, far from any medical facility.

He took another deep breath of her tantalizing woman's fragrance, unable to comprehend why the woman smelled so much like Kat, and wondered what to do with her.

She was miles from the nearest human resort. And miles in dense jungle made for a very long, difficult trip for anyone who was unaccustomed to the heat and humidity.

He couldn't nudge her toward the tourist lodge in the middle of the Amazon rain forest while trying to keep the staff at the resort from seeing him and his sister in jaguar form. Seeing jaguars prodding a human into the camp would surely give the tourists and staff heart attacks. Not to mention that he didn't think this woman could easily be herded mile after mile to safety by a couple of jaguars.

His sister also studied the woman for a moment, then looked to him to decide what to do next. As jaguars, he and his sister had no natural predators in the jungle, save man and the anaconda. And even then he had tackled an anaconda and won.

The woman would have plenty to worry about, though.

Neither he nor Maya could run through the jungle as humans, not without clothes to protect them from the mosquitoes, scorpions, snakes, ticks, and chiggers, to name a few of the problems with exposing human flesh to the elements in Amazonia. But he needed to reassure the woman that the two of them weren't going to eat her. Neither he nor Maya could shift in front of her to speak with her, though.

He grunted. They would have to herd her to their own hut deep in the jungle where they kept provisions and clothes when they came here to shift and run like the predators they were.

Night would fall soon. Jaguars normally slept in the trees during the day and hunted at dawn and dusk.

The woman probably would be horrified to see what he drummed up for dinner and how they ate it raw.

But how was he going to get her back out of the tree? He had to get her down, then nudge her along to their hut, which was about two miles away in the opposite direction from the Amazon lodge for tourists.

Once at the hut, he and his sister could shift out of view in the jungle and return to speak with the woman. A couple of days of rigorous hiking would get her to the tourist lodging.

He jumped down from the tree branch, landing beside his sister, and nudged her away from the tree. She limped away from it, which must have been why she had been roaring before. He glanced at her hind leg, encouraged her to sit, and saw two thorns sticking into her paw. He glanced up at the woman, who was watching their actions with intrigue.

Not wanting her to think they had human thought processes but unable to do anything else, he poked at his sister's foot with his nose, hoping he wouldn't touch a thorn accidentally, make her growl in pain, and scare the woman any more than she already was. Hoping, too, that the woman would come down from the tree to pull out the thorns. He couldn't get them with his teeth, or if he managed to get one, he would more than likely chomp it off and make it too difficult to pull out later. And Maya couldn't walk on the thorns for any distance without suffering pain.

They both glanced at the woman, Maya lying on her side, looking as docile as she could, and Connor sitting beside his sister, most likely appearing perfectly lethal.

All the while, the woman continued to watch them as

she sat in the tree and didn't appear to have any plans to come down soon. Which meant?

Connor was going to have to do something drastic to change her mind.

Chapter 2

IF SHE DIDN'T KNOW ANY BETTER, KATHLEEN WOULD have sworn the male cat wanted her to pull the thorn out of the female cat's paw. And then?

They would eat her. As soon as she pulled on the thorn, the pain would cause the female to growl, swing her head around, and bite Kathleen. The male, thinking that Kathleen was injuring his mate, would finish her off.

So she sat in the tree.

And they sat on the ground. No one moved.

Then it began to pour. The rain came down lightly at first, but then more heavily, dripping off smooth leaves with most of the drops never reaching the forest floor. Kathleen was already soaking wet after stepping on ground that wasn't solid and sinking into water nearly up to her collarbone, which had almost given her a stroke. All she could imagine was that a crocodile would come to investigate what delightful edible creature had dropped in to see it. After struggling to get back on relatively dry land without meeting up with a croc or two, she had thanked her guardian angel for watching over her again.

The air was muggy and as wet as she was. She figured she would never dry, just mold instead.

Feeling dizzy from the heat and realizing she hadn't drunk any water in some time, she tried to get her pack off her back to reach a bottle of water. But a twisted branch behind her caught on the bag, and she couldn't free it. She leaned forward to get it loose and immediately realized her mistake. She was too far forward with nothing to grasp on to, and she lost her balance. With her heart in her throat and unable to stop her fall, she plummeted from the tree to the spongy ground some fifteen feet below, landing hard on one knee. Pain shot through it. She didn't think she had broken anything, but she had hurt it for sure.

The jarring impact sent a shard of pain rippling through the old bullet wound in her thigh, adding insult to injury.

Now on her side, she stifled a groan and fought against cradling her knee, whimpering, cursing, or doing anything that would alert the cats that she was down-and-out for the moment. She briefly thought about how the jaguars would think she was like a wounded creature, falling from the tree and perfect for a predinner snack.

Despite not wanting to look in their direction, fearing they might approach to take a lick and a bite, she did glance at them. The female was still lying on her side. But the male was standing, watching Kathleen. She swore he took a deep breath as if he was concerned about her, surprised maybe, but then he headed toward her. That couldn't be a good sign.

She scrambled to a sitting position, groaning as the pain shot through her leg to her kneecap and short-circuited her plan to make for the tree again. This time she did cradle her injured knee, cursing herself for her folly.

As if he knew she might try to take refuge in the tree, the male jaguar loped toward her, no longer moving cautiously. When he reached her, he opened his mouth and gave her a way-too-close-up view of his saber-tooth wicked canines, which looked remarkably white and polished for a wild beast. She gaped at them but couldn't even get a scream out.

Then he licked her cheek.

His huge, wet tongue was like rough sandpaper against her skin. She knew it. He was tasting her before he ate her.

But then he pushed under her arm with his nose as if he was trying to get her to stand. She couldn't stand, damn it. If she could, she would have climbed back in the tree as fast as she was able.

When she wouldn't cooperate, he went around the back side of her and bit into her backpack. In a strangled cry, she yelled, "No!"

He stopped what he was doing for a second as if startled by her reaction, almost as though he would obey her word.

Glad her backpack had protected her from his fearsome bite, she still figured that was only the beginning. Once he found out the bag didn't taste all that good, he would take another bite, somewhere a lot more tasty.

He ignored her scream and didn't take another bite. Instead, he held on tight to her bag and dragged it. Since the bag was attached to her back, that effectively pulled her along with it. She briefly thought of his teeth making mincemeat of everything in her bag—the canines puncturing her water bottles, sinking into her granola bars, destroying and desanitizing her medical kit. Then she realized how much more serious this was. He was taking her closer to the injured female so *she* could eat Kathleen at her leisure!

She struggled with the backpack but couldn't get her arms out of the straps to save her life.

How sweet for his mate. If Kathleen managed to live through this, she could write about how caring a jaguar male could be toward his mate. Of course, after the cubs were born and only a couple of weeks old, the mother would chase the male off so he didn't eat her offspring.

To her surprise, the male jaguar left Kathleen next to the female's hind foot. Then he came around and put his nose close to the thorn. She could see now there were two, but he didn't touch either of them. She thought he really was telling her to remove them.

She couldn't believe it. She wondered if the two jaguars were like wolves that had been raised by families in the States who then grew tired of them and released them into the wild. She had heard that sometimes people in the jungle raised jaguars. Manuel, her guide now long gone, had told her about a male jaguar cub discovered on a road, his mother nowhere to be found. The people in his village took the cub in because he would never have survived otherwise. Another was kept at a reserve for injured wild animals.

Maybe these two had been raised by natives and…

She shook her head. They still were wild beasts of prey. But what if one had been Connor's pet and the jaguar had picked up a mate? What if Connor was nearby?

Kathleen didn't believe she could get that lucky.

Her hand shaking, she reached for the two thorns wedged between the pads of the jaguar's foot. As soon as Kathleen grasped the first, the female cat growled low at her.

Kathleen's heart stuttered, but she had done it now. She

yanked out the thorn, then reached for the other and heard male voices. The male jaguar growled low this time.

Kathleen yanked out the other thorn, and to her astonishment, the male jaguar grabbed her bag and dragged her back to the tree. The female quickly raced to the tree and climbed into the higher branches. Kathleen couldn't climb. She couldn't even stand, but before she knew what the male was up to, he'd jumped into the tree, carrying her by the backpack and nearly giving her a seizure. Now she was in the tree again.

His action reminded her that big cats often carried their catch—even one as large as a dead deer—into a tree to eat it later, protecting the snack from predators below.

———◦◦◦———

Connor assumed the woman thought he and his sister would eat her. At least if he was in her predicament, that's what he would have thought. But for now, they would sleep, hidden in the canopy in the rain forest, away from the human predators who were moving noisily through the jungle, cutting a swath through the tangle of vines and plants and cursing as they went. He didn't trust handing the woman over to them, not after he had found her alone in the jungle and not knowing who they were.

He assumed she was alone because something had gone wrong and that the man he had heard earlier was part of this group of maybe three or four men. They wouldn't stay out here for long because it would grow too dark for the men to see, and Connor was sure they didn't have a camp nearby. That made him wonder just what they were doing out here this late in the day.

When they could safely do so, he and his sister would escort the woman to the resort and leave her there. But the woman had hurt herself, and they couldn't easily get her to the resort anytime soon.

The woman was sitting stiffly on the branch next to him, looking tired and uneasy. She alternated between watching for the men, who were moving away from them, and looking at Connor as he quietly observed her. He was afraid she would accidentally slip off the branch if she managed to fall asleep, as tired and drawn as she looked. He put a leg over her lap and looked up at her to see her reaction. Her eyes widening, she stared at him in disbelief. She had the most beautiful green eyes, the irises flecked with gold and encircled by a ring of gold. He envisioned that she would be one beautiful jaguar.

She whispered, "You were someone's pet?"

If he could have smiled in amusement at the thought, he would have. But he was afraid smiling would show off his big predator's teeth and wouldn't put her at ease.

Her voice was sweet, in awe, and appealed to him on some deeper level. She was American like he and his sister were, but he couldn't place the region she was from. He nudged her arm with his nose to show he meant her no ill will, pretending he had been someone's pet. It would work well for all concerned if she believed it.

She put her hand on his paw, as if accepting his friendship, and he grunted in his jaguar way. But her touch was doing things to his body that he shouldn't be thinking of as a jaguar.

His sister looked down at him from a higher branch. She appeared contemplative as she turned her attention to the woman. The woman's hair was very dark brown and long and curly, the ends dripping with water. Again, he wondered how she had gotten so wet.

She was drenched, her lightweight, tan-colored clothes clinging provocatively to her figure, which he could enjoy without fear of censure because she thought he was only a cat. Dark pebbled nipples were visible under her wet shirt and bra, and he studied them with fascination. Mainly because the bra was some kind of leopard print yet sheer enough that he could see her rigid nipples.

Hell, he hadn't been with a woman in months. And right now observing this woman was taking a toll on his body.

He rested his head on her lap to make sure she wasn't still afraid of the two jaguars protecting her and would try to slip away into the jungle if he should fall asleep, or that she would accidentally fall from the tree and injure herself further.

Unable to ignore that carnal, feral side of his jaguar nature that wanted to learn just how ripe she was to have his offspring, he breathed in her musky feminine scent. Not that he normally sniffed at a woman in that way—mainly because he had never been in a situation like this before—but with his head resting in her lap, he couldn't help himself. And didn't want to, either. Yeah, she was ready. If she had been a jaguar and he hadn't been a shifter, he would definitely have been enticed to see just how receptive she would be to his advances. But he was a shifter and she was strictly human, which should have meant paws off.

She frowned at him. "Connor Anderson?" she whispered.

He stared at her. Her voice. That's what had sounded

so familiar. It… it couldn't be Captain Kathleen McKnight. For a second, he thought she knew he was the jaguar, then he realized she couldn't. So how had she known he "ran" with a jaguar out here? But she had been a blonde before and had blue eyes.

She stroked his head as if he was *her* pet. It *was* her. She was safe, healed from her injuries from that firefight a year ago. So what was she doing in the jungle again? Another undercover mission?

But then her hand rubbed his head some more, and she stole his thoughts.

If she only knew the lascivious notions he was having about her, thinking of what he would attempt if they had both been jaguar-shifters.

She finally relaxed, leaning one shoulder against the tree trunk, which helped him to relax a little. He liked the feel of her caressing his broad head, the gentleness of her touch, the way she sighed deeply. He couldn't close his eyes, though, not with the way he kept breathing in her feminine scent and enjoying the softness of her lap, even after her hand stilled and her breathing slowed until he assumed she had fallen asleep.

He couldn't believe how different she looked, but he had recognized her scent and her voice.

Why was she here?

When the dark finally came, he raised his head and saw that she was indeed sleeping. He looked up at Maya. She was watching him curiously, a speculative gleam in her golden eyes, and she knew just what he intended to do. He leaped from the branch to the ground, and she jumped down to the one Kat was sleeping on, then followed his example and rested her head in the woman's lap to make sure she didn't fall. With one last look at the two hidden in the canopy, feeling sure they would be safe, Connor loped off to his and Maya's home in the jungle.

Running as a jaguar, he didn't take long to reach the hut. He quickly shifted, dressed, and raced back to where he had left his sister and the woman. Maneuvering along the narrow path and running as a human, he hated how much time was passing, much longer than when he had run as a powerful jaguar. Even though they normally didn't chase anything down, jaguars could run up to twenty-five miles per hour if necessary. They just couldn't run for extended periods of time.

All the while on his trek back to where he had left the women, he was considering how he was going to get Kat out of the tree without injuring her knee further.

When he finally arrived and looked up at his sister, spread out on the branch as if she owned it, with the human sleeping next to her, he still hadn't reached a decision as to how to easily get Kat down. Maya stretched. Then to his surprise, she bit into the woman's backpack, pulled her with a jerk from her seat on the branch, and released her into midair. Kat screamed as she felt herself fall.

Connor quickly maneuvered to catch her and easily swept her up in his arms and cast Maya an annoyed look. That was one way to get Kat down from the tree. He would have tried something less frightening for the poor woman.

In panic, she struggled to get free from him, pushing at his shoulders with her fists and yelling, "Let me go!"

A shadowy darkness surrounded them and she

couldn't see him well, although he could see her with his cat's night vision, so he could understand her fear. One minute she was in the tree, sleeping with two jaguars that were protecting her. The next minute, she was free-falling from the tree and now secure in the arms of a man she didn't know.

"I raised the cats," he quickly assured her while cradling her in his arms, his voice as soothing as he could make it, although it sounded way too gruff to his ears. He tightened his hold on her so she wouldn't get loose, land on her feet, and put pressure on her injured knee. Although as much as she was struggling, he figured she would end up on her ass if she managed to wriggle free.

"Connor?" she inquired, her voice steady and hopeful.

"Corand came to get me, letting me know that I needed to rescue a beautiful woman in the jungle. But yeah, I'm Connor Anderson," he added, giving himself a fake name for when he was in his jaguar form.

She stilled as if she realized he was with the jaguars, that he was the man who had stopped her bleeding when Gonzales's men had shot her, and that Connor wasn't the enemy. She stared up into his face. "You're... you're American."

"Texan," he said smiling, as if that meant he was a special category of American.

"From Texas."

"Yes, ma'am. I didn't recognize you at first. Different color hair, eyes." He waited for an explanation.

She took a deep breath. "*This* is my natural look. That was for the mission."

Connor raised his brows.

She smiled a little at the astonished look he gave her.

"I was supposed to look like a cute, clueless college-age girl who was too stupid to live, but who had loads of money. Blue contacts made my eyes look like the Caribbean. I kind of liked the blue eyes."

Connor shook his head. "You're beautiful as a brunette. And your green eyes remind me of the jungle."

Appreciating his comments, she gave him a rueful smile, then sighed. "Thank you. Believe me, as a blonde, I did *not* have more fun. The guys I worked with ribbed me by repeating every dumb-blonde joke known to mankind." She swallowed hard, and he wondered if she was remembering her fallen comrades.

Not wanting her to relive what had to be nightmarish memories, he glanced up at Maya. "Come on. Time to return to the hut." Then he said to the wet, curvaceous woman in his arms, "You'll meet my twin sister, Maya, soon."

His sister dropped easily to the ground and led the way down the path to the hut, her long tail swishing back and forth.

"Your sister? Oh." Kathleen sounded relieved that his sister was here with him. She probably assumed he couldn't be all that dangerous then. Little did she know.

"Anderson? Is that English?" she asked.

"On our father's side. But he married a Scotswoman, so we're also Scottish. The Scots moved into Texas and settled a lot of the areas."

He didn't know how far back his jaguar roots went. Neither their mother nor their father would talk about it much. Just something about their father's great grandfather having been a Sir Lionel Anderson who had taken an expedition into the Amazon searching for medicinal

properties in the plant life. Rumors abounded that he had
been searching for gold. They suspected he had tangled
with a jaguar-shifter. And somehow he'd managed to
live. Return trips to Edinburgh had been far and few between until he stopped returning to Scotland altogether.
But a son took his father's place. A son who had been
born in the jungle.

The woman nodded at Connor, breaking into his
thoughts. "I'm Kathleen McKnight."

"Kat," he mused. "The captain." He wondered why
she was alone in the jungle, but if she was doing an undercover operation, he suspected she wouldn't tell him
the truth anyway.

She frowned up at him. "I... I can't see a thing any
longer. How can you find your way in the dark?"

Chapter 3

As HE MADE HIS WAY OVER TWISTED VINES AND KEPT his footing in muddier areas, Connor hadn't considered that Kat would realize he shouldn't be able to see anything in the dark, just like she couldn't. As cats, jaguar-shifters could see well at dusk and dawn. And that ability carried over to their human half once they had shifted back. Just as their sense of smell was enhanced, so was their hearing.

"She can lead us back to the hut." But that didn't explain how he could see his sister. Hopefully, Kat wouldn't realize this.

"But I can't see the jaguar. How can you?"

Connor gave the woman points not only for her astuteness but also for not allowing him to get away with attempting to bamboozle her.

Maya glanced back at Connor as if to say, "How are you going to cover your tracks on that one?" He could almost see the smile in her expression.

"I know the way back. Traveled it many a time," he smoothly said, giving his sister a superior look.

"Oh." But Kathleen didn't sound entirely convinced. "The jaguars, have you raised them from cubs?" she asked.

"Yes."

She sighed. "Orphaned?"

"Yes." Essentially yes. Their father had left their mother to raise Connor and his twin sister and never came back. And their mother had left them when they were teens with the same result.

Sometimes he thought it was because of their parents' cat-shifter half. Sometimes he thought they just weren't meant to be good parents. That was one reason he and his sister were thirty years old and hadn't settled down. Well, also partly because of the problem with finding a shifter mate. Real jaguars had been known to mate with a leopard or a lion. But their offspring were sterile. So it had occurred to him that if they couldn't locate a jaguar-shifter, maybe another would do, if such a shifter even existed. But they probably couldn't have any offspring, and something in his primal big cat makeup balked at that.

Still, neither Connor nor his sister had had any luck in locating any kind of cat-shifters, and he wasn't about to bite some poor unsuspecting woman so he could have a suitable mate. Not that he knew if a bite could cause someone to carry their genes anyway. They still didn't know if Sir Lionel Anderson was the first on their dad's side to carry the jaguar-shifter genetics or if someone earlier had carried the genes. Maybe he had been born with it and that was why he'd gone to the Amazon. Not in search of medicinal plants or gold, but in search of a shifter mate. Or like they did—to be one with their jaguar halves. They just didn't know enough about it.

Then there was their mother's side of the equation. Her great-great grandfather had been studying some of the ancient civilizations in South America and didn't return for ten years, this time settling in Texas. He couldn't stay away from the rain forest, either, and his Scottish wife began accompanying him, although everyone thought it odd. She was more of a homebody from what journal entries had said, so trekking through the Amazon seemed out of character for her. So had he been turned, then changed her?

If a wolf-shifter—although totally fantasy—could turn someone with a bite, why not cat-shifters?

Not that he was about to test that theory.

"Connor, thanks. I can probably walk now," Kathleen said.

"The tree roots and vines are hard to see at this time of night. Best if you don't twist your knee while trying to get to our place." Besides, he enjoyed carrying her, enjoyed feeling her soft curves against his hard chest, smelling her sweet, wet fragrance, and feeling the heat of her body against his. Any physical exertion in the steamy jungle would make a body hot, Connor told himself. So why was holding this woman against his body making every sexual part of him tighten with need?

Which reminded him again that he hadn't been with a woman in a damned long while.

But it was more than that. He couldn't say what it was exactly. Maybe the feel of the energy surrounding them in the jungle, the primal, feral nature of it, the fact she was here in his territory, vulnerable and yet adventurous enough to be here, that made him keep thinking about the possibilities of turning a woman.

Not any woman though. Just *this* one.

Maybe it had to do with the fact that for a year he had thought about what had happened to her, worried that she hadn't made it out of the jungle in time, and wondered if she had recovered physically and psychologically from the battle with Gonzales's men if she had.

Kat didn't say anything more, just leaned her head against his chest, and he thought she might have drifted off to sleep before he arrived back at the hut sitting high on its stilts. As exhausted as she was, he thought she probably had been wandering through the jungle for some time, unable to sleep because of all of the dangers surrounding her. He climbed the rickety stairs to the hut. When he walked across the mahogany floor, the boards creaked slightly with his weight, and she jerked awake.

"You can sit on one of the wooden chairs so that you don't put any weight on that knee. Do you have a change of clothes in your pack?" he asked, moving toward the chair. He set her down on it, then helped her off with her pack, resting it on the floor nearby.

"Yes, I have several changes of clothes."

"Good." He wasn't sure Maya would want to share her clothes with a virtual stranger if Kat had nothing else to wear.

He had left a kerosene lamp glowing in the one-room hut so that she wouldn't be so spooked when he brought her back here. The lamp cast a soft, mellow light throughout. The roof was thatched over wooden walls, and screened windows provided some relief from bugs and snakes. Mesh netting covered the two beds to keep the mosquitoes away because there wasn't any way to keep them out of the hut in the wet jungle environment.

He and Maya used a small propane camping stove to cook what they needed when they couldn't eat as jaguars, although they normally hunted their meals and ate them as a cat would—no mess, no bother. Connor and Maya came down here from Texas to be one with their jaguar halves, normally not intending to play house as humans while on a jungle vacation. But if they were worried about hunters in the area, they remained in their human forms until the threat passed, therefore the necessity to have provisions for any situation that might arise.

A basin of water was nearby, and he motioned to it. "Fresh water that you can clean up with. We don't have any real privacy here so I'll leave while you change." He glanced at Maya, who was still in her jaguar form, pacing across the hut's floor and swishing her tail. He knew she wondered why Kat had called him by name while he was still in his jaguar form. "Did you want to stay with her?" he asked his sister.

She grunted, which he took as a "yes."

Good. He nodded. "Be back in a little while."

"I'll hurry so you won't have to be out there for very long."

He smiled at the notion. Here Kat was worried about *his* safety, while he was worried about *hers*.

He just hoped the men who had been cutting a swath through the jungle weren't looking to cause trouble for any of them.

———

Maya continued to pace across the hut as Kathleen turned her back and began unbuttoning her shirt. Maya wondered just what the connection was between Kathleen and her brother. She had seen the raw attraction between them, smelled it, felt the air between them fairly sizzle. For the first time in a year, he had shown real interest in a woman. Why this one? And how had Kathleen known her brother's name? She and her brother made it a point not to get attached to humans. So where had he met Kathleen before?

Her mouth gaped as the notion came to her—the battle between the drug runners and the U.S. soldiers. When Connor had returned to the hut early that evening, Maya had been annoyed that dinner had grown cold before he had shown up. But when she smelled and saw the blood soaking his fur coat, she had been horrified and rushed to see to his injuries. Except he hadn't been injured.

Maya stared at the woman as she peeled the wet shirt off and hung it over the back of the chair. *Captain Kathleen McKnight*. Connor had been beside himself with worry over the woman's condition when she had been shot. He had tried to hide it from Maya, tried to pretend the woman had been an inconvenience, but Maya knew her brother better than that. He couldn't eat dinner that night, hadn't slept, had prowled the jungle in his jaguar form. She had followed him and discovered that he had returned to the drug dealer's encampment.

Except for the marks on the ground where a tent had been secured, blood splatters, and spent bullet casings, they found nothing and no one—no dead men, no one alive either. The jungle had reclaimed the territory as its own as if humans had never existed there. She had returned before Connor had seen her spying on him, but she had never seen him so... distracted, so bothered by human affairs.

They had even cut short their visit to the Amazon, something they never did. He hadn't been himself, totally disconsolate, and they finally had flown home. For weeks, she had found him searching on the Internet for something, but he wouldn't say what. When she caught him at it, he would shut the computer off, act irritated, and head back outside to the nursery to dig some more holes, whether they needed to plant a tree or shrub or not.

Had he been looking for Kat all that time? For word about her well-being?

Maya smiled in her jaguar way. She wasn't about to let Kat get away from her brother this time. At least her brother could have someone in his life if Maya could make this work.

Kathleen seemed the perfect woman to be his mate. She climbed trees well, even as a human. She was good at keeping her fear in check. Although she had nearly died in the jungle only a year ago, she had returned to the Amazon. Maya believed that being a shifter like them would suit Kat.

Most of all, her brother was intrigued with Kat. More than intrigued. There was no mistaking that he had the hots for the woman. Kat didn't wear any rings or have the telltale sign of a white line on her finger indicating she had worn one recently. So she couldn't already be married.

Maya paced across the floor some more. So why couldn't he have her? He wouldn't take her in a million years. He wouldn't take any woman like that in a million years.

Well, not only that, but they weren't sure how it all worked. They had been born as shifters; could they change someone who wasn't one? They suspected that their ancestors had been changed in such a way, but no one had shared the information, so they really didn't know for sure. There was only one way to find out.

Maya turned and studied Kat. She had her back to Maya, dressing modestly even though for all Kat knew, Maya was only a jaguar. Kathleen had already pulled her pants off and was buttoning a long shirt. She leaned against a table for support, keeping her weight off her injured knee. She was in great shape. Probably due to being in the military. Well-toned legs, like she was used to running, and trim everywhere else, too.

Maya already liked her. Anyone who would tackle guerrillas in the Amazon to make the place safer for decent folk and who wasn't afraid to return to the same area after nearly dying would make a great jaguar-shifter. And Kat would make a good sister, Maya thought. At least the woman seemed to like jaguars—even if she believed Connor and she were only semiwild pets when in their jaguar form.

Maya paced some more. It was now or never. She had to make her play before her brother came back. She would never have a chance like this again.

With her nails retracted, she ran up to Kat silently on her large cat paws. Then she extended her claws and raked them down the back of Kat's left thigh. Kat cried out and nearly crumpled when she stepped with all her weight on her injured leg. Maya quickly licked the wound and mixed her shifter saliva with Kat's blood, before Kat jerked around and bumped her backside against the table, her eyes wide and her mouth dropped in horror.

In a hurry, Maya flopped down on the floor, then rolled onto her back and played the docile, happy kitty. Despite wanting Kat to be one of them, Maya did feel remorse for what she'd done. She hadn't wanted to injure the woman, but Maya hadn't been able to think of another way to try to change her.

Kat stared at the jaguar, and then, as if realizing Maya was like a really big kitten that would scratch at its human companion in greeting and then lick her, she visibly relaxed.

"You need to be declawed," she said, glancing back at the injury on her leg. She didn't say it in an annoyed way, more matter-of-fact.

What a horrible idea, Maya thought. Her teeth and claws were essential for hunting prey and protecting herself and climbing and marking her scent on trees. But then without even consciously thinking about it, she swished her tail around and caught it between her hind legs with her front paws, and Kat laughed.

Kat's sweet laughter lightened the ominous mood, and Maya was glad she had amused the woman. One day, hopefully really soon, Kat would play with her own tail.

Maya didn't know how long it would take for Kat to shift. All they had to go by was werewolf lore—but none of that werewolf stuff was real. Maybe biting or scratching someone wouldn't work at all.

Her gaze shifted to a puckering of skin on Kat's left thigh, and she wondered if that's where she had been shot a year ago. Connor had really been closemouthed about what he had found at the encampment, no matter how many times Maya asked him what had happened. He had tried hard not to allow her to see how torn up he had been over the woman. She had finally given up asking, but now she was determined to know what all had gone down.

The sound of someone running through the jungle

toward the hut caught Maya's attention, and she feared
her brother had heard Kat crying out. Kat still hadn't
pulled her pants on. What if he saw the scratches on the
back of Kat's leg and knew what Maya had done? He
would be furious with her. But if she had turned Kat and
it was already a done deal, he would have a mate. And
she knew that he would love Kat. But they had to have
time to reach their own conclusions.

Then it would be Maya's turn to find a mate.

Kat pulled an antibiotic cream out of her backpack
and began to apply it to the bloody claw marks on her leg.
Any wound could be dangerous in the jungle. Although,
if the shape-shifter antibodies slipped into Kat's blood
and began to work, Kat would heal quickly—a day or
so at the most.

Kat slipped the tube of Neosporin into her backpack
and turned just as Connor rushed into the hut, his face
anxious, his breathing hard. He stared at Kat, his gaze
raking over her naked legs, then he quickly shifted his
focus to her face.

"Are you all right? I heard you cry out. You're not
dressed," he said, sounding surprised and worried at the
same time.

"I'm… I'm fine. My… my knee. I just put all my
weight on it by accident." She gave Maya a look as
though she was about to tell on her, then took a deep
breath and instead said, "I'll just wear this long cotton
shirt to bed. It's too hot otherwise." She glanced at the
two beds.

Maya quickly shoved the screen door open with
her nose and slunk onto the screened-in porch to avoid
sleeping in the other bed so her brother could stay with

Kat. She had to keep them together, let them get to know each other. Let them bond.

"Sleep in mine. I'll use the hammock," he offered gallantly, but Maya would have none of it.

The woman was his now, and Maya had every intention of making sure they stayed together. Even if this first attempt at turning Kat didn't work, Maya wasn't letting go of the idea. Kat hadn't even told on her! She knew then that if this worked, they were going to be sisters and the best of friends.

"Are you sure?" Kat asked Connor. "I could sleep on the covered porch."

He looked back at her bare legs. "No, with your injured knee, it would be easier to sleep on one of the beds. We'll talk in the morning."

"Where's your sister?" Kat asked, and Maya got the distinct impression Kat was questioning whether Connor had lied about having one. After all, she had to think it fairly unusual that he would have a sister roaming about in the jungle by herself at night.

"She'll be here soon. She's with the other cat."

"Oh."

Good save, Maya thought.

Kat sighed heavily. "Thanks, Connor, for helping me out. Again. I don't know what I would have done if you hadn't come for me when you did before. Well..." She gave a small bitter laugh. "I would have bled out. So... thanks. I've wanted to do that for a long time. *Thank you*, I mean. And thanks to your jaguars, too. I don't know what I would have done if you hadn't come along this time, either."

"You're welcome. We'll get you back to civilization

within the next couple of days," he assured her, then cast a look in Maya's direction as if he was uncomfortable with the way the conversation was going.

Maya couldn't allow Connor to take Kat back to civilization. She had to ensure that Kat stayed with them. That he got to know her. That Kat had time to turn so that he couldn't let her go.

Maya shifted into her human form and quickly climbed onto the hammock, surrounded by fine mesh netting, and pulled a light cover over her naked body. In the dark, she watched her brother speaking with Kat.

His interest in Kat was his fault, not Maya's. But he hadn't a clue how determined she could be when she set her mind to it. And matchmaking in a human-to-shifter way wasn't all she wanted out of the deal.

She was going to have a jaguar-shifter sister.

Chapter 4

CONNOR PULLED OFF HIS SHIRT AND WATCHED KAT getting into bed, her movement cautious as she tried not to hurt her knee further. Seeing her half naked didn't make him feel gentlemanly in the least.

He sat on Maya's bed and untied his boots. "Do you have some Wellingtons in your backpack?"

"Yes." Kat pulled the cover over herself, and he eyed her through the mesh as if she were a princess in another land, her dark hair spilling across his pillow, the bed surrounded by a gauzy film.

He thought about how after she left them, he would still be breathing in her delectable scent on his pillow and his bedsheets. Neither of which would be conducive to sleep.

"Good. Because of the recent rainfall, we'll be walking in mud up to our calves in some areas. Progress will really be slow at times," he said.

She was already closing her eyes, opening them, and then shutting them again as if she was having the most difficult time keeping them open.

"Sleep," he said quietly, pulling off his boots, then his trousers. He figured she had already had quite an ordeal—getting lost alone in the jungle, coming across two jaguars that had scared the pants off her, and more than likely getting very little rest for however long she had been lost. "We'll talk again in the morning." He crossed the floor to the sole table in the hut, saw his sister watching him through the screen door, and shook his head.

He knew what she hoped for, but he wanted to make sure Maya understood that he and Kat couldn't go there. Then he turned off the lamp and retired to his sister's bed. The rain began again, making a lulling sound as it hit the tree canopy above them and their own thatched roof. He thought the sounds and scents would help him sleep—the fresh smell of rain and the steady downpour, the ceaseless sounds of cicadas and other insects offering a cacophony of various pitched songs, a frog in a nearby fig tree making a knocking sound, and the scurrying of some rodent through the leaf litter on the forest floor. But he couldn't quit worrying about the woman resting in the bed across from him and wondering how he could safely get her to civilization sooner rather than later.

Much later that night, Kat's soft moans awoke him from a light sleep, and he quickly sat up and stared in her direction. A nightmare? Dreaming of jaguars attacking her? Her guide abandoning her? Fear of snakes? The threat of the men who had been slashing through the jungle? Or of Gonzales's men shooting her?

He took a deep breath, listening to her ragged breathing, and stared at her through the mesh.

Or had something else caused her to moan in her sleep? Something much worse?

——✳——

Kathleen was used to Florida heat and humidity and the feel of semitropical weather, but the Amazon was much more tropical than that. Hotter, muggier, buggier.

Being in the rain forest was like living in the primordial soup where life began. Even scientists studying Amazon plant life had to admit they had not discovered all the varieties growing in the canopy. She felt saddened at the thought that they might never have the chance if the trees were cut down and the rain forest destroyed, along with the animals that lived there.

Millions of cicadas sang through the night, reminding her of Florida. But the black howler monkeys—screeching in alarm way up in the treetops when something, maybe an anaconda, had come a'calling—brought her back to the South American Amazon far, far from home.

She tossed and turned, feeling the heat boiling her blood, the jaguar's scratches burning down the back side of her thigh, her knee throbbing with pressure—the tissue bruised and swollen—and her cheeks and hands sizzling from the sunburn she had gotten while traveling up one of the rivers by canoe. Even her old bullet wounds seemed as hot as fire all over again, scorching her from the inside out.

She moaned, miserable, soaking in sweat, and so sleepy she could barely stay awake but in so much pain that she couldn't drift off all the way.

A masculine voice intruded in her world, worried, deep, baritone, soothing. She couldn't see the figure in the inky blackness because her eyes were blurry with hot tears.

"Kat," he said again, then a cold hand pressed against her forehead, leaving an icy imprint as he cursed aloud. His soothing voice was incongruous with his angry words.

"What's wrong?" a woman's voice asked, soft and worried as she drew close.

"She's burning up with fever."

The woman sucked in her breath. The sound of rain pouring down on the roof overhead should have drowned out any other sound, Kat thought, as hard as it was coming down. But she heard the woman's audible gasp and wondered who she was. Wondered who he was. And where she was right now.

Her eyes burned and she couldn't focus, couldn't see much more than a blur. The hut was too dark to make out anything more than that.

The boards creaked as someone moved across them. Then her cover was pulled away and a wet cloth placed on her forehead.

Neither the man nor the woman spoke again, but Kat was drifting in and out of her world, thinking of all the fevers she could have contracted in the jungle—malaria, yellow fever, dengue fever—and believing she had every one of them at the same time.

"She should have had the vaccination for yellow fever before she entered the jungle," the woman said.

"She should have," he agreed.

But had she? Kat couldn't remember.

"But if she traveled into the jungle too soon after getting the vaccination..." the woman said, her words trailing off.

"Hopefully she was vaccinated early enough before she entered the Amazon. We've still got a supply of medicine for malaria, but there's nothing we can do for dengue fever, if that's what she has," he said.

Everything grew silent except for the sounds of the jungle. The doves cooing somewhere nearby. Frogs croaking. Cicadas chirping.

Kat heard men's screams, bullets showering the jungle, and felt her wrists burning where the rope tied them tightly together to the metal pole. The damnable metal pole secured deep in the hard-packed earth so there was no way for her to pull free. If she could have gotten a knife to cut through the ropes... Then she thought about the bleeding... her leg, her arm... she was going to bleed to death first. She had to stop the bleeding. She could see her Army buddies scattered around the large tent, dead and covered in blood, could smell the stench... heard Roger...

No, he wasn't here. He couldn't be here. Not on this mission.

The rain forest. She was in the rain forest. But not there. Not in the tent with the dead men. Somewhere else.

Her wet shirt lifted, and Kat felt exposed and cold. She began shivering violently.

"No rash. Probably not dengue fever. Get a fresh cloth, Maya."

Maya. Who was Maya?

"And bring me the medicine for malaria. We'll try to get her to drink some water."

Kat's eyes drifted shut.

If she had thought how miserable she would be on a second trip to the jungle... the first fighting the bad guys, the second... the second... What was she doing here again?

She wasn't fighting the bad guys this time, was she?

She should never have come here. The Army... they wouldn't let her go on another mission. The doctor said she was... was not right yet.

Tears blurred her eyes. She swallowed hard, trying to recall why she was here again in the jungle.

The doctor.

He said if she could… if she could what?

Her thoughts drifted again.

The jaguar rested his head in her lap, and she sighed, comforted by his presence. She had never visited anywhere that was as primitive and teeming with life as the Amazon. And she had found just what she had wanted to see—a jaguar, well, two of them, running in the wild— and felt the peace of the jungle when before it had just been a mission. A mission gone bad. And Connor, he had come for her before and he had come for her now.

She let out her breath hard and sucked in more soggy air.

The jaguars had even protected her in the tree. Now how astonishing was that?

But then someone was trying to cut through the ropes binding her wrists, and she screamed. Or tried to scream. Maybe the howler monkeys were screaming. Maybe it wasn't her at all.

"Kat, it's all right," the man said, his voice soothing as he held her hand and ran a cool cloth over her cheek. "It's all right. You're having a nightmare. You're safe."

Her thoughts were so random as they shifted from one to another that she could barely catch hold of one before another intruded. She thought of Manuel and losing him in the jungle. How his friendly, South American charm had won her over. He was smiling at her. Talking with her in his broken English. Giving her a great guided tour, pointing out a howler monkey watching them from a tree overhead, showing her a yellow-and-black poisonous dart frog and a strawberry dart frog on a fig leaf nearby. An anaconda was coiled around the base of a tree, nearly invisible to her until Manuel showed it to her.

She moaned and someone brushed her hair away from her cheek.

She thought of sitting in the early-morning hours at the Spanish café where she was to meet Wade Patterson, who was supposed to lead her to where Connor Anderson was staying. What had become of Wade? How had she missed meeting him in the café? She thought she'd gotten the time wrong. The place wrong. But she hadn't.

And then the sunny café faded and she was once again in the lush, green jungle, the jaguar again looming before her on a branch as if he was trying to distract her, comfort her. He nudged her with his broad head, then rested it in her lap. Immediately feeling protected in the dark jungle, she reached out to pet him.

She found her hand wrapped in larger hands.

"You'll be all right, Kat," the man said, his voice dark and low and comforting.

The chills receded, but the suffocating heat took hold again. She was in a sauna, sweating every ounce of water out of every cell in her body as she faded off into the humid, hot ozone.

Chapter 5

THE RAIN HAD STOPPED SOME HOURS EARLIER, BUT THE drums had been pounding since then. Connor was certain the local natives were having one of their celebrations deep in the rain forest, but the beating made his head throb, as sick as he was with worry that Kat would die. She had come to the jungle, gotten lost, and contracted a fever —and none of that was his fault. But he couldn't shake the concern that it would be his fault if she died on him. The immediacy of the situation—her being near death and under his care again—was like déjà vu.

He didn't want to take her to the resort any longer. He wanted to take her back to the States where she could have competent care until she was well again. But transporting her there quickly wasn't possible.

She watched him through blurry eyes set in a face that was very pale except for her red cheeks. But she wasn't really watching. She was staring through him into a world of her own once more, semilucid and then confused and incoherent again.

"Kat?"

She hadn't once spoken in coherent words since the fever had struck. Just moans and groans and a frustrated "no" when he had tried to keep her covered when she was too hot again after shivering with chills. Several times she had reached for something. What was she trying to get to? At times she seemed comforted by something and at other times, terrified.

Connor heard rustling at the table and glanced in that direction to see what Maya was doing. She was searching through Kat's backpack.

"Anything in there that will tell us more about her?" he asked quietly.

Maya pulled out a passport. "She's an Aquarius, born the first of February, and she's four years younger than us. Hmm... Mom was an Aquarius, and she said that was why she was honest and loyal..."

"Not about staying with us," Connor grumbled.

"And independent like Kat is, having come to the jungle alone. And she's friendly, too."

"The downside?" Not that Connor ever put much stock in Zodiac signs or their supposed meanings.

"Contrary, unpredictable, detached, unemotional. I think she'd fit right in with a couple of Aries like us."

He grunted.

"Sure. You and I are both adventurous and impulsive, courageous and confident—she can't help but be swept up in our enthusiasm for life."

"Maya," he warned, not wanting her to think they were taking the woman home with them like she was some kind of pet they could nurture and make their own.

"She was born in Merritt Island, Florida," she said, ignoring him. "So she's a Florida girl."

The dark side of being an Aries, if any of it was true, was that Maya was definitely impulsive. A lot more so than he was, and he knew she was trying to get him to accept taking Kat into their family.

"The injuries she suffered on her Army mission

here don't seem to have caused any serious permanent damage," he said, changing the subject to one that was more important.

"You said she was the only one who was still living when her people came to rescue her. You saved her life, Connor. She's grateful." Maya rummaged around some more in the pack. "There's nothing else in here except survival stuff and more clothes and a credit card." She zipped up the bag, then joined Connor at the bed where Kat was still tossing and turning.

Maya put her hand on his shoulder. "Why don't you hunt supper for us? I'll spell you for a while."

He didn't want to leave Kat for a minute, worried she might slip into a coma and die. But another worry consumed him. What if his sister bit Kat, trying to turn her?

But he didn't think she would. Not as sick as Kat was. Unless she thought that by turning her, Kat would get well more quickly.

He cast his sister a warning look. She regarded him as if she didn't know what he was inferring, all innocence. Maybe she was totally innocent at the moment. Maybe deep down, *he* wanted Kat turned so she could be his.

He shook his head at the notion and left the hut, climbed down the stairs, removed his clothes, and tucked them on a shelf below the floor of the house on stilts, and then shifted. He ran as a jaguar, smelling the air, searching for dinner, and wishing he had some way to get Kat to a hospital and well again.

Had she caused Kat to be so sick? Maya had been beside herself with worry. And so had her brother. Connor had only left to catch fish for them or take down a tapir, or one time a caiman, and then she had prepared their meals. Otherwise, he had stayed by Kat's side, trying to cool her down and keep her hydrated. He had barely let Maya take care of her.

Maya studied Kat's bullet wounds, tracing the scarred tissue. She wondered if the jaguar healing genetics would heal the tissue, making it like new again, when she was able to turn Kat. Did the injuries ever trouble Kat? Maya hoped she could cure her of anything that might cause her difficulty. When Kat was better, Maya intended to ask her subtly about her injuries and what had happened when Connor had taken care of her.

Connor had tired of questioning Kat about her family, so Maya took up where he had left off. Maya's questions were more important, though. "Where's your family? Do you have a husband? Boyfriend? Fiancé?"

Kat shook her head no, moaned as if moving her head like that made it hurt, and then closed her eyes. Was that a no? No what? No husband, boyfriend, fiancé, or family?

Maya had been in such a panic to try and turn Kat quickly before Connor caught her that she hadn't thought of the repercussions. Kat would have to dump a husband, boyfriend, or fiancé if she had any of those.

Maya drew nearer to the bed shrouded in mesh netting, poked her hand inside, and then held Kat's hot hand. She stroked Kat's hand with her thumb. "I always wanted a sister," Maya said quietly.

Kat's eyes opened, and despite their bleariness, Maya swore that Kat seemed to focus more on her eyes this time.

"Kat," Maya quickly said, still in the same hushed voice, "do you have family?"

Kat shook her head, almost imperceptibly. Maya's heartbeat and breathing increased rapidly. She wanted to shout for joy. Kat was an orphan, and she would be Connor's mate.

And Maya's family, too. She couldn't wait for Connor and Kat to have cubs. To cuddle a couple of rambunctious, curious cubs in her arms. Maybe as many as four. She would help Kat raise them—just like a good aunt would. Not that Kat would birth a litter of jaguar cubs. She would probably birth them as a human, like their mother did them. Then they would shift when they were little whenever their mother did.

Her mother had later explained to Maya—as kind of a birds-and-the-bees lecture—that the shifter chose which form she would take to have her offspring. And the cubs would change with the mother's shifting until they were older and understood the risk of shifting whenever humans were around.

Yes! This was just too good to be true. Then Kat could help Maya find a mate since Connor hadn't been looking all that hard.

"Kat, you don't have a brother, do you?"

Kat closed her eyes.

No brother. *No family*. Of course, no brother.

"No boyfriend, right?"

But Kat appeared to be sleeping now. Maya looked around, listening for any sound that her brother was nearby, and heard nothing but jungle noises—the birds and bugs and monkeys. She got up from her chair and walked over to each of the windows, looking for any sign of Connor. *None*. She and Kat were perfectly alone.

She returned to the bed, and for the first time since she had scratched Kat, Maya pulled aside the bedcover and moved Kat's leg to see if it was still scratched or if the scratches had faded away like a shifter's would.

They were angry and red and looked infected. Maya sucked in a breath, held back tears, and wanted to sob out loud. She had only wanted a sister, a mate for Connor. Because of the jungle conditions, she might have infected Kat, giving her a slow and painful death instead.

———

Lightning flashed in the heavens above and thunder rumbled all around them as the afternoon rain steadily tapped on the thatched roof of the hut and the broad leaves of the surrounding trees. The rainwater funneled ever downward toward the jungle floor beneath the hut, which was situated high above the ground on stilts. Connor sat beside a sleeping Kat, running a wet cloth over her bare arm while his other hand held hers in reassurance. Though he wasn't sure if he was trying to reassure her… or himself.

The next day, she was still hot, still tossing and turning, still half out of her head.

How horrible Maya had to have felt when he'd been sick. At the time, he hadn't comprehended why she'd alternately been so upset and angry with him. But now seeing Kat so ill, he felt the same fear surging through his blood. Though their shifter genes helped to heal them, some wounds could be fatal for him and Maya, and some illnesses difficult to overcome. But Kat was only human.

He breathed in the dampness mixed with the faint fragrance of gardenias from the wet cloth, a mixture Maya had made from wildflowers and hand sanitizer, as he slid the cool, moist cloth over Kat's shoulders and collarbone and throat.

Kat opened her eyes and stared past him as she had done several times already. Once again, his heart tripped just to see her eyes open. He sat forward on the chair, praying she was finally coming out of the fog.

He leaned in and whispered, "Kat," in a husky, dark voice, not wanting to wake Maya, who was sleeping on the porch.

More than anything, he wanted to hear Kat respond, to say something intelligible again. He watched for any change in her expression, any sign that she recognized him. Her hand reached up unsteadily as if to touch his face, and he leaned forward even more, not sure what she intended to do. Whatever it was, he wanted to make it easier for her.

She ran her hand over his hair with a featherlight caress. His body tightened with an uncontrollable need that he instantly resented. He wasn't about to give in to his feral craving to taste her, possess her, have her for his own—if the only reason was to satisfy the part of his nature that was a born conqueror.

She licked her lips, moistening them, her glassy eyes fixed on his mouth.

"Kat?"

She tried to say something, and he grew even closer, bringing his ear nearer to her mouth so he could hear her words. Her lips, soft from his washing, and her cheek and then her silky skin touched his ear. He quickly lifted his head and stared at her. Her gaze met his briefly before it settled on his mouth again.

"Kat, can you understand me?"

She slipped her hand down to his cheek and tried to lift her head but was unable.

"What are you trying to do?" he asked.

She murmured something that he couldn't make out. He leaned down to hear her, and again he felt the soft press of her lips against his ear. She couldn't have meant to kiss him. He had just gotten too close to her. Or she was just delirious. Her hand gripped his hair but not hard, not considering how weak she was. She couldn't want him to kiss her. He wished he could give Kat a kiss and take away her sickness.

He ground his teeth. He was already too attached to her, had been ever since he'd first found her in the jungle that fateful day.

She closed her eyes, either too tired to keep them open or in resignation.

He touched her forehead with the fingertips of his free hand, thought her fever was breaking, and closed his own eyes, silently giving thanks.

And then he did what he knew he shouldn't. He brushed her lips with the barest of kisses. Her fingers tightened on his in response, as if signifying that he'd done what she'd needed him to do most of all. But then she let go and was again lost to him.

In some dark part of his predator's soul, he felt torn. The tentative bond they'd shared was swept away as the rain fell in a steady torrent. All he could do was watch her and hope she would wake again soon and rejoin their world. But to what? He would have to return her to the one that he and Maya truly weren't part of.

Then he'd lose her—for good.

Chapter 6

KAT WAS STILL PALE AND ALTERNATING BETWEEN chills and sweating for another day. The incessant drums were beating night and day, never letting up. Maya imagined that the hunter-gatherers, led by their shaman in the jungle, were offering healing powers to make Kat well. At least that's what Maya envisioned, hoping some of the shaman's magic would suffuse the rain forest and aid with Kat's recovery.

Connor was driving her nuts as he either paced or hovered over Kat. This morning, he had seemed different somehow, as if something had passed between him and Kat the day before, but he wouldn't tell her what had happened.

He had barely spoken to Maya, and she was glad that he had never moved Kat around so he could see the backs of her legs. Whenever he took off into the jungle to hunt for their meals, Maya applied more ointment to the angry-looking scratch marks on the back of Kat's leg.

Maya hadn't had a chance yet to check on the scratches today. She had been busy building a fire in their cookstove, then washing Kat's shirt and bra and panties in the rain, and finally drying them over the stove. She had to smile at Kat's choice of undergarments—leopard print. Jaguar was better, of course, but leopard was similar and acceptable.

She scooped the dry clothes up and was getting ready

to take them to Connor's bed to help Kat into them when she heard Kat whisper, "Maya?"

Startled, Maya dropped the shirt, bra, and panties on a chair and rushed over to Kat. "What's wrong, Kat?"

"I'm ready to rejoin the living." Kat was clutching the bedcover to her naked body, her skin glistening with perspiration, her green eyes clear for the first time since she'd gotten sick.

With joy and relief, Maya smiled at the woman whose face appeared tired and gaunt, her eyes huge, her hair damp and stringy. "I have a spare toothbrush and mint-flavored toothpaste that you can use to brush your teeth. And as soon as you're well enough, we'll take you to the falls, and you can wash."

Kat's eyes widened a little, and then she gave a small smile. "I'd like that. But I do have my own toothbrush and paste."

"The falls," Connor said darkly, stalking into the hut carrying a string of fish. He eyed Kat warily, then appeared to relax marginally. "Are you feeling better?"

"I think my knee is all healed up."

Maya caught her brother's concerned look. The knee hadn't been the problem. The high fevers and the wound on the back of her leg had been the major concerns, although Connor had never managed to see the scratches, thank God. Or if he had, he'd never let on.

"She's doing much better, Connor. If she can manage to make it to the falls in a day or so, I'll take her."

"She's too weak," he said, expressing what Maya knew would be the case.

"Then you can carry her." Maya smiled brightly.

She knew that Kat would feel better if she could just

have a clean shower. Maybe she could even swim in the river with the pink dolphins one day. Maya was dying to show Kat everything wondrous about the jungle.

He grunted, then handed the fish to Maya. "Here, make yourself useful."

That was his not-so-subtle cue for Maya to butt out.

She smiled again and tossed him Kat's shirt, bra, and panties. "Sure, if you'll make *yourself* useful."

Then movement in the jungle alerted them of possible trouble—*men*. Monkeys howled and were noisy; the birds squawked and sang and chirped, too. But the monkeys and birds lived among the trees, one with nature and its environment. Men slashed and hacked and destroyed wherever they went.

Worried, Maya looked to Connor.

"Stay," he warned. Then he pulled a high-powered rifle out from under his bed and crossed the fallen tree that they used as a natural bridge to their lookout post.

Kat tried to get dressed, but she was weak from not having taken much more than sips of whatever soup Maya had managed to prepare for her.

"Here, I'll help you," Maya said in a hushed voice, joining Kat and helping her fasten her bra.

"Who are they?"

"Maybe natives, who usually are no problem. They'll be hunting, that's all. But maybe not." Actually, probably not. Maya noticed that the drums had ceased to beat. And the hunter-gatherers were usually like the jaguars, moving about just as quietly and elusively. "Sometimes the cartels use the locals to transport drugs through the Amazon jungle."

To get her mind off the men and wanting desperately

to learn if Kat was experiencing any shifting urges or changes in her hearing, smelling, or sight at night, Maya asked, "Do you feel all right? Feel any… *differently?*"

"I just feel incredibly tired and weak. I'm sure it's because I haven't eaten enough."

"Yes, you'll also need to get some exercise when you're feeling stronger. But you don't feel any… *differently* otherwise?" Maya had to be careful she didn't overtly say anything she shouldn't, but she was dying to know if she had turned Kat.

Kat shook her head. "My knee feels nearly back to normal. The bruise is fading but doesn't hurt, and the stiffness in the joint is gone."

Maya sighed and buttoned Kat's shirt. She was glad Kat's knee wasn't hurting, but that wasn't the issue. "I like your leopard panties and bra."

Kat smiled. "It was a joke from a girlfriend because I kept talking about the spotted cats and how much I loved them. They've had five jaguars born at the Palm Beach Zoo. And I was always going to the zoo to visit them. Then I wrote a couple of articles on them."

That was a good sign. "Palm Beach, as in Florida?" Maya asked, hoping to finally learn more about Kat.

"Yes."

"That's where you're from?"

"Yeah."

"So, have you got family there?" Maya asked cautiously, praying that Kat didn't have.

"No. I was raised in foster homes, which is a subject better left alone." She gave a small shrug.

The family situation couldn't be better. Maya was already feeling overprotective toward Kat, and she wanted Kat to feel as though she could talk about anything with her.

But still, important issues needed to be discussed that had to do with Connor right now. "No boyfriend?"

Kat smiled at her, as if she could read her thoughts. Yeah, she was trying to matchmake Kat with her brother.

"Connor's shy with women, if you didn't notice. And he doesn't have a girlfriend." Not that he was the least bit shy, only reluctant to really get to know a woman for fear of losing his heart to her. And then where would he be?

"Probably hard to find one who likes to vacation in the Amazon jungle on occasion," Kat said with a small smile.

"Yeah, exactly." Maya wanted to say that Kat seemed to like the jungle, but she figured that would be too blatant.

When Kat tried to stand, she wavered, nearly falling back on the bed. Maya grabbed Kat's arm to steady her, then helped her into her panties. Maya's skin prickled with fresh concern at seeing Kat still so unsteady on her feet, and she grabbed Kat's arms to steady her again. "Are you going to be all right?"

"Yes. Thanks, Maya. I'm just a little dizzy."

A lot dizzy, Maya thought. Not feeling totally reassured, she managed to get a good look at Kat's scratches, or where they had been. They were all healed up with not even a scar. Maya let out a relieved breath.

But did that mean Kat had the shifter genes now or not? If she didn't, wouldn't a small scar still be visible?

The battle scars. Maya said, "Gonzales's men shot you?"

"Um, yeah," Kat said, her expression turning dark all at once.

Maya worried that maybe it wasn't a good subject to bring up yet, at least not so soon after Kat was starting to feel better.

Kat took a deep breath. "It's classified."

Maya stared at her in disbelief. "Classified?" Omigod, she hadn't thought of it, but what if Kat was still in the military? If she had an obligation, a contract, or whatever they called it, she couldn't just quit her job with the Army, could she?

Connor would kill Maya when he learned what she'd done. What if Kat didn't show up for whatever job she had or missed her next mission and they came looking for her? Maya could just envision a SWAT team swarming the Amazon looking for whoever was detaining their fellow operative.

Kat didn't say anything further, but Maya's heart was pounding with fresh anxiety. This changed everything. Maya ground her teeth. Okay, so they could deal with this new issue somehow. They would have to. Kat couldn't belong to the military any longer. She might have to keep her other missions secret from Connor and Maya, but Kat definitely would have to keep her new condition—if she had been turned—top secret from everyone else.

Maya suddenly smelled something burning.

"The fish," Maya squeaked as they started to crackle and smoke in the skillet. She helped Kat sit safely on the bed, then hurried to scrape the fish off the pan and flip them over. She sighed. "Cajun style. Blackened."

Kat chuckled. "I'll have to remember that the next time I cook a blackened meal."

Maya smiled at her, loving that her new sister had a sense of humor. She *would* be her new sister, whether Kat was turned already or not. "Connor and I have a nursery in eastern Texas. It's really beautiful. It's surrounded by forests, and we have a huge tropical greenhouse. And a small lake is located on the property. We'd love for you to come and stay with us for a while if you'd like."

"Stay permanently" was what Maya was dying to say. The truth of the matter was that if Maya had managed to turn Kat, she couldn't go anywhere but with them, permanently. She wouldn't be safe as a shifter on her own.

"Thank you. I'd like that."

Maya relaxed. Good. Everything was falling into place. Now if only Connor didn't throw a fit...

Looking tired, Kat reclined on the bed and watched Maya cook. "Where are the cats?"

"During the day? Probably sleeping somewhere in the canopy. They'll stay out of sight. When it gets dark and again at dawn, they'll be on the prowl."

"Oh. Somehow I figured they were like big cat companions that went with you everywhere you went in the jungle. I guess I thought that because when Connor came to rescue me the first time, one of the jaguars was with him."

"One was?" Maya asked incredulously. She hadn't been with Connor when he'd exposed himself to danger that time. Although she had been angry with him for doing so without letting her know, she had been glad he saved Kat's life.

"Yes."

"You... saw him?"

"No. I was tied up. But I heard one of Gonzales's men shout something about a jaguar. I thought I was hearing things."

"Oh, so you didn't see the jaguar."

"No. Later, I heard rumors that Connor was seen with a jaguar, vacationing in these parts. And he told me himself when he came to my rescue that he was vacationing here."

"Ah." So Connor had arrived as a jaguar, then shifted before Kat had seen him. Now some of it made sense.

"So what do you do when you return to Texas? Leave the cats here?"

"Um, no, they stay with us always. It's safer for them." Maya hoped Kat wouldn't ask how they crossed the border with the jaguars. They wouldn't have been allowed to. Maybe she could say they had a special permit, but she hoped she wouldn't have to explain and lie any further to Kat.

"Wow. So do you have special pens for them back home?"

"No," Connor said, stalking back into the hut. "Maya, if the men had been trouble, they would have heard you talking." He sniffed at the fish, his narrowed gaze flitting to hers. "You burned them."

She knew he wasn't angry with her, just teasing her in his superior way.

Still resting on Connor's bed, Kat quickly spoke in Maya's defense, as if she was afraid he was truly angered. "It was *my* fault. She was helping me dress."

He glanced at Kat's bare legs and raised a brow.

"We didn't get that far," Kat said, making a disgruntled face.

But he looked concerned. He had to realize that Kat was still too weak to dress herself.

"Not that you have never burned our food," Maya said, a hint of challenge in her words. She loved how Kat had come to her rescue.

He glanced at Kat who wore a barely constrained smile, her eyes sparkling with humor.

"Why did you come here, Kat? To the Amazon?" he asked, leaning against the door frame, arms folded across his chest and looking imperious.

Her eyes widened a bit, making her appear surprised at the change in conversation, but Maya wondered if something he'd overheard spoken between Kat and herself had gotten his attention. Like the fact she might still be in the military.

"I wanted to find you, to thank you for saving my life. The doctor said if you hadn't stemmed the bleeding when you did, I wouldn't have had enough in me to make it."

He opened his mouth to speak, but she raised her hand to stop him, and one of his eyebrows lifted. No one ever stopped her brother from having his say, and Maya was more than amused to see the effect Kat had on him.

"I tried to locate you in the States. But I didn't know where you were from, and tons of Connor Andersons are listed. I posted on Facebook, Twitter, on my blog, trying to locate the man who saved my life. And was rewarded."

This time both of Connor's brows shot up. "Who would have known we come here? We don't do Facebook or any of those other networking sites. We do have a Web presence because of our garden shop, but that's it."

She sighed. "A man said he visits here and knew of you. He said he could lead me to where he thought you stayed. But he didn't meet me, and I paid for a guide who said he knew of you also."

Connor looked at Maya, who was just as astonished. "Who is the man you missed seeing?" Connor asked.

"Wade Patterson. Do you know him?"

"No," both Maya and Connor said at once. Maya had an uneasy feeling about this, but their food was getting cold. "Let's eat."

Maya served up some of the fish, bananas, plantain, and pineapple—all harvested from the jungle—on reusable plastic plates. She hadn't had a girlfriend in years. Bonding was too difficult when Maya was a shifter and the potential girlfriend wasn't. But she wondered who this man was who knew about Connor and herself. "The men who were scouting around the area were all right, weren't they, Connor?"

"They had gone way around where we live. But I don't know if they were safe or not. Thankfully, the noise of the jungle and the vegetation would have helped to muffle your voices."

The men probably couldn't have heard them because they didn't have jaguar hearing, Maya figured.

"What about this Wade Patterson?" Connor said, helping Kat to the chair.

"I met him on Facebook," Kat said. "He got interested in my articles about jaguars, then saw my queries concerning a Connor Anderson and his pet jaguar in the Amazon. I didn't tell him how you saved me or anything about the mission. Just that you had saved my life, and I wished to find you to thank you. He didn't know where you lived in the States, either, but he said he'd heard from the locals that you visited here twice a year. Wade also vacations in the area."

"But you didn't know the man before this?" Connor asked, poking at his blackened fish, his gaze still zeroed in on Kat.

Maya knew what he was inferring. How could Kat have trusted a virtual stranger with her life? But Maya also read between the lines. As determined as Kat had been to find Connor, Maya knew more was going on between them than Connor was willing to admit.

"I investigated Wade as thoroughly as I could. I discovered that when he wasn't in the Amazon searching for lost treasure, he was a respectable businessman in Pensacola, Florida—a computer programmer during the day and a game-design hobbyist at night. He was on Facebook, LinkedIn, Myspace, Twitter, and a number of other networking sites."

Connor was frowning.

Kat ignored his obvious annoyance. "I had posted about doing a feature on the new jaguar cubs at my local zoo and was searching for any information about a Connor Anderson and his jaguar who vacationed in the Amazon when Wade told me he knew of you—not personally, but he had seen you around."

"Around," Connor said skeptically.

Kat folded her arms and said to Connor, "Wade asked if I wanted to meet up with him when he visited the rain forest and said he would take me to where you stayed. I did check him out. I found a number of pictures of him—some when he was wearing a suit, some in his jungle khaki attire. They all revealed a friendly sort who liked adventure. I admit I admired his enthusiasm for the unusual and the way he seemed grounded in a real job, too."

"Like you?" Connor asked.

"Yeah. But everything began to unravel when he didn't meet me at the café at the appointed time."

Connor shook his head. "I don't know this Wade Patterson."

Maya could tell her brother didn't like that Patterson had known anything about them or their connection to jaguars. But the inflection in Connor's voice and his expression revealed more. He didn't like that Kat had been meeting with this man alone.

"Are you finished eating?" Connor asked, sounding annoyed.

Kat nodded.

"Was there any other reason you came here?" Connor pried.

"What do you mean?" Kat responded, sounding defensive.

Connor rose from his chair, looking more like a grizzly than a jaguar, and closed in on Kat like the predator he was. He lifted her into his arms, pressing her close to his body in a posture that was all too telling that she was his and no one else's, and carried her back to his bed.

"Wait," she said, clinging to him, "I want to brush my teeth."

He turned around, headed for the washbasin, and set her on her feet. Then she retrieved a toothbrush and toothpaste from her backpack. After she brushed and brushed and brushed, she finally relinquished the toothbrush and toothpaste, and he carried her back to the bed.

"I believe," he said quietly to Kat, although Maya could hear because of their highly attuned cat hearing, "there's more to your coming here than you're letting on."

Maya could have kicked him when he acted so intimidating toward Kat, but to Kat's credit, she didn't back down from him. Once he set Kat on the bed, their gazes collided and locked as if ready for battle. Maya heard their accelerated heartbeats and hoped this was only a bit of getting to know you better and not that they really didn't like each other at all.

"Like you were nearly killed here a year ago. Like you were having nightmares. Like you might still be on a mission," Connor accused.

Maya wanted her brother to back off, but she wanted to know Kat's motives, too. With her back stiff, her nerves on edge, and her lips clamped tight, Maya cleared the dishes and listened.

Kat lifted her chin and looked Connor straight in the eye. "My mission was to personally thank you for saving my life."

"And?" he pressured.

She pressed her lips together, then took a deep breath and said, "*Yes*, I have nightmares still. Sometimes facing your fear can help to put it in proper perspective."

"You're not on a military mission, then?"

"No," she said, sounding irritated, but whether with Connor or the Army, or both, Maya couldn't tell.

"She's too weak to move anywhere," Maya warned, trying to get them off this other business. She wanted them to get along, not be annoyed with each other. But most of all, she didn't want her brother thinking it was okay now to dump Kat off at a resort.

Both Kat and Connor glanced at her as if they'd forgotten she was there.

"A couple of days, Maya," he said, giving her a dark look. "Then we'll see."

Maya could tell her brother didn't trust her where Kat was concerned. Maya prayed that she had already done the deed of turning Kat and that Connor wouldn't be able to stop the process. And that he wouldn't be too angry with her.

She glanced at Kat. And that she wouldn't be, either.

Chapter 7

AFTER EATING, KAT WAS FEELING MUCH BETTER, RELA-
tively speaking. At least her head was no longer filled
with fog, and she could remember what everyone asked
her. Connor was cleaning the burned frying pan while
Maya worked on the plastic dishes and asked her all
kinds of questions.

Kat had been amused that Maya had questioned her
about whether she had a boyfriend. Connor hadn't touched
the subject. But he'd listened to every word she'd spoken,
watched her every move, and if she didn't know better,
she'd think he was listening to the inflection in her voice,
trying to determine her hidden agenda. She didn't have one!

She sighed. She didn't owe either Maya or Connor
an explanation about her personal life, but Maya was
becoming a fast friend. And although she never had
anyone to use as a sounding board before, she wanted to
talk about her ex-fiancé for some reason.

"I was engaged," she said, watching the two of them
for a reaction.

Connor's scrub brush stopped in midair, and Maya's
hand stilled on the dish she was wiping off.

"Oh?" Maya said, her tone encouraging.

Kat was fairly certain Connor was dying to know the
details, too, but he was trying hard not to show it. He had
gone back to scrubbing the pan, but much less vigor-
ously than before.

"Roger was a major in the Army, working on the same mission behind the scenes."

She was surprised when Connor gave her an incredulous look, and then his expression became one of condemnation. "Behind the scenes," he growled, not hiding his annoyance at the way her ex had treated her.

"It was the mission. What wasn't part of the plan was that my men would all die and I would be so severely wounded."

The muscle in Connor's jaw ticked as he studied her. He looked like a thunderstorm building in the jungle— sudden, dark, and dangerous.

"Roger couldn't cope with the prospect of having a future wife who was that unstable."

"Unstable," Connor said, raising a brow.

"Nope, not good for any kids that we might have someday had. I don't blame him. Well, maybe a little bit. If he had been shell-shocked during a mission, I would have stuck it out with him. Through sickness and health."

Connor looked her over with the predatory appearance of a feral animal, as if he wanted to take her for his own.

He was gorgeous and sexy, his body rippling with muscles every time he moved since he wore no shirt again. A pair of light-colored khaki pants and boots were all that he had on for now. His skin was a tawny golden color and his hair just as golden, like Maya's. And both had the most beautiful amber eyes that appeared as though they could look into her soul, read her every intention, and understand her to the marrow of her bones.

She loved his sexy voice, too. Growly at times, deep and dark and fathomless, but it also had a masculine purring sound to it. She loved listening to him talk, even when she'd been so out of it that she couldn't make out his words. Just the lulling sound of his voice, lilting at the end of sentences as if he had been asking her questions.

He had been so tender and caring. She even remembered his kissing her—when she'd wanted him to kiss her—fearing she would die before she could thank him for saving her life the first time. He'd been so gentle and unassuming. Oh, he could deny it, but she sensed his deeper interest in her.

But now that she was better, he seemed impatient and gruff. She wasn't sure what was going on with him. Did he like her or not?

She shrugged as if it made no difference, although it did and she was having a hard time hiding her feelings. "Roger stuck it out with me for a while, figuring I'd return to my former self. But I had flashbacks of the killings and night terrors so vivid that I beat on him in my sleep, trying to make the bad go away."

Connor cast her an elusive smile. Standing next to the washbasin with a soapy scrub brush and a frying pan caked with burned fish remnants, he had an appealing quality about him. Any man who would clean a frying pan that was that much of a mess had to have some good in him.

"Hey," Kat admonished him for giving her such a smug smile. "If I slept with you and began beating on you in the middle of the night, I bet you wouldn't stick around, either."

"Try me."

Connor looked dead serious. Maya appeared genuinely astonished, but then she quickly looked away, attempting to hide a smile.

Even Kat's mouth gaped before she could recover. "You wouldn't say that if you were in a deep sleep and I slugged you."

"I bet we could come to some kind of arrangement that would mutually satisfy our need to sleep."

The wicked gleam in his eyes said he wasn't thinking about sleep.

"Yeah, right." Kat quickly changed the subject. "When are you returning home?" She hoped they weren't delaying their own trip home for her sake. If they were, no matter what her condition, she would be out of here so she could let them get on with their plans. All they needed to do was point her in the right direction.

"We'll be leaving you off at the resort, then we'll go home from there," Connor said, his voice taking on a businesslike tone. It was clear he wanted her out of their lives. *Pronto*.

Feeling like a party crasher, Kat figured his attitude was because she had messed up their vacation to such an extent. How could they have had any fun out here when they were spending so much time caring for a sick person they didn't even know?

But Maya looked crestfallen. And Kat felt terrible about it. Maya seemed genuinely to like her, and Kat could really use a friend like that. She had left the Army and now was totally free—no permanent job, no home, just a few Army friends who didn't know about her final mission. But they lived so far away that she might not ever see them again. She sighed. After this trip to the jungle, she had planned to set down roots, unlike with the military that had moved her around so much. Or foster care.

Kat smiled at Maya, ignoring Connor's gruffness. Maya was as tanned as Connor, in as great shape, really pretty, and Kat's petite height. Despite Connor's male posturing, Kat would not be intimidated. He could go prune his plants, for all she cared. Kat and Maya could have an all-girls' night out. Or whatever else Maya liked to do.

"Let me know when would be a good time to visit you at your home in Texas, Maya. I'm... in between jobs right now. So I want to take the time to travel a bit before I start the job hunt all over again and try to figure out where I want to settle down."

"Then you're coming home with us," Maya said, chin up, arms folded, defying Connor to say no.

Connor glowered at his sister but didn't say anything.

"I'd love to," Kat said, assuming then that Maya owned half of the nursery and the home and also had to have half raised the cats. "I won't stay long, just a couple of days. But... I'd really enjoy that." Of course she meant to visit after she went to the resort and did everything else she had planned to do before she got lost in the jungle and came down with a fever. She really had hoped subsequent pleasant trips to the Amazon would help to get rid of her flashbacks.

Maya beamed, but she didn't dare look at Connor.

Connor growled something about leaving it alone, which Kat didn't understand. Then he left the hut, and Kat figured he was going to get away from the females who were wreaking havoc with his ability to exert his male dominance over all.

She really liked Connor, despite his need to show a gruff aloofness now that she was getting better. She couldn't help it. All along, he had been kind, tender, and caring. So she didn't believe he was truly a beast in disguise.

Maybe he had issues, like a girlfriend who had dumped him recently, or maybe he felt Kat had messed up his well-ordered life. But she didn't intend to be a bother in Texas. She'd just visit with Maya a little and then be on her way.

"Are you hungry still?" Maya asked, offering another banana. "We need you to get your strength back so we can leave. But not before we go to the falls. And I was wondering if you'd like to swim with the pink dolphins."

Loving the idea, Kat smiled. "I'd love to see the dolphins. But I'm stuffed, thanks."

She wanted to take pictures and videos of the jaguars while they explored the jungle, hopefully while it was still light out, so she could remember them always as they had protected her in the Amazon and so she could write the article about them as she had planned.

But then she thought about her guide, Manuel, who had left her, saying he would lead men he'd been concerned about away from her when they had heard them in the jungle, and then she'd never seen him again. What if he had been one of the men in the jungle earlier, searching for her?

"Maya, I've been thinking."

Maya turned to face Kat, her expression concerned.

"I wonder if the guide I had was the one who was

wandering through the jungle, maybe trying to find me and take me back to civilization."

"We'll take you wherever you wish to go," Maya said abruptly.

"All right." Kat got the distinct impression that Maya hadn't trusted the man. Maybe because he'd abandoned her.

And Wade Patterson? What had happened to him? Kat vowed to learn what she could about both men as soon as Connor and Maya took her to the resort.

~~~

The next day, Kat felt well enough to go to the falls, although she was still weak and would need Connor's assistance in getting there. She hated being indisposed and having to rely on Connor. She hoped the waterfall would not be too far away, but she wanted to clean up in the worst way.

Connor and Maya had left her alone for the first time that she could remember, some business to do with the cats, they had said. But while she was brushing her teeth at the washbasin, she heard Connor arguing with Maya in the jungle near the hut, probably not wanting to go too far away and leave Kat alone for very long. They most likely thought they were speaking softly enough with all the other jungle noises surrounding them and the way the vegetation muffled sounds, but she heard.

"Maya, you know it's too dangerous for her to visit with us at our home in Texas." Connor's voice was low and concerned… and annoyed.

The cats, Kathleen thought. Was he worried she wouldn't be cautious enough around the cats? She wasn't the one who'd forced the male jaguar to place his head on her lap in the tree and keep her there, or the female to do so afterward. Sure, she would be careful around them. She hadn't had much of a choice the first time she had encountered them. But she would have kept out of their path if she had been able. She sighed. She hadn't seen any sign of them for days—well, partly because she had been so out of it that she hadn't known who or what had been watching over her.

She stood at the window, looking out at the imposing jungle. Not even the slightest of breezes stirred the thick foliage. The rich smell of the jungle, the decaying leaves and wet plants and earth, and the smell of fish from a nearby waterway wafted in.

"I know what you're thinking, damn it," Connor continued. "I've known ever since you saw Kathleen exactly what you've wanted to do. You *can't* do it. It wouldn't be fair to her."

"But you like her," Maya said. "I know it. You were dying to know what happened to her when she was wounded. You didn't eat, couldn't sleep, and we even left here early because you were so disconsolate."

"Maya…"

"No, let me finish. You were like that for months after our return home. I know you too well, Connor. As soon as we returned here, what did you do? Went straight back to the place where she'd been wounded, and then you didn't come back for hours. I worried about you because you'd been gone so long, and there you were, just staring at where she'd been."

"Enough, Maya."

"Then you found her again. I can smell the way your

pheromones are pumped up whenever you're around her. I see it in your eyes, the way you look at her, and the way you've cared for her. Even the way you don't care for her connections with other men. You can't deny the strong attraction you have for her."

Kat closed her gaping mouth, her heart pounding furiously. She had felt his kindness and how caring he had been. He had never shown her any gruffness at all when she was ill. She couldn't believe that he had been so concerned about her when she had been wounded that he hadn't wanted to stay here any longer last year. So she couldn't understand why he was reacting like he was now, wanting her to leave and never visit Maya.

Connor didn't say anything. Too shocked that Maya could read him so well? Stunned that she would figure him so wrong? What was Connor's response? Kat was dying to know.

"She can't stay with us. That's my final word," he growled.

And in that instant, Kat thought that he was just like the jaguars he had raised. Just like a human who looked like his dog, except in this case he was a blond jaguar with a growly side to him, and amber eyes and a muscular body that suited the big cat as well. Yeah, if pet owners looked like their pets, he certainly did. So did Maya. Like one big, happy jaguar family.

What was bothering Connor so much about her visiting with Maya further? Kat didn't plan to start any kind of a relationship with him, despite how much she admired him for all that he had done for her. Or that she loved the way he cared about his sister. That he'd hunt for them and clean and... well, if she was looking to settle down, she wouldn't have looked any further.

But as far as going to their home, she just planned to visit with Maya.

Maya didn't say a word. Kat didn't want to get between the two, but she hoped Maya would stand up to her brother. No one had any right to tell her who she could and couldn't visit with. That tugged deep at the heart of Kat's own dark past.

"Maya, damn it, you know I'm right," Connor said finally.

Kat could envision him pacing across the jungle, waiting for Maya to capitulate. And Maya standing her ground, undaunted. But then she finally spoke.

"I think..." Maya said slowly with a hint of a smile in her voice, "it might be too late."

Chapter 8

IN THE THICK OF THE JUNGLE, ALL OF THE ANIMAL noises ceased to exist as Connor stared incredulously at Maya, his worst fear realized. But he had never seen any bite marks. And he had looked.

"You didn't turn her," he said shortly, his anger sifting to the surface.

"It's too late," she said quietly. "Too late, Connor, and she has to stay with us now." This time she sounded almost contrite.

But knowing how much his sister would want this, he thought she was probably damned pleased with herself.

"Hell, Maya." He paced in front of her, then turned and scowled at her. "I haven't smelled a change in her. She doesn't act any differently."

Maya gave a little one-shoulder shrug, but the expression on her face and the light tone of her voice said she wasn't as sure as she was trying to sound.

"Where did you bite her?" he growled, hoping that if Maya had tried to turn Kat, she hadn't been successful.

"I didn't bite her."

He stared at her hard. He knew he hadn't seen any bite marks. But if she hadn't bitten Kat…

Maya swallowed reflexively and folded her arms, her chin going up in a defensive way. "I scratched her."

His mouth gaped for a split second. *Scratches*. He had seen a pale line of scratch marks on Kat's leg when he had tried to wash her back the one time. He had thought she had gotten them from the wicked thorns of a jungle plant. But still, scratching Kat couldn't have turned her, could it?

"I can't believe this." He stalked back toward the hut, intending to examine Kat, question her, see if anything was different about her. He had been trying to keep his distance from her. From her feminine allure. From the scent of her. From wanting to know anything more than necessary about her. But no more. He had to learn the truth—and fast.

Maya ran after him. "We can't let her go, Connor. She has to be your mate. I want her for my sister."

It finally sank in. *Maya wanted family.* Connor felt miserable then. She hadn't done it just so he could have a mate and then she would find one. She wanted more of a family. Always had. But it didn't change the trouble that could arise from Maya's impulsiveness.

"What if she's changed and she doesn't want to have anything more to do with us?" he growled over his shoulder.

Maya looked dejected. He hated to be the one to give her the news, but what if Kat had been changed and she hated them for it? They had no idea what would happen next. She could be so depressed about it. She might even be suicidal!

And what if she didn't want him for a mate? What if they didn't suit each other at all?

"We have to keep her," Maya pleaded. "We have to make sure that she'll be all right. She can't be on her own."

Oh, yeah, he knew that. He could just see them having to build a wild-cat pen for her and keep her padlocked in it every time she shifted. Keeping her secured in a room in the house every time she came back to her human self. They had no idea what they were in for. Or how she would react to it. They wouldn't be able to let her out of their sight.

He still had high hopes that she hadn't been turned. He truly didn't think scratch marks would do it. He thought back to Kat's fever. What if Maya had brought the sickness on when she clawed Kat?

He let out his breath hard. He knew Maya hadn't meant anything bad by it, knew she had really liked Kat from the beginning. And cats didn't just like anyone. He had to admit he was already thinking of Kat as family. She didn't have any of her own. But if she had been turned, she didn't have a choice. She would be part of their family, like it or not. He couldn't let her loose on the unsuspecting population.

"What are you going to do, Connor?" Maya asked, her voice ragged with worry.

"Discover the truth." What else could he do?

They had been about a half mile away from the hut to ensure privacy while they talked, although a few hundred feet would have been good enough, as noisy as the jungle was and as thick as the vegetation was. Now he rushed back on the narrow muddy trail that led to their place to check on Kat.

"When did you scratch her?" he asked, thinking that if it had been days ago, she would have changed by now, but if it was more recent, maybe not.

Maya didn't say anything, and he glanced over his shoulder at her. "Maya?"

"Before she got the fever." Tears flooded her eyes.

"Hell, Maya." He didn't say anything more than that. He could tell his sister felt doubly responsible for Kat, and now he realized why Maya had felt so morbidly worried Kat might die. Not only might she have turned her, but she might have killed her in the process. He wanted to reassure Maya that everything would be all right. That life would go on as it had before, but it wouldn't. And they both knew it.

"She cares about the jaguars. It'll be all right," his sister said, sounding as though she was trying to reassure herself as much as she was him.

"Observing one and being one are not the same, Maya."

They grew quiet as they drew closer to the hut. He could see Kat peering out one of the windows, looking in the direction they were coming from. Had she heard their conversation?

With all the jungle noises drowning out their voices, she couldn't have, unless she had been turned.

—∿∿—

Maya was afraid Connor would scare Kat to death as he charged up the creaky steps to the hut. As soon as Kat had seen them approaching through a speck of clearing in the jungle, she had quickly moved away from the window.

Maya didn't know if the scent of her brother on his bedsheets had cloaked Kat in the feline scent or not, but Maya was certain she had smelled the scent on Kat. No matter what, Maya had hoped to put enough doubt in Connor's mind to keep Kat around long enough for Maya to figure out a foolproof way to turn her.

"Time to go to the falls," Connor said abruptly to Kat

as Maya entered the hut. He was headed for Kat like a *Panthera onca* ready to lunge at its prey. Jaguars were much more a stalk-and-ambush rather than a chase-and-take-down predator, and right now he was stalking Kat as she backed up against his bed.

She eyed him warily, wide-eyed and not entirely sure she liked his aggressive stance, Maya thought. She smiled. Kat was perfect. She wasn't trying to escape him, but she wasn't fighting him, either. Which was probably a good sign. Like she was accepting him as her mate. At least Maya could hope so.

"Can you walk?" he asked. But he didn't give her a chance to answer. He drew so close that he was pressed against her, smelling her, trying to determine if Kat had feline genes now or not.

Kat's breathing accelerated, and Maya tried to see if Kat was attempting to take in his scent, too, and analyze it. But she couldn't tell, not as tall and broad-shouldered as Connor was and the way he was blocking Maya's view.

"I'll carry you," he said without waiting for Kat to answer.

"I'm sure—" she began, but he swept her off her bare feet and whirled around, doing this his way, stifling her objection.

He looked like an alpha jaguar that had selected his mate and was letting her know just how much he was in charge. And Maya loved it. She wasn't sure Kat did, but she hoped Kat would love him in time.

"How do you feel?" Connor asked Kat as he carefully carried her down the stairs.

"As much as I hate to admit it, weak."

He let out his breath.

Did he think that if Kat was still too weak from her bout with the fever, she couldn't be a jaguar-shifter?

Maya sighed. Maybe Kat hadn't been turned. Maya would have to bite Kat the next time with a small nip to see if that worked.

Chapter 9

THE IDEA OF CLEANING UP WAS ALL KAT SHOULD HAVE cared about as Connor carried her out of the hut. She had really looked forward to washing in the waterfall ever since Maya had brought it up again. But the conversation that Maya and Connor had had in the jungle kept running through Kat's thoughts, and she couldn't quit trying to figure out what they meant by "them."

"She cares about the jaguars," Maya had said, but she sounded concerned.

"Observing one and being one are not the same," Connor had responded angrily.

His response didn't make any sense at all. Being one, as in being a jaguar? On the one hand, that's what he had to have meant if he was responding to Maya's comment. On the other hand, he couldn't be saying that, so he must have been talking about something entirely different, and Kat had missed some of the conversation. And then they were talking about mates. Mates? If they had been Australian, she could have understood. But they were Texans and a long way from Australia.

The weirdest part? Maya had said she had scratched Kat. When? And why? The jaguar had, sure. But Kat didn't remember having any other scratches that a woman might have made. Unless her long nails had scratched Kat inadvertently, and that's what she had been referring to.

"I'm postponing my visit to see Maya in Texas," Kat said quietly to Connor as he carried her down the steps and made his way along a narrow path through the jungle, the vines and trees and shrubs encroaching on the human-made trail. Although she imagined the jaguars probably also ran along here.

Wearing a backpack, Maya led the way. Neither she nor Connor said a word.

But Kat figured if Connor was that unhappy that she was going to visit with them further, it was best not to bother. She was surprised, though, when he didn't respond right away and tell her how good an idea that was. Was he having second thoughts about her not visiting? Maybe he thought Maya would be so upset with him that she would be hard to live with if he didn't let Kat visit.

Kat had never had a brother or sister to grow up with, and she admired the way the two always worked together, teasing each other with a fondness Kat had never seen between siblings. She both admired and envied their relationship.

Connor sighed heavily and looked down at Kat, frowning, his voice deep and committed. "You already agreed to go with us. To stay with us. To visit a while."

Kat stared at him in astonishment. He hadn't wanted her there. All along it had been very clear that he hadn't. Why the change of heart all of a sudden? Still, she felt something more was wrong, and, well, she didn't know anything about this man and his sister. *Really*. And the way they had been acting, she decided it was time to forget the whole deal. Although she would have enjoyed seeing their home, nursery, and tropical greenhouse— and observing how the cats thrived there intrigued her.

"I'll have to take a rain check. I need to apply for a job and figure out where I'm going to go from there. I can visit later," Kat said evasively.

Maya was listening, barely taking a breath and with her back straightening, waiting to see what Connor would say.

He didn't hesitate to respond. "You can stay with us while you sort it out. Free room and board."

He didn't make it a suggestion. He was telling her what she *would* do.

"I have a reservation at the resort. I'm sure you and Maya had other plans until I came along. That will give you a chance to do whatever it was that you wanted to do. That will give you time to enjoy the rest of your vacation plans."

"No," Connor said flatly.

Her back stiffened.

"Since you never showed up for your reservation, the management at the resort will have given your room to someone else." He shifted his gaze from watching where he was walking to her again. His golden eyes had taken on a darker cast. From the shadows of the trees or something else? "We didn't have other plans anyway, so you'll be welcome company."

Why was he making this stuff up? No way would he consider her welcome company. Not after what he had said to Maya during what they had assumed was their *private* conversation.

She didn't feel she had the strength to argue with him right now. She would politely pretend to acquiesce for now, but she wasn't stopping off at their place. She wasn't sure she would make the trip to see them later, either. Let them work out their problems on their own. Or maybe she could correspond with Maya, and when Kat had settled down somewhere, she could ask Maya to visit her instead. *Sure*. That's exactly what Kat would do.

When Kat didn't agree with Connor right away, he said, "We'll talk about it later." But he didn't sound cheerful about the prospect. More grumpily resigned than anything else.

Worse, he didn't sound like he meant for her to have a choice.

She smiled a little at that. She was the only one who made decisions about what she was going to do with her life. Ever since she was old enough to leave foster care, no one else told her what to do. Well, except for work, but she had been paid to be told what to do. Connor didn't have any right.

They reached a nearly black, deep pool of water, and she eyed it warily. Except for a tree trunk that had fallen over the width of it, there was no way to cross it. The pond looked like it could be filled with crocodiles or anacondas waiting for the unsuspecting.

The tree trunk was mossy, wet, and slick as Connor carefully carried her over it. He slipped twice, and she clung to him with all her might, although he had instinctively tightened his hold on her. The heat of his body, the feel of his hard muscles, and the way his arms held her so close raised her own thermostat to hotter than blue blazes.

Once they had made it across the tree trunk and Connor's boots had hit firm ground again, she sighed with heartfelt relief. Connor gave her a conceited smile as if *he* hadn't been worried in the least that he would get them safely across.

The path narrowed even further, and she heard the water rushing over the waterfall long before she saw it. The path looked as though they would soon reach a dead end, but the falls beckoned to her from somewhere through the dense foliage, sounding like a river rushing over a mountain. Her concern about where she was going next evaporated as they came to the edge of a pool of water and she finally saw the beauty of the waterfall spilling over ancient rock walls. Nearly every inch of rock was covered in moss and dripping with ferns and vines on three sides, while trees towered high above, making the waterfall like an enchanted, hidden shower spot just for them.

The large pool of water was brown and muddy, but the stream pouring over the top of the rock face from high above looked clean and white. She wanted to shed her clothes at once and stand beneath the falls and scrub her skin and hair clean. She stared at the tropical paradise and was so glad Connor had brought her here now.

"A cave is directly behind the waterfall, and from the back side, the water spilling over the rocks is gentler," Maya said. "The curtain of falling water is so dense that you can't see through it. You can either stand up to your thighs in the lake on this side of the falls, or wash up as you stand on a rock ledge behind the falls. We have shampoo that's biodegradable and body soap."

"I'll shower behind the falls," Kat said. Even though she would probably need the rougher water to feel clean, she wasn't sure she could withstand the pressure. She really did need to eat more to get her strength back. Standing in the muddy water didn't appeal to her, either.

What if a hungry croc or an anaconda was hidden right beneath the surface?

Carrying her, Connor ducked through the screen of a shower of gentler water to the right of the falls, and then they were behind the falls, the roar of the rushing water nearly deafening. She glanced at the shallow cave. The rock walls were covered in moss, while ferns grew nearer the outer edges where they could reach the light, like lacy green trimming. Inside, it was cooler but just as humid, the air scented with earth and rock, plants and fresh water.

"The rocks are a little slippery," Connor said next to her ear, making sure she heard him over the noise of the falls before setting her down on her feet.

Trying to keep her balance, she clung to him. His arms wrapped around her protectively, and he seemed concerned for her welfare all over again. And something more. She wasn't sure what was in his expression. Almost as if he was rethinking his earlier decision to keep his distance from her. His interest in her made her skin flush with heat again. She looked around for Maya, but she hadn't joined them behind the falls. Where was she?

Then she saw the bottles of shampoo and body soap sitting on a rock ledge. She supposed then that Maya and her brother came here on a regular basis to get clean.

"I can manage," Kat said, although she didn't let go of Connor's waist. She was not sure she could manage alone, as much as she wanted to show her independence and strength—which was normally how she dealt with any situation.

He was still holding her waist with a tight grip to make sure she didn't fall. "I'll help, if you don't mind."

Again, he said the words with authority, as if she had no say.

She assumed that was because he could envision her fighting to prove she could do this on her own when she truly wasn't able. "Maya—"

"Isn't strong enough to hold you up if you slip and fall. And the pressure of the falls will tire you. Trust me in this."

Think of him like a male nurse, Kat told herself, flushing to high heaven.

He smiled a little, and that sexy-as-sin smile warned her he wasn't a male nurse, but a man who was looking forward a little too much to his role.

"I…"

He shook his head, but he didn't make a move to do anything, waiting, she thought, for her acceptance.

She wanted to get clean. Another flush of heat spread across her skin. "Fine," she said in an ungracious way.

Again, he smiled, looking amused this time.

She reached for the buttons on her cotton shirt, but her fingers were trembling and she wasn't making much progress.

"Here," he said, not gruffly as she might have expected, but with a gentler tone like when he had tried to make her well. "I'll do it. Just hold on to my waist so you don't fall."

She didn't know which was worse, stripping in front of him on her own or having *him* remove her clothes. She tried her damnedest not to feel as though this was something much more intimate, personal, and sexy.

She looked around again, wondering where Maya was.

Connor had Kat's shirt off before she was ready, and

then he worked on her pants. He hadn't let her put on her boots before they left the hut, so he didn't have to mess with pulling them off. As soon as her pants joined her shirt on the rock floor, she expected him to hold her hand as she moved under the waterfall. But he leaned in close as a lover and unfastened her bra! As if he was used to unfastening women's bras—easily, no hesitation, no fumbling.

So maybe he wasn't so shy with women after all. Just around her... for some inexplicable reason. She would have told him that she didn't need to remove *all* her clothes. That she could have cleaned up nicely wearing her leopard panties and bra. She hadn't expected him to strip her bare. But here she was, still clinging to his waist and naked as the day she had come into the world.

"Still okay?" he asked.

"I'm okay," she said, sounding a lot shier than she wanted to.

Again, the elusive smile.

"All right. Next step. I'm going to get the shampoo and body wash, and I'm going to walk you over there to get it, so just hold on."

What had happened to Maya that she couldn't have helped?

Kat did as he said while he gripped her arm and moved them slowly over the slippery rock floor, the wet moss feeling like squishy velvet beneath her bare feet. Her heart in her throat, she began to slip. Connor held her tightly against his hard body, like a pillar of strength, keeping her on her feet.

Then he grabbed the bottles of soap and walked her slowly back to the falls.

A roar she barcly heard beyond the waterfall reached her ears. She stared at the rushing water but couldn't see through it.

"Maya sent one of the cats to watch over us and make sure we don't have any unwelcome visitors," he explained.

That's where Maya had gone.

"Did you hear her roar?" he suddenly asked.

Concern and wariness etched his voice, warning her that knowing the truth was important to him.

"I thought I did. Although the roar of the waterfall nearly drowns everything else out. But still, the jaguar's roar sounded different." Which, come to think of it, she thought was odd. She hadn't had to shout to Connor to be heard. Although initially he had spoken next to her ear so that she could hear him, he hadn't done so the rest of the time he had been speaking with her, and she had heard him.

Now he was looking at her differently. She couldn't say how, exactly. But it was as if he was looking at her with new eyes—as if she had changed in his estimation somehow. She wasn't sure if that was good or bad.

"Hold on to me," he said, his voice low.

She clung to his waist as he pulled her into the falls and doused her in the water. Every silky drop felt wondrous, and she wanted to shout her pleasure as the water ran over her face, her shoulders, and her breasts and then all the way down to her toes.

He smiled at her, and she luxuriated in the feeling of the water sluicing over her bare skin.

But then he pulled her out from under the shower of water, long before she was done with the exhilarating experience. He smiled again, seeming to understand her disappointment, and began to soap her hair. *Oh*. At first she was annoyed with his controlling nature, but this—oh… my… God—was heaven.

The soap smelled divine, like oranges—fresh and citrusy and sweet.

No man had ever washed her hair, and if the feel of the waterfall rushing over her body had given her a new high, this did even more so.

He was gentle, careful not to pull or snag her hair, which had to be horribly tangled from her sleeping and tossing and turning on it and not being able to wash it for several days. In fact, she had to look like a total mess.

That brought a fresh flush of heat to her cheeks and throat and chest.

But Connor didn't seem to notice as he concentrated on soaping up her hair, massaging the scalp, and caressing her with a gentle tenderness. She didn't know when it happened, but the next thing she knew, she had moved in closer to him. Her body pressed against his, trying to cling to him like one of the vines wrapped around the trees beyond the falls. Her bones were melting.

She figured once they were done, she would have to return to the hut and sleep for a while because she was feeling so relaxed and worn-out all over again.

"Can you manage all right?" he asked again, moving her away from him a little bit.

"Yes," she whispered. Not sure she could, wanting to hold him tight and never let go, when she had never been a clinging vine in her life.

"I'll try to do this quickly," he reassured her.

Do what quickly? she wanted to ask.

But he was already taking the body wash, which

smelled like tangy tangerines and just as sweet as the shampoo, and spreading it over her. He washed every inch of her, including the less sensitive parts that felt sensitive with his large hands moving over them and the very sensitive parts that swelled with eagerness at his touch.

She shouldn't have loved what he was doing to her, should have treated this as purely a clinical task that he was performing. Yet she couldn't help wanting this to be the real deal—making love under the waterfall in the Amazon rain forest while the colorful birds of paradise serenaded them from overhead. The mosslike emerald-green velvet carpeted their private shower, and living plants and ancient stone served as the walls. The water-fall itself was a shower curtain and shower all in one.

He was acting as though he didn't notice that her nipples were rigid and the nub between her legs was swollen as he washed her thoroughly there, too, that her breathing was becoming raggedly aroused, her heart beat pumping harder... but he had to have noticed.

Then she noticed something else. She swore she could hear his heart beating more loudly, faster, his breathing just as ragged.

His gaze shifted to her eyes, and she wondered if her eyes looked as insanely aroused as the rest of her felt. His eyes darkened.

Yeah, he wasn't immune to her, although she didn't want to get too close just to see how his body was react-ing to him touching hers.

Ha! She didn't need to. One look at his water-soaked clothes, and she could see just what she was doing to his body.

Time to rinse and get back to the hut before they did anything they would both regret.

She began to take a step toward the water, slipped, and stopped, and his arm moved around her to steady her. She wasn't sure how it happened, but the next thing she knew, they were kissing under the waterfall. The soap suds had been washed away, leaving her body squeaky clean and smelling like a medley of oranges and tangerines.

His arms wrapped tight around her, holding her against him in a hard embrace. Every muscle group outlined by his wet clothing was pressed indecently against her naked body. And damn if she didn't want him inside her now!

His kiss was so passionate, so feral, that she knew it was only the beginning.

Chapter 10

CONNOR COULDN'T DENY HOW MUCH HE WANTED KAT. He loved that although she had to know he didn't want her to visit, Kat had stood up to him to make his sister happy. And he couldn't deny he was glad to see that his sister and Kat really seemed to hit it off. He had been worried about how melancholy Maya had seemed lately because the two of them only had each other.

When he had nursed Kat back to health, he hadn't been able to help how much he had desired her, but until now, he hadn't thought he could risk giving in to the way he felt about her. As a jaguar-shifter, he knew one-night stands were the only way he could keep from falling for a woman and wanting her forever when he knew he could never have her that way. Because Kat had been in his care, he couldn't think of her as a one-night stand. And now...

He pressed his lips against Kat's again, while her arms wrapped around his waist as if she would collapse from his kissing her at any moment. She hesitated at first. And then she was kissing him back as if she couldn't get enough of him, purring like a cat would and smelling like a cat—like a jaguar cat—along with the fragrant scent of oranges from the shampoo and her mouth tasting of the sweet pineapple that she'd had for breakfast. Her soft, heated body—but not from the fever this time—pressed tightly against him, against an arousal that he couldn't have kept in check if he had wanted to. The feel of her made him want more of her than was safe.

But could he want her forever? Exclusively?

Male jaguars had larger territorial boundaries than females, overlapping more than one female's boundaries. And a male would service each of the females, not just one. Even though he was a jaguar-shifter and his human half fought against the notion of straying, Connor had never found a woman he was the least bit interested in staying with forever. And he wasn't sure he could keep his jaguar half in check if he did take a mate.

Now everything was different. Kat didn't know what she was in for, and he couldn't let her go and deal with her changed state on her own. Living alone would be too dangerous for her. If anyone were to discover the truth about her, the danger would be too great for any of them.

As Kat's tongue stroked Connor's, he shifted his hands to her buttocks and cupped them, pulling her even harder against his body. He wanted sex with her, and she seemed to want the same of him. Now. But he couldn't follow through. Not until she understood what she had become and could live with it and with knowing he meant to make her his own.

If another male jaguar-shifter happened upon them, Connor sure as hell wasn't going to give him a chance to make Kat his.

He growled with feral desire and rampant need. He wanted her. Damn it. Forget about courtship or dating rituals.

The jungle was teeming with life—from the larger kind like his own to the miniscule forms no one could see with the naked eye.

Wild and untamed, like he felt.

But he pulled away from her before he gave in to his animal instincts. Even though she seemed more than willing, he couldn't. Not yet.

"I'd better get you back to the hut," he said, his voice husky and ragged with need.

"My clothes…" Kat said when he scooped her up into his arms, as if he was going to haul her back through the jungle naked.

His other head might have been thinking for him, but he did remember he needed to help her dress.

"I'll help you with your clothes and carry you back to the hut. You need to get your strength back." He hoped now that she had some of their cat genes, she would heal more quickly, but then again, they wouldn't help unless she ate better to regain her strength.

She was still way too weak as he assisted her into her panties and then her bra. He should have thought to bring a towel. Both of them were soaking wet. And nothing dried easily in the muggy jungle.

She clung to him as he helped her into her pants, the rock floor slippery and her own weakness hampering their efforts. By the time they were done, she looked ready to collapse.

"You need to eat more," he said, worried about her, as he lifted her into his arms.

"At least my appetite is coming back," she said and sounded cheery, although tired.

Here he was, working on ravishing her beside the waterfall with no thought to her physical stamina. He shook his head at himself. He wanted her. And the way she had kissed him back, he knew she wanted him. But what would happen when she learned what he truly was? And what she had become?

He wondered if Kat had turned all the way. Could she shape-shift? If she could, would she do so at the worst of times, having no control over it? Because he and Maya had been born shifters, they could change at will. No moon dictated their shifting, like in werewolf lore. Their natural instinct to hunt during dawn and dusk normally made them want to shift at that time. Still, they usually only shifted when they were visiting the jungle or when they felt the urge while swimming at night at the small lake on their property.

He hadn't a clue what would happen to Kat regarding her need to shift. Then another thought occurred to him. What if she couldn't shape-shift at all? What if he planted his seed in her, and it didn't take root? That as a nonshifter turned, she would be unable to conceive a shifter child?

That would be the end of his shifter line—and although it shouldn't have mattered to him, deep down it did. He imagined that the primal animal in him wanted to leave his legacy behind.

But what if she had a human child who didn't have the shifter genes? And that child learned Connor was a shifter? That his mother was, too?

Hell, Maya. They didn't have a clue what might happen next.

―⁂―

Maya heard her brother and Kat coming out from behind the falls, so she shifted and rushed to dress. She hoped Connor had learned that Kat was one of them now, but as soon as he spied Maya, he shook his head, his expression ultra dark.

Normally, she knew just what her brother was telling her with his nonverbal communication, but this time she wasn't sure.

She hurried to catch up to them as Connor carried Kat back to the hut.

"Do you feel better?" Maya asked, hopeful, but she could tell by the way Kat drooped in Connor's arms that she was worn-out.

"Hmm," Kat said, sounding dreamy and half asleep.

Maya sighed. Kat still wasn't well enough. "Is she okay?" she asked her brother, hoping he would clue her in.

"She needs to eat more," was all he would say.

Maya tried to get closer to Kat to see if she smelled like a feline, but all she could make out was Connor's scent all over her, *again*, along with the fragrance of the shampoo and body wash. She would have to speak privately with Connor later.

When they finally reached the hut and climbed the steps, Connor tossed over his shoulder to Maya, "Fix her something to eat, will you, Maya, before she falls asleep?"

But the idea of a meal was already too late. As soon as he laid Kat down on the bed and Maya began to cook the tapir and plantains he had brought up earlier, Kat was sound asleep.

"Is she? One of us?" Maya whispered to Connor.

"Yeah, in part," he growled. Mostly because he was so unsure whether Kat was fully turned or only partly. And what would either mean to all of them?

"How do you know?" she asked, her voice hushed as she cooked over the stove.

"She smells like a cat. But beyond that, we haven't a clue, Maya."

"Are you going to keep her?" she asked, hopeful.

"We have no choice. No matter what, even if she's only partly turned…" He let his words trail off.

"You mean if she can't shift?"

"Yes, that's exactly what I mean. But we might not know that for some time. And what if in a year or two, all of a sudden she does?" He shook his head as he looked back at Kat's sleeping form enclosed by the netting around the bed. "We couldn't risk her being on her own."

Good. If Kat wasn't fully turned, sometime when Connor wasn't around, Maya would nip Kat just enough to break the skin and finish the process. Hopefully.

"When should we leave?" Maya asked, ready to pack up now.

"She's still not ready. And we have another problem." He gave Maya a scathing look. "What if she shifts when we're trying to get her home?"

"On the ferry," Maya said softly. She could just imagine the passengers scrambling to jump overboard into the Amazon River, running away from the hungry jaguar to join the piranha.

"Even if we drove across the continent, it could be a problem if she shifted. We'd be in trouble if we were caught trying to take a jaguar into the United States because of the law against the interstate and foreign trade of exotic cats."

"Oh," Maya said, not having thought of that. "You think she won't have any control over shifting?"

"I have no clue, Maya. None whatsoever. But I highly suspect that might be the case."

"I'm sure she'll be all right," Maya said, hoping to God Kat would be, as she finished cooking their lunch. She glanced at the bed. "Should we wake her?"

Maya would do anything to get Kat ready to leave the jungle and return with them as soon as possible. Taking care of Kat at home would be easier, wouldn't it?

Smelling the jungle and listening to the rain pattering all around her, Kat moved stealthily through the forest on four paws. Four big cat paws. Jaguar cat paws.

She wanted to hunt, wanted to climb a tree, wanted to swim. But when she heard men coming toward her, all she thought of was self-preservation. She leaped into a tree and hid in the dense foliage, her golden coat with its black rosettes making her blend into the dappled shade of her surroundings.

A monkey screeched and Kat shot up in bed. Staring into the darkness, she could see Connor asleep on Maya's bed while his sister slept soundly in the hammock on the porch.

Kat's stomach rumbled. She had missed the meal again. She sighed. They must have let her sleep instead. But now she was starving. Had they left anything for her to eat?

She stared through the netting at Connor, his face so peaceful in sleep and almost angelic. The way he had kissed her at the falls hadn't been the least bit angelic. She knew then that he had been fighting his own demons regarding seeing more of her.

She sighed. He was a master of mixed messages, but she was ready to take their relationship further.

Looking for the lantern and thinking it should be turned off since everyone was asleep, she glanced around the hut. But it wasn't lit. She frowned. Why was the hut so well lit when… it wasn't. Really. The night was still dark. So why could she see so well? Another hallucination?

She groaned, lay back down, and closed her eyes.

She couldn't stop having the unbelievable dreams that had haunted her throughout the night. She thought maybe she'd been affected by the strange foods she had been eating, like the white meat of the tail of a crocodile—better that she ate him than he ate her—that tasted like a combination of chicken and white fish. Or the tapir she had eaten that tasted somewhat like beef. Or the plantain that tasted like a cross between potato chips and a banana.

Maybe her strange dreams were a residue from the fevers she'd had. Or something about the atmosphere of the jungle itself—the earthy wet smells and the constant animal noises that penetrated her dreams.

Maybe she wasn't even awake.

She closed her eyes and drifted off again. Thunder boomed overhead and the rains began again. Streaks of lightning flashed way above the tree canopy, a distant light flickering like an on-off switch that was broken.

But when the dream took hold again, the sensations were so real that she couldn't wake herself from it, no matter how much she tried. So she quit trying and gave in to it.

One minute, she was struggling to get out of her buttoned shirt and panties, and the next, she was prowling the floor as a jaguar. Her cat claws were retracted, her paws silent as she padded along the wooden boards. Her body felt more muscled, stronger, heavier.

She yawned, curling a long pink tongue out of her mouth, and licked her lips, her mouth huge compared to her human mouth. And teeth. She ran her tongue over her pointed canines. Wicked.

And unreal.

Her stomach rumbled, which was part of what had disturbed her sleep. She was ravenous. But restless, too. She didn't feel… *right*. She had to move, test her muscles, experience walking as a jaguar. To sense her surroundings in a new form. To see and hear and taste and smell.

She wanted to run free among the rest of the jungle inhabitants, just as feral and at home with the environment. To stalk and swim. To enjoy the sensation of being at the top of the food chain.

Yet some part of her resisted. She wasn't a jaguar. She was just experiencing a very vivid dream.

She poked her nose at the screen door, opening it, and then moved onto the porch, staring for a moment at a sleeping Maya. Then she pushed through the second screen door on the covered porch and did what a jaguar might do—skipped the steps and leaped for the ground. She half expected to run into Connor's two jaguar pets roaming around at the base of the hut. Maybe she would find them as she explored the jungle. She would like that. The three of them running and swimming together while they served as her jaguar tour guides. They would know the best eating spots, the best climbing trees, the most interesting places to explore.

At a walk, she investigated the jungle, going farther and farther from the hut, deeper and deeper into the tangled mesh of vines and tree roots. She felt strange exploring on four paws instead of walking upright on two feet. Being closer to the ground, her eye level gave her a much lower perspective. She couldn't get used to breathing in all the smells that were so much more pronounced—the sweet scent of flowers, the earthy smell of wet ground, the fish in the nearby river. She wasn't bothered by bugs and heard all kinds of sounds that she hadn't heard before. And she was seeing at night, although it didn't look like night to her exactly.

With all the moving she had done growing up and in the military, she had never felt at home. Now she felt at home in the Amazon when before she'd felt like an outsider, strictly a visitor.

She kept moving, hunger propelling her forward, making her search for something to eat. Then she found a river and waded in. She kept her chin up and listened as she swept the muddy river bottom with her large paws, listening to the fish swimming about. She spied one and dove in to get it. She seized it in her powerful jaws and pulled the struggling fish out of the water, then carried it to shore. This was so much easier than the one time she had gone fishing with a bunch of Army guys and managed to pull up everything—from old fishing lines and sinkers to a grungy sneaker—but never a fish.

Not even giving a thought to how she should prepare the fish, she ate it, no cooking, just raw. And loved it.

Shouldn't she have been worried about not cooking it first? That was why she knew it was a dream. She would never have eaten raw fish.

Her appetite appeased, she continued to explore, sending a spider monkey screaming for cover. She would *not* eat a monkey, although she knew the natives did and so did jaguars. That had to mean she really wasn't a big feral cat. Otherwise, she wouldn't have any qualms about it. Right?

A blue-and-red macaw poked its head out of a hole in a tree, saw her, and instantly disappeared back into the tree. She wouldn't have eaten him, either.

She took deep breaths, smelling smells all over the place, on trees and on the ground, littering leaves and vines and mud. She swam across a number of water obstacles, not afraid of anything, ready to take on a caiman or an anaconda if it dared to bother her. She had never felt so alive in her life. Fiercely independent. Attuned to nature, one with it.

But she was getting tired again. Time to return to bed, end the dream, and sleep. But when she turned around and saw the rushing river before her, she wasn't sure how she could get back to the hut. How long had she traveled? How far? In what direction exactly? How many waterways had she crossed? Where was she now?

She was lost in the jungle... *again*.

Chapter 11

CONNOR HAD BECOME ACCUSTOMED TO KAT'S BREATHing, her soft sighs, and her moans when she was feverish. But he had been so tired after taking care of her for several days and hunting when he could that he had finally slept deeply for the first time since she had wandered into their lives.

And now he heard nothing. A sudden rush of panic raced through him. He sat up quickly in bed and stared at where she should have been, screened by the netting like a fairy princess tucked away, but he could see the bed was empty. He hurried to climb off the mattress and rushed onto the porch.

Maya was sleeping soundly in the hammock. He quickly woke her and asked, "Did you hear Kat leave?"

Had she left the hut to relieve herself? That's all he could think of. She had never left the hut before on her own. But now that she was able to, she could very well have needed a private moment to herself.

Maya sat up on the hammock, eyes narrowed. "No. She's not in bed?"

Connor shook his head and returned to Kat's bed, pulled the netting aside, and saw her shirt and panties. He cursed under his breath.

"What's wrong?" Maya asked, coming up behind him.

He lifted her shirt off the bed and showed it to Maya.

"She's shifted," Maya said, her voice nearly inaudible.

"Come on. We have to find her. Now." He was certain they could track her, but the problem was what if someone or something dangerous found her first?

———ᴡᴡ———

Kat could manage almost anything except being lost. The first time she had been lost in the Amazon jungle, at least she'd had her backpack, and she had figured Manuel would come back for her eventually if she didn't find a way to the resort on her own. But this time, she wasn't even human. What if hunters discovered her and thought she would make a nice fur coat or believed she might be interested in eating someone's livestock? Not that she had seen anyone's livestock in the jungle.

Not that this was real, either. She was experiencing the worst nightmare ever. Everything was so real that she could still taste the raw fish she had eaten.

If she was a jaguar, why couldn't she figure out where she had come from? Wouldn't she be able to follow her trail back? She was one dumb big cat.

She had crossed several waterways, but she hadn't marked a trail like a cat would do—as far as she knew from what she had read—by urinating or scratching trees. She stood still, lifting her nose to sniff the smells, hoping she might catch a whiff of Connor or Maya's smell. But how could she? She was probably miles from the hut.

Not knowing what else to do, she meant to yell—call out to them, hoping maybe she could wake them and they would find her. She opened her mouth and... roared. In a jaguar's way. A deep, rough coughing sound, over and over and over again.

And scared the shit out of herself. That was *her*? Making that unbelievably wickedly loud and annoyed sound?

She stared at her big feet, her claws still retracted, knowing she couldn't really be a jaguar. *Not really*.

She just couldn't wake from an incredibly real nightmare. She roared again, like a jaguar looking to mate, but she wasn't. Totally frustrated, she needed help to wake from the dream.

Something like this had happened to her before. Sleep paralysis was what it was called, where she was half-conscious and half-asleep, desperately trying to wake up all the way.

If she hadn't been dreaming she was a jaguar, she would have been trying to shout to wake herself from the dream. And Connor would have heard her and come to reassure her that she was just experiencing a nightmare. Only he didn't come, and she didn't wake.

She stared at the jungle, which seemed to have closed in on her. She felt alone and afraid—even though as a jaguar, she probably could hold her own in the jungle. But could she?

She let out another highly irritated roar.

The jungle was noisy whether it was day or night, but all of Connor's senses were attuned to searching for any clues to where Kat had gone. He had smelled her a couple of times, brushing up against trees, seen her paw pads imprinted in mud, the edges clear and crisp, meaning she had recently made them, but when he came to a river, he lost any sign of her.

Until he heard her roar. His heart leaped. At least he

assumed she was the one calling out in the dark of night surrounded by lush jungle.

Maya ran up beside him and looked to the west.

That was where he had thought he heard Kat, too.

And then there was another roar, farther away. Deeper. Lower. A male.

Hell and damnation. If a male jaguar tried to mate with her, she would be scarred for life. Not that she wouldn't already most likely have some issues. But what if the male was a jaguar-shifter? That brought a whole load of new problems into existence. He, whoever he was, couldn't have her.

The female that had to be Kat roared again. He and Maya called to her in their jaguar tongue. Then silence. Had they frightened her? What if she thought the jaguars would try to hurt her? Or maybe that one would try to mate with her? She was probably confused by the sound of the roars coming from all directions.

He wouldn't consider having sex with her unless they both were in their human forms and Kat was agreeable. For now, all he could do was worry about the other male in the vicinity. This was Connor's territory, although he hadn't been marking the area regularly while caring for a sick Kat.

He took off running in the direction where he thought she was. She was miles away, though, and he hoped she would stay put. Or head in their direction. Away from the other cat. But what if she was worried that he and his sister were the ones to avoid?

She didn't make a sound again, although he and his sister roared a couple more times, trying to pinpoint her location and praying she hadn't run away from them.

The other male roared again, looking to hook up with
the female. He probably assumed Maya and Connor
were a pair and that he was encroaching on their territory. But the desire to have an unattached female would
be too much to disregard.

They had traveled at least a couple of miles when
Connor stopped to smell the air again and caught a whiff
of jaguar claw marks dug into the trunk of a tree.

He stopped and sniffed and looked up.

The jaguar was lying on a branch, watching him and
not making a move to leave her safe perch. Maya ran up
behind him and looked up. The jaguar in the tree had to
be Kat. She twitched her tail back and forth, her gaze
shifting from him to his sister and then back again to
him. She was so beautiful, her sage-green eyes studying
him, her golden body covered in rosettes, that she made
him smile.

He was relieved to see her within reach. But he didn't
know what to think. Was she upset? Confused? His jaguar smile faded.

She had to be both.

The male jaguar roared again, but he was leaving the
area. He sounded frustrated that Connor had gotten to
the female first. *Good*. Connor didn't want to have to
take time to fight the jaguar, and he didn't want Kat to
witness the battle if he had to commit to one. Jaguars
rarely killed each other in the wild over territory—but
they would fight if necessary to prove territorial rights.

Although he briefly wondered if the other was a
shifter or just a regular cat. He could deal with a shifter
more forcefully, knowing they both could heal. A
regular jaguar? He wouldn't want to injure one, yet the

fighting could get rough and Connor had no intention of letting a real one get near either his sister or Kat.

He eyed Kat with concern. What if she shifted all of a sudden, and he also had to shift to carry her back to the hut? Running naked as humans through the jungle was too dangerous. Just walking through the forest, they risked poisonous snake bites—some highly deadly.

Before anything of the sort could happen, they had to get her back to the hut.

But once more, she was in a tree, and Connor was trying to figure out a way to get her down.

Kat watched the two jaguars looking up at her from below the tree branch where she had taken refuge. They were the two who had taken care of her until Connor came to get her in the jungle the first time she had met him. The two that Connor and Maya had raised from cubs. And they were in her dream. Just as real as she felt she was right now.

The other one she had heard roaring? Another, only he would have been a wild jaguar, not raised by humans.

The male beneath the branch she sat on jumped easily high into the tree, landing on *her* branch and shaking it a bit. Panic shot through her. What if he planned to bite her? She was in their territory now… an intruder. They wouldn't know she was Kat, the human they had befriended days ago.

Or what if he wanted her? As a mate. *That* sent a frisson of alarm winging through her.

He nuzzled her face with his big head, his whiskers bumping hers. How sensitive her whiskers were. His whiskers moved forward, inquisitive, exploring, testing her response.

Hers moved backward, defensive, avoiding him.

He seemed to smile, at least it appeared that way to her. How did she know what a jaguar smile looked like? She could smell something in the air surrounding him that showed he was intrigued with her. And how could she tell this?

Her whiskers felt the shift in air currents. Even if she couldn't see him moving his head closer, she would have felt the change. Again, he nuzzled her slightly.

This couldn't be happening. He'd better not be interested in her as mate potential and try anything. Thankfully, she was backed up against the trunk of the tree.

He nudged at her face this time, as if he was trying to get her to jump from the tree. She wasn't going to. What if she did, and as soon as she was on the ground, he tried to mate her? Sure, since she had been roaring, he had to think she was hot for some kitty-cat loving.

The other, the female, was his sister. She was watching and looking hopeful, worried maybe.

He pushed at Kat again, harder this time. She growled low in her throat. She wasn't going to be pushed around.

He didn't move back, though, remaining in her space and trying to intimidate her, she thought. The female down below grunted as if she was talking to Kat. Or maybe she was talking to the big guy, telling him to hurry up or back off. Kat thought the female was on the male's side. But that made sense. They were brother and sister, close to one another. She was the stranger. The newcomer.

He was so much bigger than Kat. All it would take

would be a little harder nudge, and he could push her off the tree branch. But what if she swiped at him first?

She was not going to be knocked off the branch so he could mate her.

She didn't think he would believe she was going to shove him from the tree—not as small as she was and as large as he was, so when she gave a powerful swipe with her paw at his shoulder, he was actually caught off guard and fell to the forest floor, landing on all four paws with a thud.

Stunned, she stared at him in disbelief, having not realized her own strength or that she could best him. He stared up at her for only a split second, then leaped into the tree, shaking it again with his weight, which unsettled her. Before she could balance herself and prepare for his retaliation, he swiped at her with his forearm, this time knocking *her* out of the tree.

Like him, she landed on all four paws. And planned on running to get away from the male beast. But he jumped down next to her before she could bolt, and when she tried to race off, he leaped into the air and pounced on her, effectively pinning her down. She roared, telling him to get off her. He wouldn't budge. But at least he was pinning her down across her back, not trying to mate with her.

The female cat came over and licked Kat's nose in greeting or in consolation. Kat wasn't sure which.

The female grunted at the male. He grunted back at her.

Then the female jaguar began to blur, and Kat thought the fever was returning. When the female cat turned into a naked Maya, Kat knew she was delirious. She wasn't

dreaming about being a jaguar—she was sick again.
And then the dark jungle turned even darker, blackening to midnight.

"She fainted," Maya said, sounding stricken.

Chapter 12

STILL IN HIS JAGUAR FORM, CONNOR STARED AT KAT IN disbelief, never having thought that a jaguar would faint. Not that she didn't have some heady stuff to get used to. But he never would have thought she'd pass out on them.

He had figured that Kat would be less upset if she saw his sister shift and talk with her, woman to jaguar. He thought that if he shifted and Kat saw him as a naked man, she would have had more difficulty with the truth. Not only that, but he was afraid Maya couldn't stop Kat if she tried to flee. Which was just what she had intended. With his bigger weight, he'd kept her from running.

Now, he wasn't sure what to do. He licked Kat's face, trying to nudge her to consciousness, while Maya talked soothingly to her, attempting to get her to respond.

"Kat, can you hear me? You'll be all right. But we need to get you back to the hut. Kat…"

To his guarded relief, Kat finally stirred. She blinked her eyes and looked up at him standing over her as a jaguar and at Maya, her expression worried. Kat closed her eyes as if she couldn't deal with the repercussions anymore, her tail rising and slapping the forest floor.

"Kat, the mosquitoes are eating me alive. I need to shift back into a jaguar to protect myself. Will you come with us to the hut, and we'll explain?" Maya asked, her words rushed.

Kat's eyes opened again, and this time she tried to raise her head. Again, she blinked as if she was dizzy, then stirred a little more. When she was lying on her stomach, her head up, Maya said again, "You have to return with us. It's too deadly out here for you alone."

Maya couldn't wait any longer and shifted before Kat's eyes, stretching her muscles and appearing as a blur of golden, tanned skin as she stood as a human and then with a golden pelt with black rosettes decorating her skin in her jaguar form. Maya dropped to her four paw pads as a jaguar and waited.

Connor watched Kat, worried she would bolt or faint again. She seemed half out of it still. He nudged her with his face, and she looked up at him, her greenish-golden eyes gazing into his, her expression one of confusion. He wanted desperately to tell her everything would be all right.

She seemed to want to stay here forever, gathering her wits and trying to sort out her feelings. Then finally she slowly rose to her feet as if it took the greatest effort. He still worried that she meant to run, that she was pretending to be indisposed so she could race past him before he suspected her ploy. When she had knocked him out of the tree with a swipe of her paw, surprising him to such a degree, he couldn't believe she had bested him.

If he hadn't been so concerned about what she was thinking about them and the mess she was in, he would have been amused. He admired her for her strength of character, for not allowing herself to be bullied into action. But he knew the only way to get the upper hand with her was to climb back up on the tree branch and catch *her* off guard this time.

Wavering slightly, she appeared unsteady on her feet, and he thought she was still attempting to overcome the shock of them being shape-shifters.

He nudged her with his face again, trying to head her in the right direction. At first, she balked, but then she turned, and Maya twisted around and began to lead the way. At first, Kat just watched her while Connor studied Kat's body language. Jaguars normally didn't vocalize a whole lot. More of their communication was nonverbal, such as giving off scents that would clue one another to their intentions or warn other animals off. Household cats learned to vocalize more with their human companions to get what they wanted. But jaguars didn't need to.

But Connor and Maya were also human, so they behaved somewhat differently from their big cat cousins. They were used to communicating as humans. But still, they were limited to what their jaguar vocalizations would permit. A roar, kind of a cough, grunts, meows. And though purring wasn't usually something they did, since they were one of the roaring cats—which included lions, tigers, and jaguars—they did emit kind of a purring sound when they breathed out.

And that's what Kat was doing now. Purring in a jaguar way. He liked the way she sounded, the way she moved, the way she reacted to him, no matter the circumstances.

Then as if she had no other choice, she ran to catch up to Maya. Connor breathed a tentative sigh of relief and followed close behind, watching her tail swish back and forth, taking in her heavenly sexy scent, and wanting her for his own. There was no doubt in his mind that this wouldn't be easy.

And they had a long way to go before he and Maya
could get Kat safely to their home in Texas.

—⁓—

Maya had so badly wanted Kat to be Connor's mate that
she hadn't considered all of the potential pitfalls. She
was glad her brother didn't seem angry with her. In his
usual way, he was trying to make the most of what could
be a bad situation. He truly was interested in making Kat
his mate, so how could he be too irritated with Maya
when she had helped to make it happen? Maya hoped
Kat would also want him for her own.

Except now, they really did have a problem with
getting Kat home safely without her shifting at the
wrong time and getting them all into a lot of hot water.
But Maya was sure that she and Connor could come
up with something that would get them through this
situation intact.

As for Kat, Maya was sure Kat would forgive her
once she learned how advantageous being a shifter
was and how wonderful having Connor as her mate
would be. And Maya was not forgetting how Kat
would have a sister all at once, too. Kat couldn't be
unhappy about that.

Maya was delighted when Kat began to follow her.
Before that, she'd figured they were going to have a real
fight on their hands to get Kat to go with them. They
couldn't force her; they had to show her how much they
wanted her to be part of the family. Maya was already
thinking they might have to find the local shaman for
some kind of tranquilizer they could use on Kat to
get her to comply with their wishes until they could

convince her she would be all right. If they tranquilized her, would she turn? Stay as a jaguar? Human?

Anything they did was iffy.

To Maya's relief, Kat was sticking close for now while Connor took up the rear. Kat had gone a long distance from the hut, crossed several tributaries, and hadn't left her scent much of anywhere, so Maya was glad she had roared for them and finally clawed the tree.

Maya had been worried Kat might have been injured, but she appeared fine, except for being shook up. Maya wanted to check out the other jaguar that had been roaring while he tried to locate Kat. What if he was a jaguar-shifter? For now, though, her loyalty was to her brother and Kat. Maya's own needs had to come second, considering how much of a bind she had put everyone in.

When they reached the hut, Maya waited for Kat to go up the steps first, but she just stared at them. Maya looked back at Connor to see his take on the situation. He raised his brows slightly, but then looked back at Kat and continued to wait. He wasn't going to push her.

Maya fought pacing. She wanted to sleep through what remained of the night. But suddenly Kat sat down on her rump as if she just couldn't walk another step, climb the stairs, or move a muscle.

Connor was strong, but could he carry Kat up the stairs while she was in her jaguar form? She didn't appear to be balking about being here, just that she was too tired…

No, not too tired. Kat began to blur in forms, first a cat and then a human.

Connor quickly shifted also and lifted Kat into his arms to carry her up the stairs. She was like a rag doll, all her energy spent. She still wasn't herself after being sick for so many days, and all her exertion as a jaguar had taken more energy than she could afford.

Maya raced up the stairs after them, entered the screened-in porch, and stood in the doorway of the hut, her tail twitching back and forth as she waited to see what Connor wanted her to do. Connor had already placed Kat on the bed and pulled the cover over her naked body. He slipped on a pair of boxers as he watched Kat, as if he was afraid she would try to leave again. Her head resting on his pillow, she stared at Connor, not saying a word.

The night still cloaked the jungle in inky darkness, but it appeared they wouldn't be getting much sleep.

─────

Exhausted, Kat stared at Connor, unable to believe he was what she thought he had to be. He was gorgeous, his golden eyes filled with worry as he observed her. She couldn't process all that had happened, no matter how much she tried to convince herself that none of this was a dream.

She didn't say anything, waiting for him to speak first. What if she tried to talk, and she roared instead? She still had the heightened jaguar senses—sense of smell, hearing, night vision. That she might roar when she attempted human speech seemed only logical.

Connor sat down on the bed next to her, as if he was attempting to show her that he would no longer keep any socially respectable distance from her. That she was his. Naked. Covered only in a light coverlet. And she felt vulnerable.

He touched her hair spread out over his pillow.

"Kathleen," he said formally, his words spoken softly, "you're one of us now."

One of us. What did that mean?

She didn't say anything, just stared into his beautiful eyes. She was certain Maya was watching them through the screen door, since Kat hadn't heard it open and close.

"What are you?" she asked just as softly, so... so tired, but she had to know, she had to learn all she could before she could sleep. She wondered if they could morph into anything, like on the reruns of a sci-fi series she used to watch where some aliens could change into anything—even melding into metal or wood or water. She was glad that her voice had come out normally.

What if they could become eagles and soar over the jungle? Or porpoises and swim across the oceans? Or a snake slithering in the grass? She didn't like the idea of being a slithering snake, but being a bird could be fun.

What were they really? Aliens from another planet? Any of it seemed too unreal to consider, but she had to know, although her head was pounding and she could barely keep her eyes open.

"We're jaguar-shifters," he said, his voice still quiet and reassuring, his hand still touching her hair as if it made him feel connected to her in some way or he thought she would feel comforted by his gentle touch.

She did. His touching her like this was reminiscent of the way he had taken care of her when she had been so sick. "You can only change into *jaguars*?"

He smiled... genuinely smiled as if he had never expected her to ask such a question. "Just jaguars, Kat. Nothing else. We were born this way."

"Born..." she whispered. "How...?"

He gave her a half shrug. "Just like with regular people. We had a mother and dad, and our mother birthed us at the local hospital just like normal."

"You... what... what if you had shifted in the middle of being born? Or couldn't you have until you reached puberty, or something?" She could just imagine the poor human woman giving birth to a couple of cubs—and the looks on the doctor's and nurses' faces. And then when she was nursing them. Their teeth and claws... even thinking about such a thing made her breasts ache.

"Our mother could have birthed us as a jaguar, and we would have been cubs if that had happened."

Kat closed her gaping mouth.

"When we were young, we were tied to our mother's shifting. When she would shift, we would. When we were older, we knew enough not to shift when it was dangerous to do so."

"You can control it?" she asked, surprised.

She sure couldn't control it. One minute she was staring up at the steps to the hut, intending to climb them, and then in the next instant, she was dizzy and unbelievably tired and couldn't move another inch. Couldn't even stand. And then? She turned! And then she was sitting there as a human, naked and unable to stand or climb the stairs.

And then? Connor shifted! He was just as naked as her, sexier than any man she had ever seen nude. Then he scooped her up with tenderness—if she hadn't been so tired and stressed, she would have felt much more than *just* shocked—and carried her into the hut.

God, he was gorgeous. If she hadn't been so shook up and tired, she would have enjoyed the intimacy between them more—their bared skin heated as they touched one another, and the way he was so hard, virile, and sexy. But more than that. He was kind and protective, careful not to appear brusque or annoyed, but genuinely concerned for her well-being. He had to have been irritated with her when she wouldn't come down from the tree deep in the jungle and he had wanted her to come home with them. He had to have been incensed when she actually knocked *him* off the branch. In front of his sister, too.

She was certain it couldn't have been good for his alpha male ego.

At first, Kat thought he had been aggravated with her when he jumped so quickly back onto her branch and then shoved her off. But she realized afterward that by reacting so fast, he had caught her off guard. That time, he had gotten her out of the tree like he had wanted, not that he was irritated with her. Just concerned that they needed to get her back to the hut.

She frowned. Omigod, what if she had shifted earlier? In the tree? Without a stitch of clothing on?

This was truly a nightmare.

Chapter 13

KAT LET OUT HER BREATH AND STARED AT CONNOR'S naked chest, contemplating just how gorgeous he was. All tanned muscle, with light golden hair trailing down to his boxers. No battle scars. No tattoos or freckles. Just unblemished golden skin. Before he had slipped into a pair of black boxers, she had gotten an eyeful of an erection she had stirred up, tan the way the rest of his skin was, and the golden curls surrounding it. Did he lie out in the Texas sun and soak it up?

For a second, she stared at his lap as he sat next to her on the bed, just studying her without saying a word. Then her eyes widened, and she looked back at his eyes. She had been eyeing his jaguar male package—just to determine which sex he was—when he had jumped into the tree to join her the first time she had seen him as a jaguar. She realized that had been *him*. Connor. In the jaguar flesh.

He had been checking her out when she was soaking wet, staring at her breasts as a big, old, safe cat. But he hadn't been all cat. Or safe. He had been a man who had been intrigued with a woman alone in the jungle.

She groaned to herself, trying to remember what else had happened between them when she had thought he was only a jaguar. Nothing, she hoped.

"We were born with the genes," he finally said.

Kat swallowed hard. "But I wasn't." Which meant

what? Did they know many who had been changed like her? What difference would it make in her case, as compared to jaguar-shifters who were born that way? Besides the obvious, which was that she didn't have control over her shifting like they did. "How will I be different?"

His gaze remained on hers, although she saw a shadow of concern in the darkened depths of his eyes. "Truthfully, I don't know."

This was so not good. "Where… where are you from?"

"Texas," he said, offering a small smile. "Just like I said."

"You're not human," she said, frowning at him.

"Not like regular humans." He sighed and brushed her cheek with the back of his hand. "But we're human when in human form and jaguar in our cat form. Although we retain our human thought processes while a cat and our cat senses when we're human."

She wrinkled her nose. "I ate a raw fish. I would *never* have eaten a raw fish if I had retained my human sensibilities."

He smiled. "As a jaguar, you'll want to satisfy your hunger in a feral cat's way. It's instinctive. You hadn't had dinner. You were hungry. Fishing for your dinner came naturally. Eating meat raw is usually the only way we eat in our jaguar form. No need to cook. Our stomachs can handle it. We don't need spices to make it taste better. We eat to survive."

On some level, she could understand the concept. But she was still human and the notion that she would eat raw meat didn't appeal. "So then Maya changed me?"

"She said she scratched you. I wouldn't have thought that would have done it, but apparently it did."

Kat stared at the bed for a moment, then frowned up at Connor. "She licked me afterward. I worried a little that she would get a taste of my blood and want more."

"Ah," he said. "That's how she did it."

"Why? Why did she change me?" Kat couldn't keep an upset tone out of her voice. She was something so alien to herself now that she couldn't grasp the ramifications. She didn't think she minded that Connor and his sister were different. They couldn't help what they were. But she did mind that she herself had changed.

But then she wondered—if she had discovered what they were, would they have had to resort to what Maya had done anyway? Change her? Or kill her even? Surely they couldn't let the world know what they were.

"She wanted me to have a mate," Connor said, his tone matter-of-fact.

Kat's eyes widened. Not that she was totally surprised, but still, it seemed… medieval.

Connor let out his breath. "And she wanted you to be her sister."

Kat bit her lower lip, trying to focus on one thought as millions of questions swirled through her mind. "Why me? Besides the fact that I was stuck here with you in the jungle and made for an easy target."

"Kat, our kind don't easily take in strangers and develop a fondness for them. I didn't want her to turn you, although I assumed she would try. I wanted to take you to the resort before it was too late. But you were too sick."

"That's why you didn't want me to visit you in Texas. Or with Maya, rather. You were afraid she'd try again if she wasn't successful the first time." Now his reaction to Kat made some sense. His interest in her, yet his need to keep his distance once she was feeling better.

Despite his wanting to stay away from her, Kat recalled Maya's words to him: *"You were dying to know what had happened to her when she was wounded. You didn't eat, couldn't sleep, and we even left here early because you were so disconsolate. And as soon as we returned here, what did you do? Went straight back to the place where she'd been wounded, and then you didn't come back for hours."*

Just like Kat had felt compelled to return to the Amazon and find Connor to thank him for rescuing her. She had often thought of him, bare-chested and barefooted, leaning over her, cutting the rope from her wrists, and then hurrying to bind her wounds. His eyes had focused on hers with so much concern and tenderness that she had often wondered what it would be like to be with a man like him.

Connor cleared his throat. "Yes, I was afraid she'd bite you to change you. Neither of us has ever tried to turn someone before. She knew I wouldn't do it."

Kat shifted her gaze from his muscled torso to his face. He hadn't wanted her enough to change her himself. But then again, that made him more honorable, didn't it? That he did indeed care for her but wouldn't turn her against her will. "I wouldn't have allowed it if I could have prevented it."

"So now… you're stuck with me?" That was a disagreeable notion.

His mouth curved in a predatory way. "Hell, Kat, I wouldn't have turned you, but you've got to sense the chemistry between us. If I'd met you somewhere in Texas, you still would have garnered all my attention."

"And?" She was dying to know what he would have done about it.

He shrugged. "I might have taken you out for a drink, maybe dinner, but I never would have gotten too close. Developing feelings for a human would be risky business, and I couldn't afford it."

"You would have wanted more than a drink."

He gave her a dark smile. "With you, I couldn't want less."

"But you had vowed never to turn someone."

"Yes. I wasn't comfortable with the idea of living a double life—as strictly a human in front of a woman I loved and, behind her back, as a jaguar-shifter with a sister cut from the same spotted cloth."

She still couldn't believe any of it, yet what had just happened had happened. She couldn't deny it any longer. Used to dealing with matters that didn't exactly go her way—the loss of her men on the mission, Roger leaving her, foster homes that hadn't worked out—she'd make the most of this new change in her life. Somehow.

Kat took a deep breath and exhaled. "Now what?"

"Now we need to get you to Texas and hope to God you don't shift somewhere along the way and create a real situation."

She groaned, not having considered that new wrinkle in her life.

"Sorry, Kat."

This nightmare was growing. "If we get to Texas, what then?"

"Then? We're a family. You'll live with us."

"And I have no say?" All of a sudden, she felt as though she had lost total control over her life, and at a time when she thought she had just gotten it back!

"You can't... live on your own, Kat. It's too dangerous. If anyone learned what you were, they'd lock you up, study you, believe you were some alien race. No jaguar would be safe once you were discovered. There aren't that many jaguars left in the wild. Can you imagine what kind of a sensation you'd be? They'd eventually find Maya and me. Although we're careful, some have seen us with our jaguar pets—Maya with a jaguar, or me with Maya when she's shifted into her jaguar coat."

Kat hadn't thought of that. In the back of her mind, she just thought they wanted to keep her because she would be like them. Not that she would need to be with those of her kind—for protection and companionship.

Yet she had read a lot about jaguars and their behavior, and they didn't live as a family—at least not for long. The male stayed with the female during courtship and mating, but after the mother birthed her cubs, he was out of there, by her choice. Each male serviced a number of females, their territories overlapping his bigger one. Would she be considered part of a harem? *No way, José*.

"But jaguars don't take a mate permanently. Any old jaguar will do. Just like a domesticated cat. Just like dogs," she said. She had always figured that when she settled down and married a man, like she had planned with Roger, it would be forever.

"We're human, too, and I promise if you decide to be my mate, I won't stray."

"What about others? You can't be the only ones."

That was a horrible idea. What if they were the only ones of their kind? Then Maya would have to turn a man, too, if she could. But what if he turned out to be dangerous?

What was Kat thinking? What if *she* became dangerous? What if she couldn't control what she was, got hungry, and went after the neighbor's dogs—or kids, even? Although she reminded herself that she had vowed she wouldn't eat a monkey or colorful parrot, so she must have some control over being a feral beast.

"No, we aren't the only ones. But with jaguars as elusive as they are, finding others of our kind is close to impossible."

"That's why Maya asked if I had a brother."

Connor glanced back in the direction of the screen door. "She'd better not contemplate it."

Kat harrumphed under her breath. "Yeah, one of us is bad enough."

Connor turned back to study her, compassion in his eyes. "I'm sorry, Kat. I wouldn't have done this to you, but I intend to make it up to you any way that I can."

Frowning, Kat chewed on her lower lip. "What about the other jaguar? Roaring in the jungle. It was a male, wasn't it?"

"Yeah. I hadn't been marking our territory well enough since we came back here this time."

"Because of taking care of me—because I was so sick."

"You were our first priority."

"So… is he a regular cat or a shifter, do you think?"

Maya called out from the hammock. "It doesn't matter, Kat. Taking care of you is what's important to us now."

Kat could barely keep her eyes open, but she had to take care of one little thing. "Can I brush my teeth?"

Shaking his head, he smiled. "You'll get used to the transition of eating raw meat as a jaguar, then shifting into your human form."

He helped her to the washstand where she brushed her teeth with the spare toothbrush and a generous amount of minty toothpaste.

Then he carried her back to bed where Kat closed her eyes, unable to keep them open any longer. "Maya needs a mate, doesn't she?" she whispered to Connor.

"We don't have to worry about that now. Sleep and we'll talk more in the morning." He leaned over and kissed her forehead. "'Night, Kat. If you get the urge to shift, wake me. Please. You can't roam through the jungle alone. The rain forest is too dangerous for you."

She took a deep breath, nodded her head ever so slightly, and then, unable to stay awake, she slipped back into the world of dreams.

Connor stared at her for what seemed an eternity, unwilling to leave her side. He kept worrying she would shift again and take off, unable to help herself. But now she knew something about them and what she was. If she shifted and needed to stretch her legs as a jaguar, he hoped she would wake him and wait for him to go with her.

Glancing back at the screen door, he couldn't help admiring his sister for wanting only to take care of Kat, ignoring her own needs to investigate the male jaguar and see if he might also be a shifter. He knew Maya would want to check him out.

He caressed Kat's arm. She shouldn't have run like

she did. She still wasn't well enough to expend that much energy.

He looked at Maya's bed but couldn't force himself to retire to it. Not without worrying that Kat might shift and leave again, and he couldn't help being concerned about the other male jaguar. What if he was a shifter and he found Kat alone in the jungle? Their mother had said their father would never stay with her. It didn't matter that she was the only shifter he had ever found. He couldn't stay with one woman, period. Kat didn't deserve a man like that.

Connor snorted and folded his arms. Hell, he wouldn't be like his old man.

Maya slipped into the hut and rubbed Connor's back. "She's sleeping. Go to bed. I'm sure one or both of us will wake if she tries to leave again."

She hugged him, then returned to her hammock on the porch.

Connor wasn't taking any chances. He climbed into the small bed with Kat, pulling the wispy curtains around them as though they were a prince and princess in an *Arabian Nights* tale. Intent on making sure she wasn't going anywhere without waking him first, he covered them with the light bed linen, closed his eyes, and tried to think of anything except how sexy she felt snuggled against his body.

Chapter 14

SOMETIME IN THE MIDDLE OF THE NIGHT, KAT GREW restless. The first thought that came to Connor's mind was that she was shifting into a jaguar. He wrapped his arms around her and pulled her close, spooning her, while recognizing that he might be holding a big cat in his embrace at any moment instead of a soft, silky-skinned, naked woman.

She still smelled heavenly, like the fragrance of oranges and tangerines. He'd scoffed at Maya for buying the citrus-scented soap to wash in, wanting something less… feminine. Not now. He couldn't stop breathing in Kat's unique scent mixed with the sweet citrus fruits. He'd never eat another orange without thinking of washing every sweet part of her body in the waterfall.

For some time, she lay still, quiet in his arms, as if he had chased away any urge to shift. But then she tried to get free from him, kicking with her feet though her legs were twisted in the light cover, and he again tightened his hold on her.

His heroics earned him a hard-on, and he cursed his inability to keep his rampant craving for her at bay. He tried to think of anything but the way her warm, supple body felt pressed against him. He tried to avoid breathing in her sexy feline scent, mixed with the fragrance of the shampoo and soaps he'd used to wash every delectable inch of her body. He tried not to listen to her soft murmurs like those that he envisioned she would make as he brought her to climax at some later date. But he was drawn to her, needy, desiring her to the core.

At first, he thought she might be trying to get away to shift, but when she didn't, he believed she might be having a nightmare. "Shhh, Kat, it's just me."

With her back to him still, she swung her clenched fist around and struck him in the hip. *Night terrors.* She was having a night terror, and she was trying to beat on him like she said she had done to that worthless scumbag, Roger, her ex-fiancé.

As far as Connor was concerned, Roger had deserved whatever she dished out. But Connor was determined to chase away her night terrors. Just as he had stated, she would not beat on him when they lay down together.

He took her hand and unclenched her fist, kissing the tender skin at her wrist and then the palm of her hand, though she squirmed to get loose.

"It's just me," he said again, whispering against her ear, kissing and nuzzling his face against hers. She quit moving, quit struggling, quit trying to fight him.

He took a deep breath, glad he could chase away her fear and encourage her to sleep again. But then she turned her head to stare over her shoulder at him, her eyes wide, luminous, and comprehending.

She licked her lips, making them glisten, and he watched with fascination as her tongue slipped back into her mouth.

She twisted around to face him.

"Did I hurt you?" she whispered, her eyes still wide, her expression glum.

He cast her an elusive smile, amused she would think

striking him had made any impact, and shook his head. "No. You gave me a love pat."

His comment earned him a sexy smile. He thought they'd both just sleep, although he couldn't deny he wished to kiss her and push any hint of a reoccurring nightmare from her mind, but only if Kat was willing. Then the telltale sound of Maya pouncing on the ground below them changed his mind. Having shifted into her jaguar form, Maya was leaving them alone. As soon as Maya left, Kat seemed to be of the same mind as Connor. She began to kiss his mouth lightly as if she needed his touch, his affection, some acknowledgment that everything was all right between them.

He kissed her back, keeping the same measured pressure, not wanting to take this further than she wished.

But then her hands stroked his bare chest, her movements more desperate.

She seemed starved with need, and if she was willing, he wasn't holding back, either. Their tongues intertwined, thrust, caressed, their breath minty fresh. Lips melded, brushed, kissed.

Her fingers yanked at the waistband of his boxers, trying to pull them down over his hips. He jerked them off and threw them on the floor.

She glanced down at him and took in his nakedness, his full-blown erection, his hard nipples.

He was already hot just from cuddling with her, trying to get his thoughts off the waterfall kisses they'd shared. He remembered the way she'd felt as his hands washed every inch of her, her rigid nipples and clit swelling beneath his touch, and how he had known she wanted him physically. And emotionally, he was certain. But now...

Hell, now that she was feeling stronger, he wanted to take this all the way. He wouldn't wait, not when she was so eager. He cupped a breast, kneading a nipple and soliciting a soft mew from her mouth. The sweet, sexy sound she made was his undoing.

He kissed her mouth again, but this time with a pressing urgency that revealed just how much he wanted her. He craved claiming her for his own, wanting to put his scent on her, to prove she was his to anyone who had any other notion.

She pulled her mouth from his and kissed his throat and his chest, whispering, "Love me."

Not make love to me, but *love me.*

That made him pause. He lifted her chin and looked into her eyes, saw them awash in tears, and he hugged her tight. "I will." He kissed the top of her head and added, "I do."

With all his heart, he meant it. He couldn't envision returning to the jungle without Kat. Or returning home without her, either. Nothing would ever be the same.

The kissing renewed. Their lips and tongues touched and tasted, wet and soft and eager. The fervent need to bond, to connect in only the way a man and woman could, to become one in body and soul, shook him to the core. His hands cupped her face and their tongues mated, while her body arched against his, pleading for completion.

He'd never felt that way before when he'd had sex with a woman. Because that's all it had been. A quick release and it was done.

But this… this was so much more.

He'd found his mate in Kat, and he wasn't losing her now. The cover was already tossed on the floor, the light curtains draping out the world. The sounds of the birds and frogs and bugs disappeared as all he could focus on was the blood pounding in his ears and Kat's soft murmurs of pleasure. He swept his hand down her hips, enjoying the satiny feel of her skin, the shapely curve of her flesh, the firmness of her thigh.

"Hurry," she pleaded quietly, and he wondered if she was worried that Maya was in the jungle all alone or that she might return soon.

He slipped his hand between Kat's legs and felt the silky wetness, the dark curls wet with need. She arched toward his questing fingers. His cock jerked in response as if following her lead of its own accord. Fighting the urge to plunge deep inside her, he began stroking her swollen flesh, and she looked as though she was ready to bolt from the bed.

"Uh," she said in a moan of half pleasure, half disbelief. He tongued a nipple and her eyes closed. Her tongue swept over her lips, and her hands slid down his back, her nails tracing his skin and his muscles in a gentle caress. His fingers kneaded her swollen nub until she opened for him like a flower unfurling before the sun.

The invitation given, he pressed a finger deep inside her. She startled a little at the intrusion, then pushed her body toward him, forcing him to go deeper, wanting more.

He smiled at her aggressiveness, loving it, loving her.

His thumb continued to stroke her, and his name slipped from her lips in a whimper as she reached around to cup him. Already engorged to the spilling point, he quickly clasped her hand in his.

"Not this time," he whispered.

Her eyes opened and flashed dark green with flecks of burning gold. They were beautiful eyes, luminescent in the dark. Her mouth pursed and she looked ready to protest, but he pressed the tip of his cock against her hot flesh, and she pushed against him before he was ready to end the foreplay.

Again he smiled at her and was rewarded with the most devilish smile back.

Unable to hold himself in check, he pushed into her slowly, filling her, and felt the heavenly tightness of her sheath expanding to allow him in, deeper and deeper.

Her hot, wet flesh clenched against his invasion but then eased and caressed him, holding him tight and forcing him to take it easy. Kat had stilled, her hands on his hips, her eyes wide, her moistened lips parted, her breathing nonexistent.

For an instant, he took in the beauty of their joined bodies, her dark curls splayed against the pillows, her even darker short curls wet and encircling his shaft, her skin glistening with perspiration. He wanted to memorize every detail of the sounds and smells and sights in that instant to take with him wherever he went.

Then he thrust once, twice, her body responding eagerly to his penetration, her hips angling to get the most of him. He loved the way she wanted more of him. Now. Not at his slower pace, but at her quicker one. Heels dug into the bed, she welcomed his thrusts as her hands skimmed his back and ass.

He began to stroke her again, watching her expression and enjoying the way her eyes darkened to midnight, the way her mouth parted to take in small gulps of air, the way she flowered under his touch.

"Harder," she rasped out. "More." She groaned. "Faster."

He wanted to laugh, to shout with joy at the way she was ordering him about. He knew the moment the climax hit her by the ripples of spasms clenching his cock, the way her fingers dug into his flesh, the harsh exhale of breath and the words, "Omigod, Connor," slipping out of her mouth in a breathy, sexy way.

She was a sultry siren and wickedly all his.

Kat didn't have a chance to marvel at the ecstasy Connor had made her feel with the first bona fide climax she'd ever experienced because he thrust his broad cock deeper inside her with renewed vigor as if her coming had spurred him on to finish before he exploded.

Some primal urge buried deep inside her took over, and as his chest brushed against her aroused and oh-so-sensitive nipples, she bit his shoulder.

Not hard. A love bite, but it made him pause and stare at her for a moment in surprise. She thought she'd done something wrong, although it had felt so right, so natural and instinctive, but then he smiled down at her as if she was the dearest person in his life. His eyes were clouded with lust, and his blood was beating like the drums the natives had been thumping when she'd been so sick.

He pushed inside her again, long and hard and deeper, then thrust quickly as if he couldn't hold back any longer.

She raked her nails down his skin, careful not to draw blood, just like she hadn't when she bit him. But the urge to claw and bite and claim him—to breathe in his masculine, musky cat scent and to wear it on her as he wore hers on him—overwhelmed her.

His hands were on her hips, keeping her locked in

place, not allowing her to thrust against him in a frantic need to finish this, and he felt the pleasure rising, intensifying. She was again ready to be set free, like molten lava seeking release.

His hot seed filled her just as she felt the new climax that sent her careening to the sun. She cried out as his mouth sought hers, his tongue pressing inside, their bodies still joined.

"We're not done," he promised, and she wrapped her legs around his hips, ready for more.

They all slept late, until something disturbed Kat's sleep as she realized Connor was holding her loosely in his embrace in bed. She wasn't sure what it had been. Maybe he had twitched in his sleep and awakened her. Embarrassed that she had struck him with her fist the night before, she couldn't believe that not only had he not minded, but that he had made love to her, not once, but several times during the night and, most of all, had continued to sleep with her. Roger would have gotten angry, acting as though she had done it on purpose. He had even slapped her back once, saying she had been hysterical. Which she hadn't been.

He'd used that as an excuse to get her back for hitting him and disturbing his sleep, and that was the living end for her.

What a difference there was between the two men. She hadn't meant to make love to Connor, but she'd wanted the closeness, the tenderness, the heat and raw passion. And he had been all too happy to oblige her.

She couldn't believe she'd bitten him—twice. Roger

would have had her quarantined and tested for rabies if she'd done that to him.

She sighed. Had she fought Connor again in the middle of the night? As hard as she tried, she couldn't remember. She hoped she hadn't. But then she smiled, thinking of the comment he had made. If she had slept with him, she wouldn't be beating on him. And his comment that her hitting him was only a love pat wasn't nearly the truth. But she loved him for making light of it.

Luxuriating in the feel of his hard muscles pressed against her backside, she basked in the way he kept her close, unlike the way Roger had kept his distance in bed after they'd made love.

Then she thought about all that she had learned about Connor and Maya and herself—as far as being jaguar-shifters went. Now in the light of the day, she couldn't believe it was true. At least part of her couldn't get used to the notion. Another part, that half of her that recalled her moonlight run, knew she wasn't the same as before. Now she had big, dangerous teeth and a furry body when she least expected it.

Connor stirred, pushed the hair at the nape of her neck away, and tenderly kissed her sensitive skin. She purred. Turning to kiss him back, she hoped Maya was sleeping soundly and that she and Connor wouldn't disturb her. But then she heard men's voices intruding among the sounds of the jungle. Before she could react, Connor bolted upright.

"They wouldn't give us any trouble, would they?" Kat whispered, every muscle stiffening in preparation for action. She had an instant flashback of the firefight between Gonzales's men, her own, and herself. She needed a rifle.

Connor slipped off the bed and pulled on his trousers. "Most of the time, no. Not unless they're drug runners. Even then they usually leave us alone, and we stay out of their way. But sometimes they push too far into our territory."

"Then what?" she asked, her voice still hushed.

He looked out the window. "Then we have to do whatever it takes for self-preservation." He glanced back at Kat and added, "The natives say that a man travels with a jaguar near here, but sometimes they've seen a woman with the jaguar."

"You and Maya?" Kat asked.

"Yeah. The rumors keep the villagers away from our neck of the woods. We believe they're fearful that we might do something to them if they don't leave us to ourselves. But others who are not local tromp through here from time to time. They're ruthless and we have to be just as ruthless back."

"You have to kill them?"

"It's either that or they kill us or attempt to take us hostage. They wouldn't free us for years until someone paid our ransom. And we don't have anyone who would pay to have us released. Confinement as a jaguar-shifter out here in the jungle isn't something that we could live with."

That she could agree with. "But you come here anyway."

"Most of the time it's safe enough."

Maya slipped in through the screen door, her eyes wide. "Four men. They're looking for the dark-haired American woman by the name of Kathleen McKnight."

Connor's mouth gaped, then he turned to stare at Kat. "What is this all about?"

Kat frowned at him. "Manuel... he must have come back for me." She began to button her shirt. "He must have gotten some men together to try and find me."

"And if it's not him?" Maya asked, her eyes narrowed with worry as she tied her hair back into a ponytail.

"Who else would know my name?" Kat asked incredulously.

Connor shook his head. "Gonzales."

She glowered at him. "I'm no longer in the Army."

"All right. But you can't go with this Manuel, if that's who is with the men, or anyone else. Not now that you are one of us."

Kat snapped her mouth shut. Intellectually, she had known that. Connor was right. She just hadn't wrapped her mind around the fact that she wasn't exactly *normal* any longer.

"I need to speak with them to let Manuel know I'm all right and that I'm returning to the States with you. He'll go away."

"Maybe. Maybe not. Who knows what their agenda truly is." Connor got his rifle and handed it to Maya. "Take the lookout post. I'll stay with Kat." He looked down at Kat as Maya hurried out of the hut. "You can't speak with them. We don't know who they really are or what they're up to."

She was glad that he took protecting her from any eventuality seriously, but she still couldn't believe that they would have to kill anyone to stay alive themselves. Then she instantly tossed that reasoning out. If these men were anything like Gonzales's men, she knew just what they were capable of.

Would Maya and Connor shift to take care of the menace? Or use Connor's rifle?

Killing as jaguars seemed barbaric, but she shuddered, realizing the jungle was a beast-eat-beast world. Definitely survival of the fittest.

She'd had firsthand experience with that already— one year ago, in this very jungle.

Chapter 15

HIS SENSES ON HIGH ALERT, SNIFFING THE AIR AND listening for any movement, Connor walked with Kat onto the screened porch. He had a bad feeling about the men looking for Kat and didn't like where this seemed to be headed.

Then to his astonishment, Maya roared. What the hell? She was supposed to be watching from the lookout post with the rifle aimed and ready.

He knew her unexpected behavior meant that the men they had heard talking in the jungle were dangerous. Maya must have overheard more of their conversation and changed tactics.

"Kat, can you shift?" he asked quietly.

She would be safer as a jaguar, he thought. She could climb high into a tree and stay hidden in the canopy while he and Maya took care of the men.

She shook her head, her expression schooled.

"Stay here, then."

"I can shoot. You know I was in the Army. I had rifle and handgun training. I even qualified as a sharpshooter. I can shoot."

He knew she must be able to, though he had not seen her actually kill anyone.

"I don't want them to know where you are or even be able to get close to you." His heart was pounding furiously, and he realized he didn't want her anywhere near the men. He could see losing her in a shower of bullets. Yes, he and his sister healed more quickly than humans and could survive injuries a human might not be able to. Although if they bled out too fast, their healing genetics wouldn't have time to take care of the wounds. But what if that part of the genetic change hadn't taken effect for Kat? What if she wasn't *exactly* like them?

"I can't shift," she said, her voice urgent, hushed.

He wasn't sure if she meant she truly couldn't or she wouldn't, although he suspected she didn't have the ability to shift at will like he and his sister could. Hopefully, with time, she would.

"Come on." He took her to a vine-covered tree trunk that looked as though it was part of the vegetation, a naturally occurring fallen trunk high up in the canopy that butted up against their primitively made lookout post.

It was a heavily concealed spot high in the trees that easily hid the viewer from sight, perfect for observing unwelcome visitors while staying camouflaged from view. He stood with her there now, not wanting to leave her but having no other choice. He didn't want her to see what he might have to do to the men, and he had to hurry and join Maya before she got herself into a dangerous bind.

He would judge the men while listening to their conversation and learning what they had in mind. If they turned out to be a danger to Kat or his sister or himself, he would take care of them.

Maya was already stalking the men, listening and waiting for him to join her. That's what her roaring was all about. He hoped she wouldn't act until he was there to watch her back.

"Maya's out there," he warned Kat, as if getting permission from her to take his leave.

Kat looked determined to see this through and scooped up the rifle lying where Maya had left it on the wooden floor of the small lookout platform. Maya's clothes were sitting in a pile in one corner where she had shifted.

"Go," Kat urgently whispered. "I'll be all right. I've done this before. Protect Maya."

Her raw concern for Maya touched him. If he'd had any doubts before about Kat's loyalty to him and Maya, he now knew Kat was truly one of them. Part of their little jaguar-shifter team.

He cupped her face quickly, kissed her, and hugged her, wanting to hold her forever and protect her from the evils of the world. Beyond a doubt, he knew she would be his. He might have a time convincing her they were meant to be together, but he would do whatever it took.

Then he released her. He was out of his clothes in no time, feeling Kat's eyes on him the whole time, and then he shifted into his jaguar coat. After giving her one last lingering look, feeling torn by needing to keep both Maya and his sister safe and not being able to be in two places at once, he leaped onto the tree branch above Kat. She gazed up at him and gave him a slight nod, telling him she would be okay.

No matter how much he wanted to believe it would be so, he had his doubts. Anything could go wrong in the rain forest. All he had to do was think back to that day a year ago when Kat had nearly died.

He leaped to another branch and then another, the adrenaline speeding through his blood, propelling him to seek out Maya and the men and determine what they intended to do next.

He didn't want to kill them if he didn't have to. But if he needed to kill to save Maya or Kat's life, or even his own, he would have no qualms about doing it.

—∿∿—

Maya had been following the men, who were still a distance from the hut. They were walking along one of the paths that Maya and Connor had made, so the trek wasn't all that difficult for them. She counted five men, all dark haired and bearded, unwashed and armed to the teeth.

"I still don't know why the hell you left her behind in the jungle, Manuel," one of the men said in Spanish.

Manuel. The man Kat said had been her guide.

"I told you. I was trying to lead Juan's men away from her. If he'd found her, he would have ransomed her. You wouldn't have been able to turn her over to Gonzales, who would have been most generous with all of us. I was doing what I thought you wanted."

"Then later you couldn't find her, damn you. By now she's sure to be dead. If we can find her body, we can give it to Gonzales to prove she's dead, but he won't like it. He had plans for the woman."

"I didn't think it would take me that long to get away from Juan's men. I was afraid they suspected I worked for you and Gonzales. When I returned for her—"

"Yeah, what? Two days later?"

"I couldn't get back. But one of the local villagers swore he saw a man carrying her to the falls in the area. Kathleen had to be the woman, from the description the boy gave of her."

Hell, Maya thought to herself. She had been guarding the falls in her cat form while Connor was helping Kat to wash, but she had never seen anyone watching them. When had it happened?

"The same villager who said that a jaguar god lived near there? That the god had found a new mate?" The hefty man shook his head.

A shiver stole up Maya's spine. These men thought that a jaguar god existed? Had the natives actually seen Maya or Connor shape-shift? This was so not good. She and her brother could hold their own against these men, but Kat could be in real danger.

Movement in the jungle was constant—lizards scurrying across branches, monkeys swinging into nearby trees, birds taking flight, but the large spotted cat that sifted in and out of shadows like a feral predator on the hunt caught Maya's eye. Connor leaped to a branch opposite the tree she was in, acknowledging her with a slight bow of his head. Then his ears perked and his gaze focused on the men.

"What if what they say is true? That a jaguar god lives here? Hunts here? Kills here? What if she's with him? What if he has taken her for his own woman? That would explain why she's still alive," Manuel said.

Hmm, Maya thought. A jaguar god and a goddess, too. *In fact, there are two of us now*. She gave a big cat's version of a smile.

"You sound like you've been getting into our stash," the one who seemed to be in charge said.

"Yeah, but we heard its distant roar late last night all over the damned place. He could be here, watching us now."

"And he will die if he shows his spotted hide here."

Manuel looked nervously about, but he didn't see either Connor or Maya sitting high above them in their jaguar forms, watching them and ready to strike when they had the advantage, if Connor decided it was necessary.

"Besides, didn't you say he lives in a hut on stilts? Why would a jaguar god live in a man-made dwelling? A crummy hut?"

Manuel slashed at a vine with his machete. "He's a man sometimes. I told you. He was carrying the woman to the falls."

"Maybe we can ransom him, too. Surely someone would pay good money for a god," the man said, sounding as though he was making fun of Manuel.

Connor was ready to take the men out because they intended to turn Kat over to Gonzales, and Connor and Maya couldn't get Kat to safety quickly. He motioned to Maya to go after the last man, who was trailing way behind on the path and would soon be out of sight of the other men. Was he afraid to keep up and face what Manuel feared? A jaguar god?

And what had the villagers really seen? Either Maya or him shape-shifting at some time or another? As careful as they had been and as thick as the foliage was, screening them from long-distance viewing, he hadn't thought anybody had ever seen them. He supposed being a jaguar god would be all right as long as the villagers kept it to themselves and the word didn't spread. But the word already seemed to have spread, at least to these men.

What would happen next? If anyone in the scientific

community believed there was any truth to the rumors, Connor could imagine teams of biologists descending on the area to search for the jaguar god. Forget Bigfoot or werewolves. Here, they could have the real thing. Not the stuff of myths or legends, but a true jaguar-shifter.

As far as Connor knew, the big cat-shifter genes had been passed on from generation to generation and had been part of ancient cultures. The problem was that too few jaguars existed, and wherever the jaguar-shifters were, they were too elusive to band together and help each other. Besides, communicating with each other didn't seem to come naturally to their kind.

Maya leaped from her branch to another and continued to move through the canopy until she could come up behind the last man in the group.

He couldn't see what she was going to do next, but he was ready to target the next man who fell behind. Connor had sent Maya after the one who was farthest from the group so she wouldn't have to face several if any of the men sounded an alarm.

As if nothing was amiss, Connor moved through the trees, getting closer to his prey as the primal need to hunt raced through his blood. He prepared to jump from the tree, stalk the man, and pounce.

———

Maya had smelled the wretched man long before she attacked him and witnessed the array of weapons on him—the belts of bullets, the rifle, the guns, the long wicked knives, and the machete. He smelled of weed and sweat and fear.

He was falling farther and farther back from the

others. She assumed that he hoped the other men would encounter the jaguar god first and take it down before he had to deal with it, if such a creature existed. And if things didn't work out for the other men and the jaguar god came out on top? The man she was stalking would vanish into the thick rain forest, pretending he had never been with these thugs. Then he'd hotfoot it out of there and tell the world what he had witnessed.

The moisture from the ground was rising into the steamy atmosphere like primordial mist as it always did in late morning, forming clouds that filled the sky high above the canopy. Thunder booming in the distance warned of an impending storm.

Water from a nearby tributary had overflowed its banks, and the water on the path came to halfway up the man's calves. He sloshed along, the mud sucking at his black boots and gripping them as he struggled to pull one foot out and then the other, his progress slow. He looked warily about, a bearded man with hard, black eyes and the smell of blood on his person. He had killed or injured people and drawn blood; his clothes reeked of it.

Maya could tell from the way he moved that he wasn't injured, so she knew it wasn't his blood. Besides, the blood smelled like it had come from at least three different people.

He kept looking around like an owl, his head twisting back and forth, searching for the jaguar god, she suspected. But she was the goddess of the equation. Connor would take out the man in front of him.

This man wasn't even keeping the guy in front of him in view, although he could hear the men talking up ahead. She suspected that made him feel confident he wasn't getting too far behind.

Suddenly, he tripped over a tree root in the muck and fell to his hands and knees in the muddy water, cursing out loud. That's when she saw the tattoos on his bare shoulder, identifying him as one of the members of a southern drug cartel.

Well, one less now.

She leaped from the tree closest to the path and pounced on him. Pushing his whole body into the water and mud, she kept him buried. He fought to get out from under the weight of her jaguar form, trying to get air. She remained in place, jostling her position a little to keep him under. Until he ceased to struggle. She waited a moment to be sure he was dead. Nothing. Not a flutter of activity.

He was finished.

With her teeth, she grabbed his belt of bullets and dragged his body out of the water. She hoped she could get him to the river—where he would add to the cycle of life by feeding the piranhas once they smelled the blood on his clothes mixing with the river water—without being caught doing it. All his weaponry would eventually fall to the muddy river bottom, with no one knowing anything about it. And none of it would be used against another living soul. He would never torture or kill another human being.

She just had to make sure no one spied her dragging him to the river.

That's what she was thinking when she caught sight of a native boy, maybe twelve or thirteen, scrawny, with wide, dark eyes and carrying a bow and arrows, tipped

most likely with the poison of one of the deadly poisonous frogs that lived in Amazonia.

He was out hunting, and now he had seen her out
hunting, too.

—— ✺ ——

Connor heard the splash on the path behind him, followed by cursing, although what was happening was out
of his view because of the dense foliage and the way the
path twisted and turned through the trees. The man in
front of him hadn't heard the splash, or he might have
called out to see what had happened to his comrade who
had been following him. Like the other man, he was
slowing his already slow-as-a-snail pace as he slogged
through the muddy water.

Connor twisted his head to the side, thinking he heard
the faint sound of Spanish music. But then he realized
the man he was stalking was wearing small earbuds, the
cord attached to each hanging down into a pocket as
he listened to music. *Dumb move.* In the jungle, a man
needed all the senses. Sure, it was noisy and the jungle
sounds never seemed to quit, so a man might think that
nothing would change to alert him that something was
wrong anyway.

But a flight of macaws took off, and the observant
person would have heard them take wing, looked up,
and realized why. A jaguar had been spotted.

Or the splash in the water might have been noted, and
if the man had been all that concerned, he would have
gone back to find a female jaguar hauling his friend off
to be dinner for a bunch of hungry piranha. Just where
this man was bound to end up.

The tattoos on the man's arms indicated that he was part of a gang, and he was armed as if ready to fight in a war, not just take a woman hostage. A shrunken head dangled from a chain at his left pocket, and smears of blood mottled his shirtsleeves.

The man had serious issues. But before long, he wouldn't have them anymore.

He began singing the Spanish words to the song and nodding his head to the beat while trudging through the water at a slower pace. His eyes were on his boots when Connor took him out.

The man would never know what hit him as he went from walking along with a tune in his head to being buried in water with a 250-pound cat pressing his body into the mud. He choked on the water and mud, writhing to get free, but he would never be able to budge the jaguar.

Connor was too heavy, too muscled, too powerful, too determined—a jaguar god. He shook his head at the notion, which was bound to get them into trouble if the villagers shared what they thought they had seen with the rest of the world. Yet he hated to give up his and Maya's jaguar retreat in the Amazon.

He left the dead man floating in the muddy water, eager to stalk the next man before the last three reached Kat. This one would stay put until Maya could return for him and dispose of him in the same manner as the first. Even though he and Maya could use their powerful bite to eliminate the threat at once, it was better if they could terminate the men in a way that didn't make the local populace believe that jaguars were responsible for the men's deaths.

What would happen then? Possibly hunters would

descend on the area and attempt to destroy the jaguars that had a taste for human blood. Even if the jaguars didn't eat the men, they would most likely be considered man-eaters. He and Maya, and now Kat, couldn't afford that kind of trouble.

He hadn't moved very far when he heard muffled shots ring out from the direction of the hut.

Kathleen.

His blood on fire, Connor bolted in her direction.

Chapter 16

THE WAITING WAS KILLING HER AS KAT WATCHED FROM the lookout post. Every movement—a butterfly settling on a leaf nearby, a monkey scrambling through a tree, a lizard raising its nose in the air—caught her attention, though she attempted to remain rigidly focused on the path that led to the hut.

She heard the men slogging through muddy water, figured they must be on a path she hadn't walked before, and listened to see if she could hear any sound that would indicate Connor or Maya was near. That was why every little thing in the trees distracted her. She kept thinking she might see either of them appear as a jaguar, watching her from a tree branch and protecting her, as she was ready to protect them, just as if they were members of her special Army team.

She couldn't make out how many men there were, other than the one who had been talking and Manuel. She still couldn't believe Manuel had planned to hand her over to men who would ransom her, or worse. But she was American, a woman, and had been all alone. He had asked her a million questions while they hiked through the jungle, and she had thought that in his smiling, friendly way, he had just been interested in her Florida roots. But it hadn't been that at all. He had been trying to learn just how valuable she might be.

How well connected.

She had money, sure. Or she wouldn't be down here in the first place. But she certainly hadn't said anything to him about her finances or that she knew how to use a gun. Or that she had been in the military.

But she didn't have anyone back home who would pay her ransom. *She* was the only one who could pay it!

"Where's Miguel?" the leader of the group suddenly asked. "And José?"

Kat's heart hitched to hear them speaking again. They were way too close to her location.

"Waiting for us to do all their dirty work, Carlos," said the other man, who she hadn't heard speak before. He was gruff and annoyed, but he was sticking close to Manuel and the leader. "I told you before, this is how they always act on a job. They wait for us to take all the risks. You wait and see. We'll get the man and woman all bound up, and then here they'll be, as if they'd been with us all along."

Kat strained to see any sign of the men. Had Maya and Connor eliminated the other two? She wanted to pace, wanted to shift—no, she didn't want to do that. As a jaguar, she wasn't sure what she could really do. She knew how to shoot a weapon. Knew how to pursue an enemy with deadly intent. Knew how to wound a man to ensure she could take him prisoner. She just wasn't sure if she could face an enemy if she was in her jaguar form.

Carlos snorted. "The two of them are easy to re-place." He sounded like a cold-blooded killer, which she was certain he was.

The problem was that there were three men. If she shot one, the others would shoot a barrage of bullets in her direction, and she wasn't sure she could manage to shoot anyone else if she was under fire. Actually, she was sure she couldn't. If Maya and Connor were too far away, she would be on her own. Even so, she didn't want them running as jaguars into a gun battle. They wouldn't survive, either.

She had to play it cool, keep her head, and not fire any shots unless it became absolutely necessary.

More thunder rumbled overhead. Glints of lightning flashed through the intermittent spots in the canopy where light filtered through. It was nearly afternoon and very dark with the black clouds hovering overhead. Soon, the rain would fall.

Then the men appeared in her sights. Three of them, Manuel being the shortest of the three—wiry, lean, and much meaner looking than she remembered him. He had put on a facade of sweet South American charm with her, had cleaned up and was shaven and quite handsome in fact. But now he looked hard, his face covered in a mottled dark beard, his dark brown eyes narrowed, his clothes soggy and dirty and... she stared hard. Bloodstained?

Had he been injured? Or had he injured someone else? How could she have been so naive?

Because he had charmed her into believing he was who he said he was, a native from the area who knew passable English and who guided tourists into the rain forest for an interesting and informative visit. Only in his case, he had never planned to guide her back out.

When he had taken her on her trip, he had worn the minimum of weaponry—a machete for chopping at the vegetation to clear their path, a gun in case of venomous snakes, a knife for survival. But now belts of ammo crisscrossed his chest as if he was a wild bandito from the Old West, while double pistols sat at his hips and a rifle rested on his shoulder. His face was streaked in mud, his long hair matted and grungy. His eyes were the scariest, though. They showed no remorse, no pity, no heart.

The others looked just like him, dressed in light-colored clothes that were filthy, their faces bearded, their dark skin speckled with mud. They smelled of sweat and blood and…

She wrinkled her nose. Marijuana, she thought.

They suddenly stopped and all smiled in a menacing way as they looked at the hut high above on stilts. Then Carlos motioned toward the hut, signaling to Manuel to take the stairs and the other man to go underneath the hut. Carlos stayed in place, rifle ready.

The two men quickly moved forward. Manuel didn't hesitate to take the steps. Did he think that the jaguar god couldn't be too scary if he lived in a hut? Probably.

He would soon find the tree bridge to the lookout post, and then she would be forced to use the gun. She hoped to God she wouldn't end up in a firefight she couldn't win, and that Maya and Connor would remain safe.

"No one up here," Manuel said but twirled one of Kat's lace bras on his grungy finger. "But the woman's been here."

Carlos gave a dark laugh. "Then we wait for them to come back. Gonzales will pay us well."

Her heart tripped over hearing his name. *Gonzales?* The devil himself. Instantly, her thoughts returned to the firefight at his encampment some distance from here. The killings, the shootings, the smell of blood.

Her breathing grew even more ragged. This was truly a nightmare, and to her horror, she'd dragged Connor and Maya into it with her. That meant she had to quickly rectify the situation before Gonzales came after her himself.

"Wait, here's a bridge into the trees." Manuel deftly began to make his way up the bridge into the canopy. When he saw her with her weapon trained on him, he quickly raised his assault rifle and told her, "Put the weapon down now, *señorita*."

He took a step forward, and she knew that if he got too close, he would force her to give up the rifle, and then she would be doomed. He began to move quickly toward her, seeing her hesitation and knowing she wouldn't shoot him.

She hated to shoot him. She kept thinking of how cheerful and charming and helpful he had been.

But he wasn't stopping, and she had to do it. She couldn't afford to be taken as a hostage and put Maya and Connor at risk.

She fired a shot straight at his chest. The rifle recoiled hard against her shoulder blade, bruising it.

He jerked backward with the impact of the bullet, his red blood spreading across the front of his dirty, light-colored shirt. His eyes widened and his mouth gaped in surprise.

An explosion of bullets shot out of his gun, hitting the vegetation all around her.

She slammed hard against the vine railing to avoid the barrage of bullets. The vines gave way with the impact, just before she felt herself falling from the tree.

Maya had to warn Connor that a native had spotted her when she dragged the man to the river. She ran as fast as she could through the jungle, not taking the path, but close enough to it so that she could find Connor, knowing that he would be attempting to take out another of the men. When she saw the man floating dead on the flooded path, she knew Connor had eliminated him. But a shot rang out close to the hut, and that sent her blood racing. *Kat.* She could be in a world of trouble on her own against the three men who were left.

And then a volley of shots was fired, as if the rain forest had suddenly become a war zone.

Kat.

Connor had to be well on his way there. But still, he was only one jaguar against three heavily armed men, and the element of surprise could be lost.

Her heart in her throat, Maya shoved her way through the tangled vines and brush, sinking into mud and racing through ankle-deep water.

"Hell! Manuel?" the man who seemed to be in charge shouted.

"He's here, dead," the other man called out. "She must have shot him."

Kat had shot Manuel? Maya's estimation of her new-found sister went up another 100 percent. Kat might not have her shifting under control, but she was a valuable asset to them anyway.

"Where is she, damn it?" the man in charge asked.

"She fell from the tree, too. She's around here somewhere."

The news slammed into Maya. Her heartbeat thundered in her ears as she moved swiftly around trees, drawing closer to the men. *Kat had fallen from the tree*. Had she been hit? Several gunshots had been fired in the same general area. Was Kat even alive? She had to be.

Where was she? Where was Connor? Why wasn't he killing the men before they found Kat? She would kill both of the bastards all by herself if they had hurt Kat.

Kat was unconscious but breathing, Connor found as he located her on the forest floor while he was in his jaguar form. He couldn't tell if she had injured herself when she had fallen, but he smelled no blood on her, so she didn't appear to have taken a bullet, and she didn't look as though she had broken any bones. Hopefully, she had just knocked the wind out of herself when she fell.

The men were moving closer to her, spread out a little and poking at the thick vegetation with their rifles.

Then Connor saw Maya coming in for the kill. But before she could take out the leader, he slapped at his neck, stopped dead still, and crumpled to the ground. Connor went for the other man, but the guy repeated the other man's bizarre actions. Connor stood next to the man, staring down at him.

A blow dart was lodged in the man's neck, just like on the other's neck.

What if the native hunters tried to kill Maya and him, too? What if they went after Kat?

He saw no sign of the hunters, who were as elusive as jaguars moving around in the rain forest. No one did anything further. But he knew the hunters were watching, waiting.

Connor returned to Kat and again nudged her, trying to get her to wake. She groaned and he felt a modicum of relief in hearing her breathy response. He licked her cheek, and she wrinkled her brow.

He licked her again and she opened her eyes wide. "Oh, oh, the men," she whispered, her voice worried.

He nudged her to sit up, and with reluctance, she did. And groaned again. With a great deal of moaning and hesitating, she finally rose to her feet. Maya was watching the woods in the direction the hunters must have been, protecting Connor and Kat if they needed it, while he tried to move Kat to the hut. Connor encouraged her to climb the steps, and once she made it inside, he and Maya joined her. Both quickly shifted and dressed.

"Are you all right, Kat?" Connor asked, making her sit down on his bed.

"Yes, I just… ache all over. I hit every tree limb I could find when I fell. But the men. What happened to them?" Her voice was nearly inaudible.

"The two that were left? They're dead. The natives used them for poison-dart practice." He took her hand and crouched in front of her, looking up into her sage-green eyes. "Are you sure you're all right? You took quite a fall, and you were unconscious." And she appeared pale and distraught.

"Bruised and I hurt all over. But I really am fine," she tried to reassure him. "Nothing like when I hurt my knee. Just a little sore."

"We have to move the dead men," Maya warned.

Rotting bodies in the jungle would soon provide a feast for scavengers. "Yeah, we do. We have to get Kat home, too," Connor said.

Maya spoke up again. "The hunters know about us. One saw me take the first man and dump him in the river."

Connor let out his breath. "That's why the hunters ended up here. But they didn't try to kill you, Maya?"

"No. It was a young boy. He ran off, and I imagine he went to tell the elders and their shaman. And then they must have followed us back here."

"We have to go," Connor reiterated. "The men who came here after Kat most likely would have told others of their plan. And if the natives know what we are, it's not safe for us here any longer."

"They killed the men," Maya said. "They killed them with poisoned darts. They aided us."

Connor didn't know what to think. Did the locals feel responsible for telling Manuel about the jaguar god and had come to help him and Maya and Kat if they needed it? They had seen them on occasion, the hunter-gatherers living off the land. But they were almost as mysterious as the jaguars.

Connor looped a curl dangling against Kat's cheek and tucked it behind her ear. Maya was right that they needed to get rid of the bodies quickly. "I'll take care of the men. You stay here with Kat."

Maya looked as though she wanted to object, like she wanted to help him dispose of the bodies, but then she observed Kat's pale face and nodded. "I'll stay with Kat, but don't take long or we'll both be roaming the jungle to look for you."

He gave her a stern look. "You stay here. I don't want to have to try to rescue you both later." Then he gave Kat a warm embrace and kissed her forehead. "Keep my sister here."

She smiled up at him, but her eyes were still a bit glazed over, and her smile had only a fraction of the brilliance it usually had. He hated to leave her, to leave either of them behind. But this business had to be taken care of.

Connor left the hut and crossed the bridge to the lookout post, meaning to shift there before he took care of the men. He looked down at the leader's body, but it was gone. He stared at the location, but no matter how hard he looked, he just didn't see the body. Where the hell was it? He knew scavengers would come for it, but not this quickly.

Maybe from this vantage point, he was off in his calculations as to where the body rested. He climbed down the steps and began searching for the man and his companion. Neither were there, nor was Manuel. But they had died. He knew they were dead.

He looked up at the forest. The *hunters* had to have hauled them off. He smelled other men, seven or eight of them. They had moved as silently as he and Maya did.

Connor returned to the hut, and both his sister and Kat stared at him in surprise. Their expressions quickly turned to alarm.

"The hunters removed the bodies. I've got to see to the other one I left on the path. I'll be back soon," he said quickly, wanting them to know what had happened before he left.

He returned to the lookout post, stripped off his clothes, and shifted into his jaguar form. He leaped from one tree to another, then jumped to the ground and moved swiftly through the jungle to locate the last of the dead men. When he reached the area where he had left the man floating on the water-covered path, he found that man's body had also been removed. He sniffed the air. Several men had been here.

Connor tracked the hunters' scents until he reached the river. Hidden in the foliage, he watched the hunters depositing the bodies in the river and chanting over them, condemning them for attempting to kill the jaguar god and his mates. They made it sound like Connor had a royal concubine.

He smiled at the notion. He imagined Maya and Kat wouldn't.

For now, the natives appeared to be on their side. Maybe they had been angry that one of them had told Manuel about seeing the jaguar god and his woman, and that Manuel had promptly led his thugs to take Connor and the women hostage.

But no matter what, he and Kat and his sister needed to leave. For now. Life was getting too complicated for safety's sake. Although they would return. This was their second home, and the jungle drew them back as if it were a homing device genetically engineered into their blood.

He wished they could travel as jaguars, but that wouldn't be a viable option since they needed to get out of the country in their human forms. As jaguars, they wouldn't have clothes, money, or passports once they reached the States. He loped back toward the hut, and when he arrived, he found Kat sleeping in his bed. He was grateful she hadn't been wounded or, worse, killed.

After shifting, he took Maya aside. "Are you sure she's all right?"

"Yes. The fall did her in. She's also upset about killing Manuel, but she'll be fine, Connor."

"Yeah, but can she travel like we need to do to get out of here?"

"She can. What about the men?" Maya asked, changing the subject.

"The hunters took them to the river and dumped them, and now the dead men are feeding the piranhas and a caiman or two. The hunters seem to be on our side for now, thinking I'm the local jaguar god."

"Jaguar god." Maya snorted. "If you're a jaguar god, we're jaguar goddesses."

He chuckled. "They believe you're part of my harem."

She laughed at that but quickly turned to make sure she hadn't disturbed Kat's sleep. She whispered, "I'll have to pick up my own cache of jaguar men."

He was glad he knew Maya better than that. He could just imagine her clawing or biting a bunch of Texans and turning them. But she wasn't that kind of woman.

That night, he had meant to sleep on the porch and make Maya stay in her own bed so that he would be their first line of defense if anyone had a notion to attack. When his sister wouldn't cooperate, he cuddled with Kat in his bed so that Maya would remain in the hut with them, sleeping on her own cot.

He wanted to keep his "harem" close, in case they had any more trouble.

Chapter 17

RELIEVED THAT THEY HAD HAD NO MORE DIFFICULTIES during the night, they planned to leave early the next morning after they packed their backpacks and dressed for the long trek. Kat was quiet, subdued, and Connor wasn't sure what was bothering her. Well, besides the fact that Maya had turned her into a jaguar-shifter, men had tried to take her hostage, she'd had to kill one of them, and they still faced the difficult task of getting her back to the States without any further difficulties.

"Anything wrong?" Connor asked for the third time that morning.

She shook her head, but he knew better. He still assumed her concerns had something to do with the man she had killed. The man she had thought highly of. But probably she was also worried about the trek ahead of them. Would she make it to the States before she had the urge to shift again?

Or maybe she was worried about another hostage-taking situation.

He ran his hand reassuringly over her arm. "We'll be all right." He meant it, although he wasn't sure how much trouble they would get into before they truly were all right. But together, the three of them would make the best of their situation. "He would have taken you hostage, Kat. You had no choice."

Maya had been quietly listening to them. He had

hoped maybe she would speak to Kat and see what the problem was, but although they were both women, they weren't alike. Not when Maya and he had been born shifters. He figured Maya didn't know what to say to Kat to ease her mind, any more than he did.

"We'll make it, Kat." He pulled her into his embrace, but gently, worried she might still be a little sore from her fall the day before, although she had seemed fine when they made love last night.

She squeezed him hard and looked up at him with the determination to see this through. "I'm no longer sore. I won't break."

But she seemed fragile to him, despite her strong words.

"You're just worried about what will happen."

"What if I shift? I can just envision being the Incredible Hulk, tearing out of my clothes to change, but instead of bright green skin, I'd have gold fur with black spots and very big teeth."

"And you'd be beautiful."

She snorted.

"You would be. You were."

She sighed. "But what if it happens?"

"If we're in the jungle, no problem. We'll hide our packs in the trees and join you up there to sleep a while until you shift back."

"And if I do it at a border crossing?"

"You won't. Think positively." He wanted to tell her to think like a human, but he had no idea what had triggered the shift in her the first time around.

"I can't quit thinking about Manuel, either. He seemed so nice and then…"

Maya harrumphed. "He wasn't nice, Kat. Nice guys

don't come into the jungle armed to the teeth, intent on taking a woman hostage for ransom."

"I know but… I've never shot anyone when I wasn't on a combat mission. I close my eyes and still see the blood spreading across his shirt."

"Before or after we heard a ton of shots fired?" Maya reminded her.

"Have you had to kill men like this before?"

"Yes," Connor said. "They're a plague on mankind. Rule of the jungle. Eat before you're eaten. Come on, let's get on our…"

They heard movement below, and all three of them headed for the window. Flowers encircled the hut, and a tapir, freshly killed and cooked, with pineapples and plantains surrounding it, was laid out on umbrella-sized palm fronds, a peace offering of sorts, it appeared.

"Do you think the natives believe they offended you?" Kat asked quietly.

There was no sign of any of the hunters, but he suspected they watched, waited, and were hopeful that the jaguar people would accept their offering.

"It appears to be so," Connor said, so surprised that he couldn't believe it.

"Should we invite them? Like at a Thanksgiving feast?" Maya asked.

Connor rubbed Kat's arm. "What do you want to do, Kat?"

"What if another one of them tells someone else like Manuel that we exist?"

"We're still leaving the area."

She nodded. "Then let's invite them. Maybe the

gesture will give them some peace of mind, and they did come to our aid yesterday."

"If they appease a jaguar god and his goddesses, that will give the tribe power," Maya said.

Connor chuckled softly. "No one said anything about jaguar goddesses."

"No one had to," Kat said. "Maya's perfectly right."

He shook his head. He could see where this was going. Kat and Maya would always gang up on him. Not that he couldn't handle it. He smiled darkly.

They descended the steps and crossed to the small clearing where the feast was spread out. Kat sat down before the cooked tapir.

Connor brought out a knife and motioned to the jungle, then to the feast. "Come, join us," he said in Spanish. "Eat with us. Share the feast."

"Tell them the jaguar god and his goddesses have spoken," Maya said.

He chuckled and carved off a slice of meat for Kat, then Maya.

"You can laugh all you want, Connor, but goddesses galore exist in South American lore. Not only did the Mayan culture worship the jaguar god of terrestrial fire, but it's said that the jaguar goddess of midwifery and war might have been his spouse," Maya said, her chin tilted up.

Even though they half watched to see if anyone would, no one ventured forth from the jungle.

Kat ate a slice of pineapple. "I agree. We're just as important as any jaguar god." She whispered to Connor and Maya, "Why don't they join us?"

Connor cut off another slice of meat. "Most likely

they're afraid. Maybe they think we might still be angry. They've never made direct contact with us before. We've seen them on occasion, but they have always quickly disappeared as if they believed we'd be angry if we saw them watching us."

Movement in the vegetation to their right made them all look that way.

An elderly man headed toward them, speaking in some unknown tongue. His gnarled hands were out-stretched as if coming in peace and to show he had no weapons at his disposal. Connor was about to stand but thought better of it, afraid that towering over the slightly built man might intimidate him. Instead, he waved to the food and made a motion telling the old man to eat with them. "Sit and eat."

The man stared him in the eye as if judging Connor's sincerity, then nodded several times and sat cross-legged before the beast.

Connor handed him the knife. The old man hesi-tated, then smiled a little. Connor was offering his only weapon. But the old man probably knew that if Connor had felt threatened, all he would have to do was shift. Of course, all the man and his people would have to do was bring out their blowguns.

After the man chewed on a bite of the tapir for several minutes, he glanced back at the woods and motioned for others to join them. Several men came out of the woods and walked toward them, and Connor attempted not to show how much it bothered him that these people knew about them. He was still worried that the natives might take some action against them, and he feared for Kat's safety the most because she couldn't shift. Although if the men wanted to take them down with poisoned blow darts, he wasn't sure their shifter genetics could counter the poison quickly enough to keep it from killing them before they could race off to escape.

But the men sat down and began to eat the meal, nodding and speaking softly to themselves as if they normally shared a meal with a jaguar god. The older man offered Connor a flask to drink from, but he declined and handed it back to the man.

"The drink might be drugged," he warned Maya and Kat.

"They want to harm us or take us hostage? Is this like the Trojan horse offering?" Kat asked, sounding surprised.

Connor shook his head. "I venture it's more likely that they want us to feel good and stay. Having a jaguar god—"

"And goddesses," Maya interrupted.

Connor smiled. "...in residence could improve their status."

"Improve their fishing, crops, livestock, their living," Kat said. "Oh yeah, and the first big drought, the first failed crop, the first cow that drops dead, we'd be the ones responsible."

"That's true. And it's another reason we're leaving. I'll tell them we're leaving but we'll be back, just like we've done in the past. I think they've watched us for years, Maya. But with Kat joining us, they believe we might be expanding our jaguar clan. Maybe they wanted us to know that was fine with them. I don't want them to try and keep us here, and I'm afraid that's what they'll have in mind."

After another hour of visiting, Connor stood and everyone else did, too. He told them that he, Maya, and

Kat intended to leave and asked the villagers to watch over their home. He suspected now that the villagers had been doing so for years because no one had ever disturbed it while they were away for months at a time.

The elder blessed them, hoping they would be most fertile. He knew Maya understood him as she quickly looked at Kat. Kat didn't understand, but the look Maya gave her made her suspect something important had been said.

"Come on," Connor said. "We need to get moving if we're to make any headway today."

They thought that was going to be it—the men would take the leftovers back to their village—but instead the men picked up their staffs and began to disperse through the jungle. They were hidden from view, but Connor assumed the men were escorting them safely as far as they could go.

Connor took up the rear, Kat in between, and Maya led the way. He heard some noise behind him and turned to see women from the village carrying away the remaining tapir and other food that hadn't been eaten. He was glad it wouldn't go to waste.

Maya sighed. "We can't fly home this time, can we?"

They always flew home. Even at that, a flight would be between eighteen and twenty-four hours. He worried that Kat might not be able to control shifting for that many hours or even sit in airports waiting for the next flight out. But going by boat would take forever. "If we took a flight, we'd go from Santa Marta with a stop in Bogotá, Colombia, then on to Houston. That's where our SUV is," he said.

"You don't come here all the time, do you? Just a

couple of times a year, right?" Kat asked. She sounded worried. Like she would have to risk doing this a lot with them.

He smiled. "We live near lakes and national forests or state forests in eastern Texas and enjoy visiting them in the middle of the night when we need to. We just come down here a couple of times a year to be one with the jungle like the jaguars are. But until we sort things out with your abilities, we'll stay closer to home."

"We can't fly, can we?" Kat asked, looking as though she thought that was a really bad idea but still wished they could do it. The sooner they could get home, the better.

Connor took a deep breath. "Maybe we could charter a boat. I don't see any other way around this. We've never had a problem with flying, but if you had to shift, I doubt you could do so in one of the lavatories. They're pretty small. And then what if you weren't able to shift back for several hours? We'd be in trouble." He could just envision poor Kat, her tail in the commode, her paws up on the sink, fighting the urge to growl or roar in her distress, and the flight attendants pounding on the door when the line for the other bathroom grew too long.

"Maybe we could travel cross-country," Maya said. "I know it can be dangerous…"

"And take forever," Connor reminded her with a hard look. Though he wouldn't have wanted Maya to turn Kat at any time, he wished she had done so at their home. Not here.

Maya let out her breath hard. "All right, so we have to charter a boat."

Smugglers and pirates could be a problem, and Maya became deathly ill in a rocking boat.

"Or... what if we could take a short flight to somewhere north of here, maybe Belize or Costa Rica, stop, maybe stay overnight, then take another short flight the next day?" Kat said.

Connor shook his head. "We've done that. Even with the extra stops, it was still seven hours for one flight."

"Cancún?" Maya asked, sounding hopeful.

That was where they had planned on going originally before Maya messed up their plans by scratching Kat.

"We checked the schedules. It's about nine hours if we can get a flight out. And then it's another six hours if we could still get the one flight to Houston after that," Maya said.

"I'm all for it, if we can make some stops like that," Kat said. "Though who knows if I can make it even that long on a flight. Then again, I might not change again until the next full moon."

Connor and Maya shared looks. Shifting had nothing to do with the full moon. That was werewolf lore. The problem was not having any idea when Kat might have the uncontrollable urge to shift.

Much later that night, after traveling for miles in the jungle, they set up hammocks in a tree. Early the next morning, they began the long journey all over again. They saw another tribe in the Amazon while they were trekking through it, but like the one that had adopted them, this one just watched them, half-hidden in the shadowed foliage and not making any effort to greet or deter them. Connor hoped word had not spread to the farthest outreaches about the jaguar god and his harem.

They had traveled for miles already, and Kat was keeping up with the steady pace. He assumed that was in part because she'd had to be physically fit while in the military. But even so, he could tell she was weary by the way her shoulders slumped, and she was breathing too hard.

"Kat," he said, catching up to her. "Let me take your bag." He had already offered several times, but this time he wasn't going to be dissuaded.

She looked up at him, her face tired. "No. We always carry our own weight in the military."

"You've been sick," he said firmly. "Let me take your bag." This time he was insistent.

Maya had stopped and was watching them.

Kat sighed and handed over her backpack. "At the risk of sounding like a whiney child bored with traveling, will we be stopping soon?"

He smiled. "You have been anything but. Another two hours, though I believe Maya had an idea."

Maya's expression brightened. "We can stop and swim with the pink dolphins?"

"The river's only a couple of miles from here. We can swim for a while, get something to eat, and continue on our way. That will give us a much-needed break."

Kat's spine straightened, and she even gave him an elusive smile. "What are we waiting for?"

Chapter 18

WHEN CONNOR, MAYA, AND KAT REACHED THE RIVER, Kat began pulling off her shirt and boots and pants, eager to swim, to cool off a bit, and to wash off some of the sweat. Under the broad canopy in the thick of the jungle, the temperature was around eighty degrees and muggy without a breeze. Out in the sun, it was closer to one hundred, but a humid breeze swept across the river. Kat's wary gaze examined the jungle. They had company, she thought uneasily.

She sensed more than saw that they were being watched. Were her jaguar senses making her more aware of her surroundings? She wasn't sure.

"I don't think we're alone," she said to Maya and Connor as she waded into the river. She was wearing just her leopard bra and panties, but they looked enough like a bikini bathing suit that she felt comfortable in them even if they had an audience. As long as they weren't being watched by drug runners.

"You're right, Kat," Maya said. "I'm sure they're hunters from another tribe. They've been following us for miles, ever since we left the other tribe's territory."

"Do you think they know about us?" Kat asked. She knew the jaguar-shifters had to remain a secret to society in general, and she didn't feel comfortable that some tribes in the Amazon knew what they were. The information could prove disastrous in the wrong hands if anyone believed the natives' tales.

She wasn't at ease with what she was, either. Concern about having a sudden urge to shift had plagued her all day. Nothing had come of it, but she still had been anxious. What if this group of natives didn't know about Kat, Connor, and Maya's jaguar-shifter traits but all of a sudden saw Kat ditching her clothes and turning into a jaguar?

Would they revere her or want to kill her? And Maya and Connor, too?

She also couldn't get used to the way her senses were so attuned. It was unnerving to be hearing so many more sounds than she could before, seeing the slightest movements that she wouldn't have noticed before, and smelling the jungle in a new way. The jungle was even richer than she had noticed earlier—full of scents she couldn't even begin to recognize, but she figured Maya and Connor could. They had been coming here for a long time as shifters, and they had learned from birth how to identify odors that her human nose couldn't yet.

Connor had already stripped to a pair of boxers and joined Kat in the river. He ran his hand over her arm in a soothing caress. "I'm not sure if they realize what we are. Maybe like the others, they do know what we are like. Or they're just curious about who we are and why we're traveling through their land. We don't have a guide, and we're not hunting or gathering information or doing anything except moving through their territory, so they have to wonder what we're up to."

Wearing just a black bra and bikini panties, Maya joined them, then swam deeper into the river.

Kat knew that the freshwater dolphins swam there, but

so did the piranha. She tried not to think of that. People didn't get bitten by them all that often, she didn't think, and she wasn't bleeding anywhere, so she felt she should be safe enough. Even tourists were taken on excursions to swim with the Amazon River dolphins. She had seen numerous pictures of gray-haired grandmas floating with orange preservers strapped around their chests while reaching out to pet the pink dolphins, their noses up in the air as if delighted to see the human tourists.

Kat felt a soft-skinned dolphin glide close enough to brush up against her as if in greeting, and she grinned. They were beautiful and huge. And amazingly pink. Not all of them, though. Some were gray with a pink belly, or pink with a mottling of gray on top. The four she glimpsed rising out of the water and then diving back in were much bigger than she had imagined them to be. These were freshwater dolphins, not like the ones at the shows she had seen. But actually being in the water with them was both exhilarating and intimidating.

Connor stuck close to Kat as if she might need his rescue at any moment. She loved the way he was so protective of her and of Maya, too. He knew his sister's capabilities better than he did Kat's, so he seemed more concerned about Kat than she thought warranted. Except for the sickness, she normally was extremely capable on her own.

For now, she felt rejuvenated. Clean, refreshed, loving the water as she always had. And as she stroked the good-natured dolphins, she was thrilled they had stopped to swim and play.

"A male," Connor said as she ran her hand over an even bigger dolphin.

"But females are usually bigger."

Connor shook his head. "Not among these dolphins. The males are bigger and are more likely to be all pink."

Maya swam on her back and said, "Some call them *botos*. Did you know that some claim they have supernatural powers? An Amazon legend states that a sexy man seduces a girl, gets her pregnant, and then returns to the river in the morning to become a boto again. Some believe that it is bad luck to kill one. Some believe that the spirits of drowned souls enter the boto's body."

"I wonder what they would say about us," Kat said, watching the dolphins swim near, then disappear again underneath the dark water.

Maya smiled. "I believe they're already making up tales. Connor has his own harem."

"Which," Connor said to his sister, "if it keeps you out of trouble with the men, suits me fine. Not that you're part of my harem, but just that the locals think so."

Maya grew thoughtful. "Do you think the other male jaguar we heard was a shifter or just a regular jaguar?"

"It's hard to tell," Connor said, although from the odd expression on his face, Kat wondered if he really did know but wasn't committing himself. "I hadn't been leaving a scent around the area like I normally do to let other beasts know that I've claimed the territory, what with Kat having been so ill. So it could have been either."

Kat hadn't thought about it much, but now she realized that Maya must want to check the other jaguar out. She'd said they hadn't been able to locate any other jaguar-shifters. What if the guy was one, and Maya and he hit it off? She could have a mate without having to bite anyone to make it happen.

"Do you want to locate him and determine if he is?" Kat asked Maya. She figured that Connor didn't want to look for the male jaguar, or he would have suggested it already. Was he worried *Kat* might be interested in the other male jaguar if he was a shifter?

Connor drew in a deep breath as he stood near Kat. "He's stalking us."

Kat's mouth opened, but she didn't say anything. He was following them and Connor knew? She glanced at Maya. His sister sighed. "At least we're pretty sure he is."

"As a jaguar?" Kat asked, amazed at the news.

Why hadn't she seen any sign of him? She knew they were being followed, but she couldn't say exactly what had alerted her. Maybe that sometimes a flock of parrots would shoot heavenward into the canopy some distance in the jungle, or that monkeys would titter and squawk at each other in warning, alerting the others of trouble. She had believed they were being followed by the native people who lived here, not by anyone who might wish to take them hostage. The thought that more of Manuel's kind might be around still bothered her, but she figured anyone else like him would have made a move by now.

She had thought Connor was pushing them through the jungle so relentlessly to get them somewhere safe as soon as possible. But now she wondered if it was because he worried about another jaguar—or jaguar-shifter.

"A jaguar's been following us," both Maya and Connor said at once. Apparently they didn't know for sure if he was a shifter. If he was running around as a man, they probably wouldn't have thought he was a shifter.

Kat looked at the trees lining the banks of the river. "You've seen him?"

"In a tree, two hours ago," Maya said.

"How did I miss him? Why didn't you tell me?" When neither answered her right away, Kat asked, "Is he trying to figure out our relationships?" She assumed Connor didn't want her thinking he was so controlling that he wouldn't let her get to know another shifter.

"I'm sure of it, if he's a shifter," Maya said rather wistfully.

Connor had a harem, so who was with whom? Were both the females his? Like a regular jaguar who claimed a couple of females or more within his territory?

Kat hadn't had a real family. Not one that had looked out for her. And she had never had a man care for her to such an extent, someone who was willing to take care of an unknown woman alone in the jungle who hadn't been the best of company. She had been sickly, looking like death warmed over, so he was probably figuring she couldn't have been very bright to be there in the first place.

She'd had her share of relationships; none of them had worked out. Either the guys were too busy making rank and enjoying the freedom and money as single men in the service and didn't want to be tied down to a wife and kids, or there just was no spark. Until Roger came along. But that engagement had been short-lived after her aborted mission in the jungle. He didn't even have to tell her it was over between them. When he began giving her the third degree about her mission while she was still so out of it her injuries, she knew the mission was all he cared about. And she had been the one who ended it between them.

With Connor, it was totally different. She was certain

that if he had been able to save her life and take her with him that day she had been shot up so badly, he would never have questioned her about anything until she was ready to share what had happened. But in truth, if he had known her beforehand, she was sure he wouldn't have allowed her to go on a mission that would have endangered her life in the first place.

Even now, the way he stood so close to her made her feel sparks and heat and sizzle. A dolphin bumped gently against her leg, but Connor, looking down at her and trying to read her feelings, was the one who stole her attention.

She wanted to wrap her arms around him to prove to the other jaguar, if he was watching, that she already had a shifter she was interested in.

That's when Connor smiled at Kat in the most devil-ishly sinful way, cupped her face with his wet hands, and pressed his mouth against hers.

Everything—the flow of the river, the dolphins swimming nearby, Maya and anyone else who might be watching—faded into the distance as if none of them existed. Only Connor's hot lips against hers held her attention. It was just like at the waterfall, as if noth-ing mattered but his touching her. She treasured it and needed it—the closeness and the feeling she wasn't someone who had no one, had never had anyone in her life, and was wanted now for the first time ever.

But it was more than just want. It was a craving, something primal, instinctive, necessary. Not just an urge to have sex—although she was already thinking about the room arrangements when they reached the city. She wasn't sure Connor would want to leave his sister alone in a room of her own, while Kat and he shared another. She wasn't sure she wanted Maya off by herself, either.

But she did know she wanted Connor alone to cure this growing need to have him. Ever since he'd begun sleeping in the same small bed with Kat in the hut, with his body pressed indecently against hers, she had wanted more.

Standing in the river, he pressed his fully aroused body harder against hers. If another shifter was watching, she was fairly sure he would realize that Connor wanted her and she wanted him. Unless another shifter figured she might be fickle. As cats, they would be. But she wasn't that way.

Still, she didn't know Connor well enough to know if he would stay with her in the long run. What if he found another female jaguar-shifter who had been born to this way of life like he had? Wouldn't he prefer someone who was able to control what she was? Knew what to do as a shifter? Wasn't such a neophyte like Kat was?

She normally didn't feel unsure of herself. She had a will of her own, and once she had left foster care, she had lived her own life. But now, she couldn't help but feel somewhat insecure. She had no idea how to live this life as a jaguar-shifter.

In part, she wanted to do her own thing, plan her own life, be her own person. She had known what she was capable of—but now, she wasn't sure.

"Your thoughts are somewhere else, Kat," Connor whispered, kissing her ear and her throat, his hands around her waist, holding her in place, tight against his body.

Her body pooled with liquid heat at the feel of his warm mouth on her skin.

Yet, he must have felt the tension in her, the hesitation, and seen the way she glanced again at the woods because he said what she thought he was afraid to say to her: "He can't have you." His eyes were dark with desire, his words determined. "If he's a shifter, he can't have you," he repeated, as if he wanted to make it perfectly clear to her that he wanted her and wasn't giving her up.

Loving a challenge, she smiled and moved her hands down his back to his buttocks, the boxers clinging to his hard muscles. She tilted her lips up and replied in a hushed voice, "I take it you're going to prove to me why I should want you instead?"

His mouth curved into a lazy smile, the skin beneath his eyes crinkling in wry amusement. "If that's meant as a challenge…"

Absolutely.

He let his words trail off, right before he nibbled on her ear, and she arched against him. God, Maya had to get a separate room from them when they arrived at the city or Kat would never manage.

As if Maya had read Kat's mind, she said good-naturedly, "You two need to get a room. Let's eat so we can get back on the trail and reach the city before it gets too late." She waded out of the river and onto the bank.

Connor gave Kat another heartfelt squeeze. "I accept the challenge."

Kat chuckled under her breath. "I've never had two men fight over me before. You do realize you might not have any competition anyway. I mean, if he's a shifter, he might be interested in Maya, not me. And if he's not a shifter, there would be no competition at all."

Connor shook his head. "No matter what the situation is, I won't chance it."

He sounded dead serious, and she took his hand and walked with him to the shore. "All right by me. So where shall we go for our first date?"

Grinning this time, he looked down at her. "How about a cookout in the Amazon rain forest? We could go for a nice long hike through the steamy jungle until we reach a city. Check into a room—"

"Dinner first, though," she said smiling.

His eyes glittered with amusement. "Dinner first, then we have to work off the meal and then get a room."

"Once we get to the city and before we get booked on a flight, can we go to the beach?" Maya asked.

"Sounds good to me," Kat said, as long as they swam late at night, just in case she had the sudden urge to shift. Then she sobered. "If you've recently shifted, will that stop you from having the urge again for a long time afterward?"

Maya looked at Connor, like she felt bad for not knowing the answer to Kat's question, then sadly shook her head. "We change at will, Kat. I'm sorry. Did you have a feeling that warned you that you had to shift the first time?"

"I was asleep," Kat said, helping Connor to gather kindling for a fire. "I didn't think I was awake. I'd been dreaming about being a cat most of the night, thinking it was because I had seen you and Connor as cats in the jungle earlier, and maybe also as a byproduct of the un-usual foods I'd been eating. Then before I knew it, I was tearing off my clothes, desperate to get out of them, and I shifted. After that, I still couldn't believe it, thinking I was having a very vivid nightmare. So if I had any warning about shifting, I was too sleepy to know what it was."

Maya and Connor exchanged worried glances, which didn't bode well for Kat.

When they had a good fire started to cook the meal, Connor disappeared into the jungle. "Where's he going?" Kat quickly asked.

"To get us something to eat. It's easier if we shift so that we can hunt. But he didn't want to do it in the open, here by the river. He'll try to find as secluded a spot as he can."

"What about the other shifter? If he is one. What if he tries to visit with us while Connor's gone?" Kat knew Connor would be ready to tear into the man, jaguar to jaguar, if he returned and found the man with them. She didn't want to see that. Not if the other shifter wasn't a bad guy.

Maya poked at the fire. "If he's a shifter, he'll know not to come near us. He'll know Connor won't like it. And the guy couldn't really speak with us unless he shifts. Without a set of clothes…" She shrugged. "So he'll do what he's doing now, continue to stalk us and try to learn where we're going. Although I assume, considering the direction we're headed, he'll figure we're off to the city. If he finds me alone when we split up to our separate rooms for the night in the city, he might approach me then."

"That's what you're hoping?" Kat asked, worried that the man might be a problem. Even if he was a shifter, he might not be anyone Maya would care for.

Maya smiled and squeezed Kat's hand. "Don't look so worried. Not only can I take care of myself, but I highly doubt Connor will let me stay in a room of my own alone. He's really a worrywart when it comes to me. I'm sure we'll get a room with a bedroom and a foldout couch in a suite-type arrangement. I'll sleep on the couch, unless you want Connor to." She smiled as if knowing just what Kat wanted. "Then again, I doubt I'll have much say about it."

Kat took a deep breath, then let it out. She had never confided in another woman about her interest in a man before. Certainly, it seemed strange to be talking about this with Connor's sister. "You've always wanted us to be together, so it's not only Connor who might wish it," she said smiling.

Maya sighed and pulled on her pants, then a shirt over her damp undergarments. "I didn't want you to be angry with me for turning you, Kat. You aren't, are you?"

Kat began to get dressed, too. "For turning me?" She shook her head. "I don't know what to feel yet. I understand why you did it. Not that you were mean or vindictive or anything. You wanted Connor to have a mate."

"Not just him. I wanted you to be my sister," Maya said quickly.

Kat couldn't help but give her a small smile. "I believe we're blood sisters now." She sat before the fire. "What if Connor can't stay with me for all time? What if he gets tired of me?"

"He won't." Maya frowned. "I know he won't."

"But cats don't stay with one mate. They're... fickle."

Maya smiled. "We're human, too. Believe me, he didn't like it that our father strayed and then abandoned our mother and us. So Connor won't do that. He's stuck by my side since we were little, never wanting to leave me. Our mother even left us when we were young adults. We don't feel the same as the big cats or our parents."

"Wow." Although Kat didn't know why she was so surprised. She had seen enough of that growing up. She picked up a twig and scratched it in the dirt. "What if *I* can't stay with one mate? What if with this jaguar gene, I have the uncontrollable urge to stray?"

"All right, for the sake of argument, let's talk about it. How many boyfriends have you had?"

Kat's brows rose. She didn't speak about stuff like that with just anyone, well, with anyone, period. And although Maya was to be her sister, she didn't know her well enough to tell all. In truth, she hadn't been with more than four guys, and none had had any desire to set up a homestead until Roger. After bouncing around between foster homes herself, settling down was damned important to her. But she still didn't feel like exposing her whole past life to a virtual stranger.

Maya shrugged. "If you've had a ton of boyfriends, then maybe you would be fickle. But even so, it doesn't mean that if you found the right man, you couldn't settle down. The others could have been just a case of experimenting, trying to locate the right guy, testing the waters, so to speak. So how many have you been with?"

Kat's mouth parted, but she couldn't say. Would Maya think there was something wrong with her because she had been with so few guys? She wasn't really outgoing when it came to meeting men.

Switching the focus, she said, "What about you? How many guys have you been with?"

Chapter 19

AFTER FINDING THE SCENT OF THE MALE JAGUAR ON A tree that had a great view of the river where Connor, Kat, and Maya had swum, but not locating the jaguar now, Connor left his pack and his clothes in the jungle near a stream. He shifted and climbed onto a fallen tree in his stocky jaguar form to search for their meal. A giant river otter jerked his head around to see the jaguar, then quickly slipped under the water with his belly exposed, sweeping his tail and legs until he dove under a stack of downed tree trunks in the water and disappeared. Not that Connor had any interest in eating the otter.

Then Connor spied a pirarucu, the air-breathing, carnivorous catfish, one of the most ancient prehistoric fish from two hundred million years ago, that would eat fish, small animals, and birds. It was the largest freshwater fish in the world.

This one Connor estimated to be a couple of hundred pounds and about six feet long, although he had heard of one that had been caught weighing nearly 675 pounds and measuring ten feet in length. From his tree-trunk perch and with his spotted tail slashing the air, Connor watched the catfish swimming through the brown water. He was ready for dinner.

He leaped into the water and pounced on the pirarucu, which swiftly continued downstream and slipped out of

Connor's grasp. Connor waded after the catfish, ears perked, whiskers and tail twitching, muscles bunching as he readied himself for another try. He leaped again, his claws raking down the carnivore's tough scaled skin, which was capable of protecting it from caiman, freshwater dolphins, and other predatory fish. But not jaguars. The scales of the catfish were sandpaper rough, so much so that the natives used the three-and-a-half-inch scales as sandpaper and a scraping tool.

The catfish slid away from Connor's grasp again, turned, and headed upstream this time. The water Connor was wading in was jaguar-shoulder deep. He jumped straight out of the water again and leaped for the fish, his head submerging when he landed on his prey so he could get a grip with his teeth. The pirarucu wriggled free again, its tail waving in the water like a giant paddle and propelling it forward.

Connor stalked the Jurassic-era catfish again, wading through the water, eyeing the movement of the fish, and calculating his best timing for an ambush. He jumped straight out of the water, landed on his prey's back, grabbing its head this time, and held it under the water.

The catfish struggled, and the fish's tail slapped the water once, twice, and then it grew still. Connor released his hold on the fish, ready to grab it again, but the pirarucu was no longer moving. Now for the difficult part—getting it back to the campfire.

He would drag it back nearer the campfire so he could make sure the women were okay, and then he would return for his backpack and clothes, and shift.

~~~

When Kat asked if Maya had had a lot of male friends, Maya grinned, and Kat was relieved that she hadn't taken offense.

"Not enough boyfriends for me," Maya said. "But you see, I really have a terrible time getting close to men. I'm like Connor, worried I might become attached to someone and then have to turn the person. What if it didn't work out? So I meet men far from home, stay with them for a few hours, and leave them. They prefer it that way anyway. No strings attached. No whining woman who wants to get married and have babies."

Kat didn't think of herself as a whining woman, but she did want to get married and have a couple of children someday. "But you do, don't you, Maya? You want to have babies."

Maya looked into the fire. "Yeah, I do."

"So, what have you done to locate others like yourselves?"

Maya shook her head. "We've searched some out here and in Mexico and Belize, but we haven't found any who are shifters. Just regular jaguars."

"What about social networking sites?"

Her expression a little surprised, eyes wider than normal, brows raised, Maya glanced at her. "Like…?"

"You know, Facebook, Myspace, other networking sites."

"Hmm," Maya said, calculation in her golden eyes. "We have our garden nursery on a website, and we're on Facebook, but we use it strictly for business."

"Do you ever talk about your hobbies? Take pictures of the wildlife in the Amazon? Share pictures of yourselves as jaguars? You could show you support their cause. Have a blog about them. Provide subtle hints about being shifters. Something maybe only another shifter would recognize." Not that Kat would know how to find a secret society of jaguars, but surely Maya and Connor would know how to do it. "Heck, you can scare up just about anything on Twitter."

"Connor would say no, that it's too risky." But Maya looked hopeful that Kat would be in her corner on this.

Kat smiled. "I have a website and blog that I share pictures and stories on. But there's no real focus to it. Maybe when we reach your home, we can come up with something that even Connor wouldn't mind."

"What wouldn't Connor mind now?" he asked, stalking into their makeshift camp for lunch with nothing to show for his hunting expedition, his hair wet, his shirt open, and water droplets cascading down his well-toned hot body, his voice as dark as his expression.

"Did you locate him?" Maya asked, not even mentioning the lack of food for the meal.

Kat frowned. Him? She thought he was scaring up their food.

"I was fishing," he said, not looking Kat's way, his clothes sticking to his damp skin.

"Yeah, and I know damn well you went in search of the jaguar also. So did you find any sign of him?"

"Yeah, Maya. He'd been watching us from one of the trees close to the river when we were swimming. But he moved off, probably as soon as we came into shore." He glanced at Kat. "So what wouldn't Connor mind?"

She had forgotten what she and Maya had been talking about until she saw Maya glance her way with a

worried expression that said, "The ball's in your court—
you deal with him."

Leaving Kat and his sister alone in the jungle near
the river, even to go fishing, was difficult enough. But
Connor had had to search for the jaguar to learn what he
could about him. At least now, Connor had picked up
the other jaguar's scent and would know him if he ran
across the cat if he was in human form later.

But now Kat and his sister were up to something he
assumed was related to Maya's idea of trying to secure a
mate for herself with Kat's help. And that could get both
women into a lot of trouble.

Back stiff and not looking in the least bit intimidated, Kat lifted her chin. "We thought we might do a
little social networking to see if we could locate another
cat-shifter."

He shook his head and motioned to the jungle. "I left
dinner back there because I wanted to be close enough
that if you had any trouble, I could be here quickly. I'll
go cut it up and bring it to the fire."

"What did you get?" Maya asked, following him as
Kat hurried to join them.

"Pirarucu," he said, then added for Kat's benefit
in the event she had never heard of it, "one mother of
a catfish."

"Good, I'm starving," Kat said. "I could eat the
whole thing."

"How big this time?" Maya asked, grinning. She
knew as well as he did that Kat wouldn't be able to eat
even a tiny fraction of it.

But they would cook it and leave it for the natives
who were following them. Maybe even the jaguar, if he

cared to eat the remains, although Connor wasn't feeling magnanimous about giving him a free meal.

"Wow," Kat said when she saw the giant fish lying in the dappled shade of the trees. "That's a *catfish*?"

"Leftover from prehistoric times," Maya said. "I think that's the biggest one you've ever hunted, Connor."

Kat looked at the fish with such awe that Connor smiled. Then she looked up at him with such disbelief that his smile broadened.

"Wow," she said. "How could you have managed such a huge fish? Why even in your jaguar form, it was bigger than you."

"It wasn't easy," Connor admitted, not knowing why, when he normally wouldn't have acknowledged to a woman—any woman—that he had struggled to handle any task. "But in the end, my teeth are much bigger."

"And we're persistent," Maya said, "if we want to eat."

"I fished when I had turned into a jaguar that one time, but I didn't go after anything this huge. The fish I pulled out was… little. I don't think I would have tried to hunt something half as big as this," Kat said, still sounding astounded.

"No need to. You were hungry, caught what you needed, and that was that," Maya said. "So, do we all carry him back to the campfire or carve him up here?"

"Let's carry him to the campfire. We can skin him there," Kat said. "I was hungry but if I could freeze the rest of him, this would have kept me in meat the rest of the year. What will we do with what we can't eat?"

Connor took the most weight as they all three carried the catfish to the campfire, where they set about skinning him. "The natives who are following us will have a feast." Then he looked up at Kat. "About the networking sites for meeting those of our kind… we have to be careful that no one ever learns what we are. I heard you mention Facebook and Twitter. Any open forum like that could mean real trouble for us."

"Couldn't we disguise it enough? I don't mean to say that we would have a jaguar lover's dating site or anything."

He couldn't help smiling at that. Maya chuckled.

For the first time, he felt real relief. Kat was accepting them as family, ready to help Maya find a mate. Although that could be a dangerous venture, he appreciated that she wanted to assist his sister. And of course, Maya was beaming with enthusiasm. But he was still against doing anything like that on the Internet.

Wondering about the jaguar following them and if he had some connection to Kat, Connor asked, "Do you have any correspondence from that Wade Patterson?"

"Several emails." Kat let out her breath. "Why do you ask?"

"He comes here to the Amazon on trips. Contacted you because you were writing about jaguars and interested in locating me, a man who has a pet jaguar."

"You don't think he's a shifter, do you? The jaguar following us?"

Connor stabbed at another chunk of fish. "An American had corresponded with a woman who was interested in jaguars, lured her into the Amazon, and intended to show her the jaguar cats and get her in touch with me? How? The jaguars don't make regular appearances for anyone's sake. And I don't recall ever having smelled another male shifter in the area."

Kat let out her breath. "I don't think he's a bad guy."

"What if this Wade Patterson was planning on selling you off as a hostage? Taking advantage of you himself? What if he *is* a shifter and thought since you're so fascinated with jaguars, *he* would turn you himself?"

But then why not meet her in Florida first? Get to know her better, then turn her there?

Unsettled, Connor fisted his hand around the knife as he continued to carve up the fish.

"What if this Wade Patterson is the one following us now? Angry that he had missed his opportunity, that another shifter was claiming you instead? And here I was one of the same jaguars that Wade had enticed you to come to the jungle to see."

Now that would be ironic and would serve Wade right for luring her here in the first place with dishonorable intentions.

"I don't know," Kat said, looking thoughtful and frowning as she stared into the fire.

Connor would find out all about the man as soon as they had the chance to read over her emails. Then he would look into the man's background in Florida. But he had one other thought that had bothered him, too. "What if he's one of Gonzales's lackeys?"

She chewed on her bottom lip, then shook her head. "I don't think so. Wouldn't he have already relayed where we were to Gonzales? I don't think we'd be hiking free out here if he worked for the drug lord."

Connor had to agree with that and nodded stiffly.

After cooking and eating as much as they could of the catfish, Connor called out to the natives he was sure were hidden from their sight, motioned to the fish in a gesture of giving, and then situated his backpack over his shoulders and grabbed Kat's, too.

"I can carry my own weight," she said, "now that I've had a nice rest." She looked determined as she reached out her hand to seize the strap of her bag.

He shook his head, not about to allow her to carry the pack. "We have a long hike ahead of us. Besides, we're on our first date. Remember? I wouldn't think of letting you carry your own backpack while we're on a date."

"In an environment like this, everyone has to carry their own weight. And really, I am better," she said as Maya looked at her, appearing concerned Kat might not make it, either.

"We can set up camp along the way if we need to," Maya said. "Hell, I might not be able to make it to the city before it gets dark. And I haven't been recovering from being so sick. Appreciate Connor's gallantry. He doesn't often offer it."

"Oh?" Kat said, sounding like either she didn't think Connor could ever have been anything but gallant, or maybe she was fishing for a story.

Connor smiled a little at Kat.

Maya immediately began sharing the tale with way too much enthusiasm. "We were swimming in a Texas lake when a snapping turtle grabbed my big toe. Scared the shit out of me and hurt like the devil. As soon as I started screaming, Connor shot out of that lake like water demons were after him, leaving me behind, I might add."

Her brows elevated, Kat glanced back at Connor, who shrugged.

"I didn't know what was getting her. I figured it was every man for himself, although we were only eight years old at the time. If I'd been a jaguar when it happened, I would have made mincemeat of him." His voice commanding, he said to Maya, "Tell her the *rest* of the story."

Maya cast him a slip of a smile. "He did make mincemeat of the turtle. Well, turtle soup. He returned as a jaguar that night, once the park was closed and no one was about, so he could hunt the turtle that could have taken my toe off."

"So he ended up being gallant after all," Kat said, backing Connor up, which he thoroughly appreciated, until Maya spoke again.

"Right," Maya said in a sarcastic way. "He hunted the turtle because he didn't want to swim in the lake as a human with the turtle hunting *him* the next time."

Kat laughed.

Connor loved the way she laughed, loved that she didn't seem to mind that at least once in his life he hadn't been perfectly heroic.

Maya said, "Then there was the time—"

"Enough, Maya, or I'll tell about all *your* foibles."

Maya laughed. But Kat looked back at him, grinning, and he was sure she was dying to know what else he had done.

They trudged through the jungle for hours, taking breaks to sip water because of the heat and humidity, and even Maya looked done in. She finally stopped in front of Kat, turned, and said, "As much as I wanted to keep going until we reached the city, I can't make it."

Kat looked worried that Maya might be ill but at the same time relieved that they could stop.

Connor had wanted to spend the night with Kat in a

room of their own more than anything in the world, but he couldn't push the women any further. Maya was right about stopping for a while. "We'll make camp here and set up the hammocks in this tree."

Maya dropped her backpack on the ground as Connor ditched his and Kat's and began to set up a hammock off the ground. Before long, they were lounging in the hammocks, covered in netting, their backpacks secured in the tree.

"Do you think the natives are still following us?" Kat asked, fanning herself with a broad leaf, although it was cooler now than it had been earlier in the day.

"Yes," Connor said.

"And the jaguar?"

"Yes," Connor said in the affirmative again.

"He's going to have a hard time following us in the city, wearing a jaguar skin," Kat said, shifting in her hammock.

"Unless he's got provisions somewhere outside the city, I agree."

"He has to be a shifter, doesn't he?" Kat asked.

"Yeah, I'm sure he is." Connor knew at this point that the jaguar couldn't be anything other than a shifter or he wouldn't be following them.

"Then if he is and he's been following us as a jaguar all this time, he must have a place outside the city where he can sneak in and shift and dress. Maybe we should try to meet up with him, talk to him, see if he... well, just find out what he wants," Kat said.

"No." If the man was Wade Patterson, he had lured Kat to the Amazon under false pretenses. He had to know that Connor and his sister were shifters, but he thought they were a mated pair, not siblings, so he hadn't approached them.

"Sleep, you two," Maya grumbled. "How's a girl going to get her beauty rest?"

Connor grunted under his breath. He knew Maya wanted to meet the man. But she had to know the reservations he harbored.

Much later that night, he heard gunshots deep in the jungle and instantly realized two things—he had fallen soundly asleep, and Kat wasn't in her hammock.

Chapter 20

As soon as the gun blasts reverberated in a muffled way through the rain forest, Kat scrambled into a tree, her heart leaping with her jump as she secured a perch on a branch higher up.

She was a jaguar again, although until the shots had been fired, she hadn't realized she had shifted or that she'd been running through the jungle all alone. She groaned. Connor's words came back to haunt her. They would keep their human sensibilities while in human form, and that meant, damn it, she would still sleepwalk when she was overwrought or exhausted beyond measure.

Peering through the branches of the tree, watching for any movement, she listened, her ears twitching back and forth like antennae, attempting to figure out where the gunshots had come from and how close they had been. No one would be foolish enough to travel through the rain forest in the dead of night so she assumed someone had set up a camp somewhere and something had slithered into it — maybe a poisonous snake, an anaconda, or a wild boar.

Her pounding heart began to slow, and she took a deep sniff. Unwashed bodies, sweat, wood smoke from a campfire, and the scent of recently fired gunpowder lingered in the humid air.

But which direction were the smells coming from?

She let out her breath. If the gunshots had awakened Connor and Maya, they would be frantic about her. Should she roar to get their attention? She would no doubt scare whoever had been firing a weapon, but she was sure they were too far away to venture into the woods in the dark to search her out. They would never reach her in time before she could vacate the tree, and if they ran into her, she would be a deadly adversary, since they wouldn't be able to see her.

She opened her jaws to roar and alert Connor and Maya where she was, then hesitated. What if the jaguar-shifter who had been following them found her instead?

Not a good idea.

Hoping Connor and Maya wouldn't be too worried about her and that she could make her way back to their campsite all on her own, she leaped from the tree and landed on the ground. She poked her nose at the earth, attempting to find the scent trail she'd left with her footsteps. She caught the scent, smiled in her jaguar way, thrilled that she was getting the hang of this, and headed back the way she'd come.

Until something big pushed aside the thick foliage nearby. And she froze.

His heartbeat quickening, Connor saw Kat's shirt hanging half off her hammock, her bra clinging to one branch, her jeans on another, shoes on the ground, panties right next to them.

Cursing himself for not watching her better, he jerked off his clothes and shifted. As a cat, his sister was right behind him. They both sniffed the ground and lifted their heads, taking a good whiff of the earthy smells of the jungle and Kat's sweet jaguar scent. They searched for any signs as to which way she'd taken off. Hell, how long had she been gone before the gunfire had awakened them?

He prayed she wasn't the cause of the gunshots having been fired.

He and Maya split up, searching for any signs of Kat and trying to locate the scent of her footfalls. After what seemed like nearly a quarter of an hour, he discovered Kat had raked a tree with her nails. He grunted for Maya to join him. She loped through the thick vegetation and smelled the tree. They both looked up, hoping Kat would be reclining on the branch, maybe asleep. No such luck.

Hurried, they began to sniff the ground again, moving in every direction away from the tree to pick up her trail.

Another quarter hour had passed when Maya grunted to get Connor's attention. He raced to see what she'd discovered. Pug marks of Kat's front paws were imprinted in the muddy earth. The fresh impressions indicated she had come this way recently.

But now he was catching the odor of men, of a campfire, of the shots recently fired.

He swung his head around as another smell assaulted him. A male jaguar's urine sprayed on a tree.

Connor's blood ran cold as he continued to follow Kat's trail, glad that the male jaguar must have passed this way before Kat had. He didn't appear to be tracking her… yet.

And then more gunshots rang out.

Damn! Connor ran in the direction of the gunfire, ready to kill any bastard who might be shooting at his mate.

That's when Kat roared from a different direction. They couldn't have been shooting at her. Maybe at the other jag.

His heart beating as fast as possible, he turned. She was close by, and he roared to let her know he was on his way, just before he bounded to intercept her.

Maya had to be running parallel to him through the foliage nearby, although he couldn't see her.

Another cat raced through the jungle toward them, and Connor was sure it had to be Kat.

Eyes wide and looking grateful, Kat broke through the foliage that had hidden her. Relief washed through him as soon as he saw her, a vision in rosette-covered fur. The two quickly bonded, rubbing their bodies against each other with affection and as a sign of belonging. Maya joined them, caressing her cheek against Kat's in greeting, their tails twitching, before they headed back to camp.

The relief he felt at Kat's safe return was so pronounced that he could barely think straight. When they arrived back at the campsite, he again nuzzled Kat's face, wanting to hold her tight and never let go. But they had to leave soon.

He grunted to Maya to let her know he was going on a hunt, and she bowed her head slightly to let him know she understood.

When Connor again took off into the jungle, Kat was afraid he was going after the men with the guns. But once she had shifted and dressed, and Maya had done the same as quickly as possible, Maya explained what her brother was up to as she gathered firewood.

"It's still dark out and will be some hours before dawn, but Connor wants us to eat, then get on our way."

"But what about the men?"

"They're shooting at something else."

Kat took a deep breath. "We're leaving because I ran off as a jaguar." Kat gathered kindling.

She still couldn't get over having heard something in the brush near where she had been, but not seeing any sign of it. She didn't care to admit how scared that had made her.

"Yes, in part. He's afraid of losing you in the jungle. But in part, it's because we *can* travel under the cover of darkness, and when we reach the city, it'll be time to get a room. He doesn't like it that men are firing guns out here. They could be from the drug cartel. Even biologists who study jaguars in the area often take an armed escort. It's better if we go soon." Maya lit the fire.

"You made a mistake in turning someone like me," Kat said.

Maya looked up from the fire, the flames dancing off her irises. She barely breathed, then finally said, "What do you mean?"

Kat sat down before the fire. "I haven't done so since I first joined the Army, but while I was at one of the officers' summer training camps, I tried to climb into another woman's bunk. Everyone was shook up because they called my name and tried to find out what was wrong, but I didn't respond. I just kept trying to climb into the other bunk. Mine was on the bottom across from the one I was trying to crawl into. I was sleepwalking."

Maya's lips parted, but she didn't say a word. Then she cleared her throat. "Sleepwalking?"

Kat nodded, staring at the fire, hating to have to tell anyone her secret. "I read about it once. Experts say that often family members have the same predisposition. But since I never knew my real family, I don't have any clue. Most times, the condition doesn't persist into adulthood. But I still experience problems with it from time to time."

"You were sleepwalking?" Maya asked, sounding incredulous.

Kat squirmed to get more comfortable on the rough ground. "Yeah. At least I figure that's what happened. I didn't remember anything until I heard the gunshots fired, and I leaped into a tree to get away from the danger. That's when I realized I had shifted and wasn't back at the campsite. I had no idea how I had gotten there or where I was."

"Wow," Maya said, sounding more than worried.

Kat let out her breath hard. "I don't do it all the time. Only when I'm extremely tired. I remember one of my foster mothers calling out for me to come in and see something. Except she wasn't calling for me but my foster dad to see something on the television. I watched it without really seeing anything until the program was over, and then she put me back to bed."

Maya just stared at her with wide eyes.

"Wow," Maya said again.

"One time, I spent what seemed like an eternity trying to make a bed in another room. I was staying with another foster teen, and she and I didn't get along at all. I barely remember struggling to make a bed on the floor of the unfurnished spare bedroom. I woke up to find myself in there the next morning, sleeping on all the bedding on the floor. That's when I began to have a hazy recollection of it. Even this time, I kind of remember struggling to get out of my clothes before I shifted. Then the gunshots must have wakened me from my sleep-walking state."

Maya chewed on her bottom lip. "I'm sorry, Kat. I didn't mean to put you in any danger."

Kat didn't look at her. She didn't resent Maya for turning her. She wasn't sure why, but she really liked Maya. Maybe because she had never had a friend who would risk all to be there for her. Maya never put her down, never judged her. If anything, she seemed in awe of Kat.

Maya reached over and patted Kat's shoulder. "Are you okay?"

This time Kat looked over at her, heard the tears in her words, and saw the tears shimmering in her eyes. She knew then Maya was worried she might have put Kat in real danger, and she feared she would lose her new friend through her own folly.

"I don't know how I'd feel if I'd been in your jaguar skin, Maya, as to whether I'd ever turn someone to have another sister or to try to ensure my brother had a mate. I've never had a sibling, never thought I'd ever experience such a thing. I've done enough stupid things in my life, so I don't mean to judge you. Regrets would eat at me forever, and the best any of us can do is forge forward, learn from our mistakes, and make the most of them."

Maya nodded, but she didn't seem any more appeased.

"I don't know what's ahead for me, Maya. All we can do is take it one step at a time." Grand words, Kat thought, when deep inside she was scared to death of traveling on a plane. She was sure she would never make it to their destination before she shifted. A jaguar on a plane would definitely not be conducive to a safe and pleasant flight.

But she was not going to stew about the changes in her life because she was stuck with them, one way or another.

They heard movement in the brush, and both turned to see Connor with breakfast. Relieved to see him, she peered at the offering clenched between his teeth. *Another caiman.* She couldn't wait to get back to civilization and eat something normal like a juicy slab of steak or a lemon-pepper-seasoned piece of baked chicken, a lettuce salad with tomatoes and olives and lots of blue cheese dressing, a baked potato with butter and sour cream and chives, and of course something chocolate to finish off the meal. *Nothing exotic.*

Her stomach rumbled.

She didn't say anything about the sleepwalking, but she knew Maya would mention it before long. The issue was too important not to discuss.

Connor cooked the meal as Maya and Kat packed up their belongings.

After eating, they hiked along a dirt road headed toward civilization.

From what Connor had said before they had stopped for the night, the trek to the city would take hours still, but she couldn't wait to get a room. She wanted to clean up and sleep in a bed, make love to Connor, and never get up.

Maya interrupted Kat's thoughts of a soft bed and a hard-bodied Connor as she said, "Kat was sleepwalking." She spoke matter-of-factly, not spitefully, nor did she sound worried.

Kat closed her eyes briefly and waited for Connor to say something as he trudged down the road behind her. She took a deep breath of the humid air. At least at this time of morning, it was still cooler and the air was easier to breathe.

"Sleepwalking as a jaguar," Connor finally said.

From the neutral tone of his voice, Kat couldn't tell what he was thinking. Although she thought a smidgen of dark humor accompanied his words. She was certain he'd never thought a jaguar could sleepwalk. They probably didn't. But a jaguar-shifter?

Maya finally answered in the affirmative.

Kat thought she heard Connor swear softly under his breath. Yep, if they hadn't thought she was trouble before, they'd know she really was now. But he didn't say anything further, and they kept hiking at a steady pace through the outlying area approaching the city. Houses sprung up here and there. A few people sitting on porches stopped their conversations to observe the three Americans trudging along the road.

They must have made a bedraggled, unusual sight.

In the distance, Kat could see the picturesque, snow-capped Sierra Nevada de Santa Marta peaks. They discovered a quaint bed-and-breakfast near Tayrona National Park, which featured jungle and white sand beaches and blue waters on the Caribbean coast of Colombia. Cabanas with thatched roofs were built up a slope around huge boulders and surrounded by tropical plants that made Kat feel as though she was still in the jungle. She loved it.

They walked into the lobby where the owner greeted them with a wide smile and dark brown eyes that studied them, but if he was judging them by their appearance, he didn't let on. "Everyone calls me Garcia. Welcome, welcome! Americans?" he said in a thick Spanish accent.

"Yes," Connor said. "We'd like two cabanas near each other if you have any available."

Kat knew from past experience that if you were a tourist, you paid more. But they couldn't mask what they were so they were prepared. Having a bed to sleep in was worth just about any price for now.

Garcia must have wondered about them arriving on foot, carrying backpacks with all their belongings and no suitcases. And grungy like they had made a thousand-mile hike through the Amazon rain forest, through mud, rain, wind, and sun.

"I built the whole place by hand myself," he said, looking proud. "We have excursions to a nearby waterfall." He raised his brows in question as he took Connor's money to pay for the room.

Kat didn't attempt to hide a smile at Connor as she caught his gaze. After he'd washed her in the waterfall, she would never see another in the same way again.

"I can drive you to the park tomorrow so we can hike through the nature reserve and see all the wildlife."

"Uh, no, thank you," Kat said. They had seen all the wildlife she needed for the time being, and as for hiking any further? She was ready to be transported somewhere closer to home without having to slog one booted foot in front of another on any more long hikes.

Garcia watched their expressions as if he was trying to determine just where they had come from and why they were here. Finally, he mentioned the beaches and at that Maya nodded. "Yes, we must take in the beach."

Garcia seemed to sigh with a bit of relief, maybe worried they were trouble.

"We're biologists," Connor offered. "We spent some time in the Amazon to do research."

"Ah." Garcia looked as though he could believe that.

When Kat offered to help pay for the accommodations, Connor gave her a macho look and shook his head. The intimation was that he paid, she enjoyed. She raised a brow at him. He looked smug.

"You'll have cabanas close to each other. But privacy also." Garcia handed them their keys and gave them directions.

They hiked up the path to Maya's cabana, which was surrounded by dense foliage, trees, flowers, and colorful parrots, and even a monkey clambered up a tree high above. Now this was more like it: jungle fauna and flora, but also air-conditioned accommodations.

"Come see us in an hour after you've cleaned up and changed," Connor said to Maya. "We'll have breakfast, and then you can return here and we'll all get some much-needed sleep."

She heartily agreed, gave them both a hug, then closed her door and locked it.

After leaving Maya at her place, Connor and Kat continued up to the cabana at the top of the path. Maya's was near enough that if they encountered any trouble, they could easily get together in a few seconds via the stone path that wound its way down to the main house and restaurant.

Inside the cabana, exposed stone walls and polished bamboo floors and a real bed covered in a hibiscus floral spread made Kat feel like she was in a swanky resort. A private balcony that overlooked the jungle had an adobe tile floor for the patio and a hammock strung across it. Floor-to-ceiling windows covered with white lacy curtains let in filtered light. And air-conditioning blasted them with cool, dry air!

A shower in the bathroom was even open to the sun, which was why Connor had picked the one at the top of the group of cabanas for Kat and himself.

A small restaurant was situated next to the main lobby, and nearby was a freshwater swimming pool, which Kat was hoping they could avail themselves of later that night.

Dirty and sweaty, Connor pulled Kat in for a hard embrace, kissing her lips with a searing kiss. "Let's get cleaned up and then we can share breakfast on the patio with Maya."

Kat loved how he didn't want to leave his sister out, even though Kat was fairly sure he would have loved spending the rest of the day and night alone with her. He dumped the contents of his bag on the table and pulled out the shampoo and body wash.

"Come on, Kat. Let's take a shower."

"Don't tell me... together, so we can share the hot water." She ran her hands underneath his shirt, her fingers tracing his muscles.

"Nope." He started unbuttoning her blouse with a glint in his eye and a curve to his lips.

She cast him a mock frown and then began to peel away his trousers. "No?"

"The water's cold. We'll have to share it to keep warm."

She chuckled. "If I didn't know better, I'd say you planned it."

He laughed and quickly began dispensing with her clothes, as if he wouldn't last or was afraid they wouldn't have enough time before Maya joined them.

He scooped her up. "Grab the soaps, will you, Kat?"

"Eagerly."

And then he carried her into the bathroom and leaned down so she could turn on the water. It splashed her arm and she squealed, not intending to, but he was right. The water was cold!

The sun streamed into the shower, making it seem like a cleaner version of the waterfall. And she was excited about getting clean and whatever else they could come up with.

The scene was reminiscent of when Connor had washed Kat under the waterfall, except this time, he would be naked, too. That was much, much better because he could finish what they had started the last time. He lathered up his hands with the silky body wash and began to soap her up.

She smiled up at him, her hands already covered in soap as she smeared it all over his chest. She looked like a feral cat who loved the water as much as he did, who relished it and was emboldened by it.

The water *was* cold, but the sun and friction between them warmed them as he slid his hands all over her satiny skin, enjoying her soft curves and the way she smiled up at him as she began to soap all his body parts, making him hard as steel. He should have skipped the soap and just gotten down to business.

But spreading the silky soap over her skin turned him on just as much as it aroused her. He loved seeing her arousal, her sage eyes darkening to jungle green, the way her nipples tightened and her breasts swelled, the way her clit grew with his strokes, and the way she purred like a cat. He loved the way she barely breathed as he continued to stroke her sensitive G-spot, loved how she arched against his fingers, wanting him to touch her harder and faster and more.

She was like malleable heated clay in his hands as she melted under his ministrations, barely able to stand while he supported her with one hand around her back. He kissed her mouth as the water sluiced down their heated bodies, washing the soap off them and leaving them clean and smelling of tangerines and oranges, and musky female and male cat sex.

He might feel he had conquered the she-cat, but she had him panting, craving and savoring the feel of her, the smell of her, the sweet sexy sounds she made. As he bent to kiss her lips, her mouth parted to let him in, and he plunged his tongue inside the way he wanted to sheathe his cock between her legs. They slid their bodies against each other, bare skin to bare skin, her softness feeling so right against his hardness. Her belly pressed against his thick erection, and he cursed his need to fill her now as he tried to take it slower. But he was already ablaze, his loins on fire.

Every move she made against him turned the furnace higher.

Her hands were drifting lower, her nails lightly scratching his back and down and down. His cock moved against her soft stomach as if it had a mind of its own, soliciting a smile from her lips. Yeah, he had no control over it. Every tantalizing touch—the way her tongue probed his mouth, the way she rubbed affectionately against his body, like a cat would, only with a mission in mind—forced his body to respond with eagerness.

"You… are… mine," he groaned against her lips, desperate to hear her say she loved him, too, that she would stay with him forever, that she felt the same rampant need to be with him exclusively.

But she seemed so lost in his touch as he renewed stroking her sweet spot that she didn't say anything. Her eyes were closed, her fingers grasping his hips as if she was about to come unglued if she didn't have something to cling to, her breathing shallow and labored.

He loved her, loved the way she responded so eagerly, became so wrapped up in the act that nothing would deter her. "You… are… beautiful," he whispered, licking a trail down the water droplets spilling over her skin until he latched on to a nipple and sucked, his finger still stroking her into ecstasy.

She cried out before he'd expected it and he smiled against one nipple, then suckled the other before he lifted her, angling her so he could enter her easily. Her legs wrapped around his waist, her heels pressing provocatively against him. He slowly penetrated her sheath with his cock until she could accept his size, then thrust deep inside her, wanting her, needing her, feeling the climax she had just experienced gripping his cock tightly.

Harder, faster, deeper he pushed into her narrow passage, claiming her, his shifter mate, different from him and yet the same. She licked the water off his chin and his cheek, seeking his mouth, and tangled her tongue with his in another mating dance.

He was reminded of the waterfall where he had kissed her, feeling her heavenly body rubbing against him, the torture of her naked skin pressing his erection when he was still wearing clothes and trying to keep some distance. He could hear the same jungle sounds, only this time from the national park next door. The monkeys and birds and bugs communicating in their way, the smell of the rain forest, sweet and decadent, and the taste of citrus fruits on Kat's lips and tongue all reminded him of being back at the falls. Only this time, God, she felt so incredibly tight and feral, but most of all his.

He felt the end coming but knew that with her, it would never be the end. That she would always be at the edge of his awareness, whether he was sleeping or awake, and he would want her like this, close by, within easy reach.

He thrust hard and furious, and finally let loose his seed and groaned with spent pleasure. He leaned her against the bathroom wall, feeling satiated and more at ease than he had in years. All because he had found Kat.

And yet, it wasn't over. He wanted her, wanted to keep her, to have shifter babies if they could. But she still hadn't said the words that meant she was willing to stay with him forever.

Chapter 21

KAT KNEW WHAT CONNOR WANTED, BUT SHE COULDN'T give it to him. Not yet. What if she said "I love you" and "I want to be with you forever"—like she'd done with Roger—and that was the turnoff in their relationship?

Maybe just being there for one another, loving and caring, but not making the "I do" commitment was better. Maybe their relationship would last longer.

For now, while she was still testing the waters with her new abilities and still unsure what her future might hold, she didn't want Connor to believe that he had to be tied down to her if he found someone else who had been born a shifter.

Her heart wouldn't be broken again if she reserved some part of herself by not making the commitment.

Once they had cleaned up in their suite, they had breakfast on their patio with Maya. They watched the antics of the birds twittering about the flowers and greenery surrounding the cabana, butterflies fluttering about, a brilliantly colored poisonous frog sitting on a broad leaf, humming birds drinking from the long-throated red flowers, and even small monkeys clambering through the trees.

They intended to sleep around the clock. Although, Kat said, "If they have beef steak on the menu, that's what I want for dinner."

Connor gave her a light squeeze and kissed her

forehead. "No more Jurassic-era catfish?" He said to Maya, "Warn us if you have any trouble at all."

Looking beat, Maya nodded. She left their cabana and made her way to her own, while Connor took Kat's hand and led her into the bedroom and shut the door quietly behind them.

Connor released Kat's hand. "If you sleepwalk this time, you'll wake me. I'm not risking that we'll lose you again."

He rested his hands on either side of her head and placed his forehead against hers in a sign of relief.

Kat wrapped her arms around him and held him close. "Maya didn't have to tell on me."

"Yes, she did." He let out his breath. "What other secrets do you have that we should know about?"

Kat snorted and released him, but he seized her arms and wrapped them around his neck, then encircled her back with his and hugged her close.

"I could say the same about you. Who would have ever thought you hunted caiman with your teeth?" Kat said.

He smiled a little at her comment. "We're fabulously wealthy."

She raised a brow.

He took a deep breath. "Part of the fun in getting to know one another is learning all about each other's… secrets. Come, let's get some sleep."

Connor had turned the air conditioner on high. After having lived in the jungle for a week in the heat and humidity, Kat was freezing. But when she tried to leave the bed with the intent of turning the air conditioner down lower, Connor pulled her into his arms and whispered into her ear, "Leave it. We'll warm up after a bit."

She just hoped they were far enough away from Maya's cabana that she couldn't hear them if they got a little noisy when they were supposed to be napping.

—⁓—

Hot, Connor thought as he slid his hand over Kat's T-shirt covered body and the soft fabric moved over her lithe form. He wasn't sure about her, but he definitely needed the air conditioner on high to cool his fevered blood. They had slept for some time, but he had awakened with Kat pressed hard against his body, clinging to him for warmth. Her heat and softness and delightful scent had triggered all his senses to take their fill of her. But he wanted more.

His painful arousal jutted against her belly, and he was surprised that his prodding her with it as she pressed closer hadn't awakened her. At some point while he was sleeping, she had slipped away from him and pulled on a long shirt. That bothered him a bit. Not that she had gotten cold and put something on, but that he hadn't awakened when she'd left the bed.

Now he lifted her shirt so he could run his hands over her silky back and lower to her naked buttocks. He squeezed them, his own balls tightening.

He hadn't really had a plan except that he would sleep with her and ensure she didn't shift and sleepwalk right out of the cabana. He couldn't believe they had this additional problem to worry about.

But now he wanted her again, just like he had craved making love to her when they were standing in the waterfall—kissing, stroking, and working each other up—and again every night since they'd made love at the hut. Even when they'd kissed in the river with the dolphins swimming near them, he'd wanted to take this further with Kat.

Now, he wanted to wake her, ravish her, and encourage her to ravish him right back. He kissed her forehead, licked her cheek, ran his hand up the front of her T-shirt, and cupped a breast. It was warm and malleable, the tip turning hard and needy against the palm of his hand. He massaged to feel the hard nipple teasing his heated flesh.

He rubbed his stiff cock against her belly, making her smile. He *knew* she *hadn't* been asleep. Had she wanted to see just how hard he would try to wake her?

He leaned down and kissed her smiling lips. "Vixen."

She opened her eyes and grinned at him. "I didn't think you'd *ever* wake up," she whispered. "Even though part of you seemed wide-awake."

He chuckled low. "How could it be otherwise, the way you cuddled against me so tightly?"

"I was cold."

"And now?"

"You're heating me right up."

She smelled divine, like a she-cat and mandarin oranges and tangerines, a sexy citrus delight. The humming of the air conditioner couldn't drum out the jungle sounds surrounding the cabana. It felt right to be here like this with Kat as he kissed her mouth with a raw passion that he had never felt with any woman before. It most likely had to do with the way she kissed him back, just as aggressively, just as needy, punishing his mouth with bruising kisses while she ran her hands down his backside and kneaded his ass.

"Hmm, Kat," he said just before she licked his

mouth, and he smiled, then plunged his tongue between her parted lips that welcomed him to take his fill. She tasted sweet, of citrus fruits, her tongue teasing and touching his.

She was panting, pressing against his arousal, her fingers raking down his back.

He slid her T-shirt up her body, exposing her mons, her belly, her breasts. He kept moving the shirt upward until he pulled it over her head and tossed it onto the floor. Running his fingers through her silky hair, he took in a deep breath of her, smelling her sex and her readiness to have him.

He kicked off his boxers and kissed her mouth softly this time, his hands cupping her breasts, glorying in the feel of the soft mounds, the hard nipples, the way her body arched against him, seeking more.

He kissed her harder and moved his hand down her soft belly and through her short dark curls, and then slid his fingers into her sex. She was wet and ready, and she smiled a willful, half-lidded smile. He stroked her clit, wanting to see her come, wanting to make it happen.

She purred and arched, and he had to will himself to take it slowly with her, not to rush it. But when she tugged at him to join with her, he nudged his penis at her tight entrance and slid in slowly.

He felt hot, silky, wet delight as her flesh surrounded his, welcoming him in, but he paused, wanting to see her come first, although it was killing him to put on the brakes. He stroked her again, his erection still filling her. Seeing them joined made him even hotter.

From the look of desire and craving, and from the way her heels dug into the mattress as she pressed herself harder against his fingers, she was near the edge, which made him even hotter. Before the climax hit her, he pushed his advantage and drove deep into her tight passage. She arched in climax, calling out his name in a half purr, half growl as he continued to slam into her, driven to possess, to conquer, to satisfy the need to have her.

He kissed her nipples, licked and suckled, then kissed her mouth again right before he surged inside of her. He felt the end coming, held his breath, and let go, bathing her womb with his hot seed. She was exquisite, sexy, loving, and generous. And he was one lucky damned jaguar god. She cuddled against him and seemed to drift off to sleep as he pulled the bedcovers up over them.

He had never thought of himself as a possessive man and had always kept an emotional distance from the women he'd had sex with, but not with Kat. He felt like he was a part of her, like their souls were connected in some ancient, mystical jaguar way. Not really knowing for sure whether she had lived or died after the Army ambush had nearly killed him. As if even then they were linked by some invisible magical thread of existence.

Deep down he told himself it was fate that had made them cross paths, providence that had brought them together again. She had said she had come to thank him personally for saving her life, but he suspected there was more to it. That she had felt the same compulsion to see him again that he had felt about seeing her.

From the moment he had seen her again, he had craved being with her. Now she was his. He still couldn't believe it. Jaguars didn't mate for life. But as far as he was concerned, it was a done deal for him and Kat. She was unique and special. She had fought the drug runners fearlessly;

she had worked as part of a team the way he and his
sister did; and she was compassionate. Not only had she
accepted him and desired him, but she had accepted his
sister's friendship despite what Maya had done to her.

Everything about Kat compelled him to want to keep
her for his own. She was his mate. She completed him.

He had never really given thought to having jaguar-
shifter children of his own before, except maybe in a really vague way. Now he wanted them, wanted to prove
to his parents, to Maya, and to himself that he could be
the kind of father his own couldn't be. That he wouldn't
abandon his mate or children the way his father had done.

He rolled over onto his back and pulled Kat against
his chest, wanting to discuss something that had bothered him since the day she'd had the fever and he had
seen her bullet wounds. They should have no secrets
between them, even though Maya had warned him that
she had asked Kat and had been told the mission was
classified. He didn't buy that she couldn't share her
whole life with him. Not with what they were and how
they needed to confide in one another while keeping the
secret about what they were from the world.

Connor kissed the top of Kat's head, and she purred.
He loved the way she did that. He sighed. "What really
went down in the jungle that day you were hit?"

He didn't want to ever leave the bed as long as he
had Kat to hold close. He had never felt that way about a
woman, always wanting to distance himself both physically and emotionally after he'd had sex. He'd never
thought he would enjoy the exclusive company of a
woman and regret the notion of leaving her for anything.

The heat of the day was upon them, and everything

in the city would be shut down anyway. Later, he would call to get plane reservations. Tonight, they would go to the beach.

"It's classified," Kat said quietly, yet he heard the metal in her voice, as if she was ready to tell him her name, rank, and serial number—and nothing more.

He smiled, then frowned, running his fingers over her bare arm and loving the feel of her silky skin. "Are you still in the military?"

She shook her head, her hair tickling his chest.

"Good."

She snorted.

"What? The Army mission went wrong," he said, not willing to let it go. He had to know what she'd had to deal with. When she was wounded, she must have been scarred both physically and emotionally.

"Yes. The mission went horribly wrong," she whispered against his chest.

"I take it you were one of the lucky ones." He hadn't had time to check the other men. Some might have survived around the perimeter of the camp. He just hadn't known.

A tear splashed on his chest, and he felt mortified. "Kat…"

"I was the only one of my team who made it out of there alive, Connor."

He stroked her hair and kissed her cheek. "I'm glad you made it. God, I'm glad." He took a deep settling breath. "And, although I wouldn't have condoned what Maya did to you, I'm still grateful she did."

"Hmpf. That remains to be seen." Kat sighed. "You don't know the half of it," she said softly. "I have flashbacks. I don't know when I'll have them. I don't know what will happen when I do, either."

He didn't say anything for a time, just stroked Kat's silky hair. What kind of flashbacks had she been living through? He wanted to take them and crush them with his bare hands. More than anything, he wanted to help her get over them.

"We'll deal with it," he said firmly. He intended to help her get over them any way that he could. But he had to know what was causing them, and he wasn't sure how someone could deal with that kind of trauma.

She gave a disparaging grunt. "And I walk in my sleep."

He chuckled low. "Yeah, well, I'm not letting you out of my grasp at night or whenever we chance to lie down together."

"Controlling, aren't we?"

"You bet. What about the flashbacks?"

She sighed. "Everyone has flashbacks of memory. A song that you love might trigger a memory of… dancing with someone in the past. Or the scent of jasmine might remind you of a botanical garden you visited when you were a child."

"Your fragrance," Connor said. "When I came upon you in the jungle, I recognized your special scent."

"Yes, that's exactly what I'm talking about. But when a traumatic event has occurred in your life, something in your everyday life can trigger the memory."

"Like?"

"A car backfiring."

Connor kissed her cheek. "Which sounds like gunfire."

"Yes. So I wouldn't necessarily have to hear gunfire to have some stimuli trigger another bout of a flashback."

"Hell, Kat, you must have felt terrible when Manuel shot at you."

She gave a ladylike snort. "Hardly. The sound of gunfire was terrifying only because the bullets were winging right past me—way too close. I was afraid for you and Maya, and terrified I'd fall out of the tree and break my neck when I landed on the ground. I might be a cat sometimes, but I still don't land on my feet when in my human form."

He heaved a sigh because that hadn't been too far from his own thoughts and pressed a tender kiss on her forehead. "But the gunfire didn't trigger a flashback?"

"No."

"Has anything triggered one while you've been here?"

"Yes. The voice of one of the men. The leader. Something about his voice made me think of the man we were trying to take down. But what I'm worried about—what will happen if I have a flashback when I'm in my jaguar form?"

"You'll be fine, Kat." He stroked her cheek and looked down into her eyes. "Have you been given any treatment for it?"

"Yeah."

"What can I do for you if it happens again?"

"Hold me close. Tell me it's just a flashback. That it isn't real. Or I can stomp my feet and tell it to go away. Or talk to you and Maya about it." She shrugged and smiled a little. "The doc said a nice warm bath could help. Breathing in deeply. Reminding myself that I survived. That it's over with. And it will get better."

Connor still couldn't get his own anger under control over what had been done to her, although for Kat's sake he tried not to show it. "You don't work for them any longer, right? Not undercover or anything?"

She finally said, "They gave me a medical discharge."

"Hell."

"They do that when they believe you've cracked under pressure."

"What gave them that idea?"

She smiled up at him sweetly and innocently, but deep down, full of the devil.

He raised his brows. Once again he found himself admiring her.

"I had it together for about three months after the… *incident*. Really, I thought I could keep it all in, bury it where I never had to deal with it again, pretend that the men I had trained with for years who had families, well, that none of it mattered because we'd had a mission to do. We'd signed up, and that was our way to bring down the scum of the earth. But the intelligence was dead wrong, and we walked right into a trap." She hesitated. "I'm not really telling you all this, you know."

"Hell," Connor said again. He couldn't help it. His muscles bunched with tension as he felt like turning into his jaguar form and tearing into the men who had injured her. He would have loved to force the men who gave them the false intelligence to take their place on the front line instead of Kat. "Why did they have you go? A woman?"

"I was supposed to be the bait in a hostage-taking situation. The man in charge was supposed to take me into the camp, and my men would come in afterward, guns blazing, and free me. But the drug leader knew who I was all along. They pretended complacency, and when my team came in to rescue me, they found themselves fired upon from every corner of the camp. We'd been set up."

"But your people got you out."

"Yeah," she said sarcastically, "after everyone else on the team was dead. I was interrogated before I went into surgery and after I came out, despite the fact that I was mostly out of it the entire time. Who knows what I really said. I knew it was my job to tell them everything I could about the mission, but I was so emotionally and physically exhausted that I finally told them where they could take their future missions. I think I bloodied Roger's nose when he tried the 'I'm your fiancé and you can talk to me' ploy."

She kissed Connor's cheek. "I wouldn't have been a suitable Army wife or career Army myself. Not after I had a mental breakdown."

"Why did you really come back here, Kat?" Connor asked, thinking that a woman who had experienced a mental breakdown shouldn't be alone in the Amazon.

She let out her breath in a huff. "If I tell you all my secrets, you might just decide I'm too much to handle."

"Ha! You say that to a jaguar god?"

She chuckled but then grew serious. "I was under a doctor's care. He suggested I visit a place similar to where I had experienced my trauma. He thought it would help to cure me of the flashbacks. At least that's what I got out of the sessions. Go someplace that was relatively safe, but that might trigger the feel of where I'd been. Of course I was supposed to take a reliable friend or two with me. I couldn't find anyone like that who was in the least bit interested in going to the Amazon rain forest."

"Has it helped?" Connor shook his head. "Here Maya changes you, and you already had a nightmare to deal with."

"I feel... different. I don't know exactly how to explain it, but when I first arrived here intent on dealing with my problems and trying to find you to thank you, I loved the jungle, but I was more like a vacationer just here to observe. And I have to admit I was a little on edge, as if the enemy was hiding behind every tree. Now it's almost as though this is my second home."

Relieved that she would feel that way, Connor nodded. "I understand the sensation. As jaguars, we come home to roost, so to speak, from time to time. It's as though the craving to be here is in our blood."

He would hate it if she didn't want to return with them when they came here in the future. Yet, the fact that they had no idea how often she would shift or when bothered him. What if it took years before she could get it under control? What if she could never control it? He couldn't imagine how difficult it would be to visit the jungle then. Maybe they could buy a boat or visit a location closer to home. Belize bordered Mexico. A rain forest existed there, too, and it was closer to Texas and another haven for jaguars.

"I'm not sure about flying home," Kat finally admitted.

"I understand," he said, running his hand over her arm. He was worried about it, too, not at all sure they would make it. He was thinking of checking into other options in the meantime. "I'll get dressed and call the airlines to see if we can book a flight."

"All right. I'm going to take another shower."

The water was cold, even though the sun would warm

them somewhat. Thinking of the water sluicing down her tan skin in the shower brought a smile to his lips. He couldn't help thinking how he could warm her up in there again. Trying to get his lascivious thoughts under control, he slipped into his boxers.

He pulled out his phone and called the airlines while Kat disappeared into the shower. One flight would accommodate them best, a one-and-a-half-hour trip to Bogotá, Colombia, from Santa Marta. One stop. He was certain that Kat could make that trip. Then they would have a five-hour layover in the city. Maybe they could find someplace to hide out for a while. After that, it would be a little over a five-hour flight to Houston. It was the shortest flight plan he could find.

He heard the water shut off and cursed softly under his breath. He had wanted to join Kat in the sunny shower before she finished.

He walked into the bathroom to see her wearing only a towel around her head. He smiled, hurriedly ditched his boxers, and gathered her in his arms before she could escape. "Don't you need to… rinse off a little more?"

She laughed. "No, but do you want me to soap up *your* hard-to-reach spots?"

He pulled the towel off her head and tossed it on the towel rack, then turned the water on and moved her under the showerhead with him. "Only if I get to soap up all *your* hard-to-reach spots."

"Hmm, jaguars love to play in the water," she said and stroked his swelling cock.

Chapter 22

MAYA HAD TAKEN A NICE LONG NAP IN HER COMFORT-able air-conditioned cabana. She thought she had heard Kat and Connor making love, if the muted love cries were from them and not from howler monkeys or some-thing else that was imitating them. She smiled, satisfied that she had brought Kat and her brother together and that her plan had worked. She'd had some iffy moments over the past few days.

Now if they could only get Kat home to Texas with-out further incident. Early evening was upon them, the blue sky and wispy clouds turning violet as the warm yellow sun sank beneath the brilliant foliage, and Maya was starving.

She didn't want to disturb Kat and Connor, but she wasn't waiting.

She dressed in jeans and a flowery shirt and strappy sandals. Feeling more human, she left her cabana and headed down the quaint stone path that wound among more cabanas hidden away in the dense jungle foliage. When she reached the white building with blue awnings stretched over its long narrow windows, a toucan was sitting in a cocoa tree near the entrance and Spanish music drifted from the building.

Her mouth watered at the aroma of cheeses and fish and chicken and beef cooking in the kitchen.

When she stepped inside the large tiled room, which

was bustling with tourists and what looked to be regulars, a hostess seated her at one of the empty square tables for four. The air-conditioned air felt good, but circulating fans whirling high above helped to move it even more. She felt like she was in a breezy, chillier place than South America.

The sound of laughter and splashing came from outside where the pool was located, though she couldn't see it as she took her seat. She smiled up at the dark-haired miss who handed her a menu, but the owner of the establishment, Garcia, caught her attention. His face was dark and grim as he listened to a man speaking to him, the stranger gesticulating at the resort. Garcia's forehead was sweating, his hands clenching and unclenching into fists at his sides, and she caught a whiff of the smell of sweat on him as the fans carried it to her.

Three other men were crowded around Garcia—all of Spanish descent, dark haired, and scruffy looking— standing too close, in his space, and extremely intimidating. The one who was speaking shoved a photo at him. The owner looked at it for a long moment, then shook his head and handed the picture back. Did the interrogator see the fleeting look of recognition on Garcia's face like Maya did?

That's when she noticed the man had a gun half-exposed by his camouflage vest. This was bad news.

The waitress returned with Maya's glass of water.

"Are those men from around here?" Maya asked, knowing she shouldn't stick her nose in where it didn't belong, but she was both curious and annoyed that the men were bullying Garcia. He had been so pleasant toward her brother and Kat and her, and so

accommodating, making sure they could have their cabanas right away despite their grungy appearances, the
odd hour when they had arrived, and their having had
no reservations.

She would have loved to have taken the men on in her
jaguar form and scared them like they were scaring Garcia.

The waitress glanced back at the men and quickly returned her gaze to Maya, her eyes huge. She vehemently
shook her head.

Did that mean she knew them and they weren't from
around here? Or that she didn't know them but just knew
their type?

"What are they doing here?" Maya asked.

The woman shook her head again, too afraid to speak
and draw the men's attention.

Maya wanted desperately to take them to task, but
she knew it was best to cool her heels. No sense in making waves that could involve Kat, who didn't have her
shape-shifting abilities in hand.

"Are you certain Kathleen McKnight is not staying
here? An eyewitness said he had seen her come in here
to…" the man said to Garcia, his voice dark and threat-
ening, prompting Garcia to finish the statement.

Maya's blood chilled to ice.

There were only two things Kat might have done
when she arrived here—eaten at the restaurant or taken
a room.

Maya glanced back at the owner, fearing he would
tell the men where Kathleen was staying, but he just
shook his head, saying no.

Oh, God. He was helping them, but it could get him
killed, she feared.

She had to warn Connor and Kat.

Her heart thundering, Maya said to the waitress, "I'm afraid I'm not feeling well all of a sudden. Can you cancel the order?"

The waitress looked bewildered.

Maya repeated her words in Spanish, but the woman still seemed surprised. Maya rose from her chair, trying not to catch the men's attention. "I'll be back later, if I can."

She handed a tip to the woman, then with a forced easy stride, she left the restaurant, raced up the path to Connor and Kat's cabana, and barged in without knocking first.

Connor and Kat were dressed at least, both their mouths gaping as they turned to stare at her in disbelief.

"Someone's asking about Kat. Men like the ones we saw in the jungle. The owner is buying us some time, but they're at the restaurant now, and he told them he'd never seen the woman in the photo they had of her."

"We have a flight out of here at 5 p.m. tomorrow," Connor said, quickly stuffing his things in his bag, while Kat put her clothes in her own bag.

"What if we drive to Bogotá tonight and take a flight to Houston from there instead of waiting for the flight tomorrow night to fly us to Bogotá? Then there would be no stops. Just a straight flight into Houston," Maya said.

Connor zipped up his bag. "It's the red-eye flight. It'll leave tomorrow at midnight and arrive at 5:30 the next morning. But it's a long drive to Bogotá and can be dangerous."

Maya nodded but only commented on the flight.

"Hopefully everyone will be sleeping on the plane during the middle of the night and the lights all out, just in case Kat shifts. Did you get the very back seats?"

"Yes," Connor said.

"Maybe we should make a stand," Kat said, her voice quiet as she stared out the window, her back rigid. "Maybe we shouldn't be running away."

Maya was shocked that Kat would even say such a thing, and she wondered if it was due to Kat's military training or her jaguar senses or a little of both.

Kat continued, "I've endangered you both."

"What are we going to do, Connor?" Maya asked, rubbing Kat's arm in reassurance.

"I'll go down and take a look at the men while you pack. Kat will go with you. We'll leave our packs at your cabana in case Garcia changes his mind and tells the men we're staying there."

"I'll go with you," Maya said, "in case the men aren't speaking to Garcia any further and you won't know which men they are."

Kat turned to face them, her expression all business. "I'll go with you and see if I can identify them."

"No," both Maya and Connor said, causing Kat to raise her brows. But then they heard footfalls on the path below the cabana moving toward one of the lower cabanas, and Maya, Kat, and Connor all headed for the window to peer out through the sheer curtains.

But they couldn't see who was walking up the path. The thick vegetation hid each of the cabanas from the view of the others, giving welcome privacy for the guests.

"Shit," Connor whispered, grabbing his and Kat's packs. "Let's go." He motioned to a window that faced the park and boulders behind the cabana. "We'll climb through the window."

Kat already had slid the window up as quietly as she could, but Maya felt the slight grinding sound had alerted everyone in a one-hundred-mile radius of their plans. The problem with their sensitive hearing was they often felt as though everyone else had it also.

Kat climbed out the window and then took her bag from Connor, and then his. Maya joined her outside, and Connor climbed out last, shutting the window as quietly as he could. They moved quickly through the vegetation, avoiding the stone path while making their way to Maya's cabana. When they reached it, Maya went to the front door and unlocked it. Kat and Connor stayed hidden in the tropical vegetation behind her place.

Maya went inside, shut the door, and then hurried to the back side of her cabana and opened the window for them. They slipped their bags to her, and Connor boosted Kat through the window, then climbed into the cabana after her.

Maya was already cramming her clothes and other personal effects into her backpack.

Connor glanced out a front window and saw three men on the path headed for a different cabana. Kat drew close and watched them, her eyes widening with recognition.

This is so not good, Maya thought. "Kat," she whispered, though the men wouldn't hear her in the enclosed cabana. "Do you know them?"

"Some of Gonzales's men," Kat said. "One of the ones who shot me." She switched her attention from the men to Connor. "How could they know I was here?"

"What about this Wade Patterson you were supposed to meet here?" Connor asked, as they grabbed their bags and he guided Maya and Kat out of the cabana through the back window.

"I don't know," Kat admitted, sounding anxious as she jumped to the ground.

"We'll talk about it later. For now, we need to get a rental vehicle. We're paid up at this resort. And we'll do what Maya suggested. We'll drive to Bogotá. We can take the red-eye flight to Houston from there tomorrow night since it might be safer in the event you have the urge to change. Or we might be able to catch an earlier flight."

"Do you think Garcia told on us?" Maya asked.

"No. If he did, they wouldn't have been searching all the cabanas. Maybe they assumed he hadn't seen you, that we slipped Kat into a room. I believe someone must have seen Kat at some point and reported she was here."

"Do you think that they've been following us all along?" Kat asked. "On our long hike through the jungle?"

"I don't know. Not for sure. If so, they probably couldn't make contact any more than we could, with no satellite towers to make cell phone calls." Connor said.

"They'd wonder about us, don't you think?" Maya asked her brother.

"We rescued her in the jungle. They probably figure we're just getting her to a city for her own safety." He glanced at Kat, who looked like she was going to be sick, her face ice white. "Kat? Are you going to be all right?"

Chapter 23

"I'm fine," Kat said to Connor, but she didn't feel fine at all, and from the expression of disbelief on his face, he knew it, too.

Kat felt sick to her stomach, not just because the man she had tried to take down on her last mission was out to get her again, but because she had now endangered Maya and Connor. They didn't seem to be worried about that prospect. Just about her. And that made her feel worse.

These men were ruthless. How could she have let this happen?

Was this Wade Patterson's doing? Was he working with Gonzales? The FBI profile on Gonzales said he didn't like to lose. That he would go to considerable extremes to punish those who angered him. But she hadn't thought she would be a prime target.

However, when she had been rescued, he had lost the control he had over her fate. And she had infiltrated his camp, so she supposed that could be enough to count her as one of the bigger targets.

What if the Army psychiatrist was in on it? What if he had suggested she go to the jungle to relive the experiences because he was in Gonzales's back pocket? And Wade Patterson was to encourage her to return to the Amazon, too, except he would give a location that Gonzales knew about.

She shook her head at herself. The doctor had said she

might feel that everyone was out to get her. Wasn't this the ultimate paranoia? When she believed the man who had taken an oath to help her was out to get her, too?

She was torn between being glad Connor and his sister wanted to stick by her side to protect her and wanting to push them far away from her so they wouldn't be in any danger. Neither Maya nor Connor seemed to want to let her go her own way, but Kat couldn't do this to them. They didn't deserve it.

After taking a bus to the city and locating a rental car, Kat balked at going any further with Maya and Connor. She intended to get hold of one of her points of contact in the Army, let him know what was going on, and then hope a team would arrive in time to take Gonzales out. But she had to leave Maya and Connor and do this on her own, hoping to God she wouldn't shift at the worst time. She could get together with Maya and Connor again after this was all through. "If we split up…"

Maya's jaw dropped and she frowned, then quickly looked at Connor and said, "No," at the same time he did.

Their expressions were unyielding as Connor took Kat's arm, made her get into the passenger side of the compact black rental car, and shut her door for her. Then he tossed their backpacks in the trunk.

Her passport and credit card were both in a zippered side pocket in her backpack, and she couldn't go anywhere without them.

"We stay together," Connor said as he slid into the driver's seat, while Maya climbed into the backseat. He locked the doors.

"If we split up…" Kat said again, hoping she could convince him that her plan was reasonable. She really thought that the military could handle Gonzales and his men better than two jaguar-shifters and one ex-Army officer who couldn't control her jaguar half.

Connor shook his head. "Hell, Maya, she's as stubborn as you."

"We have to stay together, Kat," Maya said in a consoling way. "We can't do this any other way."

"You're not safe with me," Kat reasoned. "They'll kill you. They'll kill me also, but I'm sure Gonzales will first draw my death out for his own pleasure, just because I helped get so many of his men killed."

"You're not safe *without* us," Connor said. "They're not going to get the upper hand. Like Maya said, we stay together. As pure jaguars, we wouldn't hunt in packs, but we're not pure jaguars so we stick together." He gave her a dark look. "We'll do whatever it takes, Kat, to keep you safe. You're part of the family now. We're not giving you up."

Kat let out her breath in a huff. These men meant business. She and Connor and Maya had gotten lucky earlier when they encountered Manuel and the others in the jungle and the hunters had stepped in to help them. She wasn't sure they would get that lucky again.

"They have guns and lots of them. They're brutal."

"*We* know how to deal with them." Connor tightened his hands around the steering wheel. "They'll never know what hit them."

But Kat didn't want to rely on that. "I need to contact someone in the Army so they can handle him and his men. If I just call them—"

"No," both Connor and Maya said.

Connor continued, "Your men barely got you out of

the situation alive the last time. You're not going to be their bait again. That's exactly what you'd be. We're not going to allow it."

But she *was* bait no matter what she did, whether she went on her own, stuck it out with Maya and Connor watching her back, or asked the Army to do so. She knew now Gonzales wasn't going to let her go.

He had contacts everywhere. Had he had her watched for the past year, waiting to see what would happen? Where she would go? When she would be within his striking distance again?

She sank into the passenger's seat, resigned to the fact that Connor and Maya wouldn't let her do this on her own, yet unable to let go of the notion that she had gotten them into this potentially deadly mess.

"Tell me everything you know about this Gonzales," Connor said.

Kat didn't say anything right away as they drove south to Bogotá on the winding roads edged by steep cliffs. She was glad she wasn't afraid of heights.

She thought about Gonzales and his men. All that she knew was classified. But in truth, what did she really know? Only what the top echelon had fed her as the truth, and now she wasn't certain how much of it was true. Except that he was one of the bad guys.

"Gonzales is a leader of a drug cartel. He's contracted hits on several DEA bigwigs, and the Army finally got involved by sending in a special undercover unit."

"You and your team," Connor said.

"Me. I played the perfect naive tourist who ends up at a bar his men were known to frequent. The head shed had tried all kinds of different attempts at locating him but was never successful. So someone came up with the idea of an American college-age girl who had tons of money, was estranged from her fiancé, and decided to get away from high society and visit the Amazon on a whim.

"The plan was that the word would be sent to one of Gonzales's operatives, and once Gonzales learned of it, he would want to take me hostage. The powers that be thought it was a way for one of us to infiltrate one of Gonzales's camps, with the idea that he would eventually visit the camp to see the proverbial golden goose.

"My team was closely monitoring my movements the whole time I was at the bar. As soon as I sent them the signal, they would know I was in. We got lucky. If you can call it that. I ended up in the camp where Gonzales was actually staying. Then I fed the coordinates to my team. You know what happened after that."

No one spoke for some time, then Maya said, "Okay, so you came here because Wade Patterson offered you an opportunity to meet up with Connor, maybe to document jaguars in the rain forest, and… your doctor intimated that revisiting a jungle could help you to cope with your night terrors. But didn't you worry you might run into Gonzales's men somewhere in the rain forest? Or that you might end up seeing the beast himself?"

"No. My identity was completely changed for the mission. I'm no longer in the military, just a tourist. I don't even look the same."

Maya frowned at Kat. "Are you sure the Army isn't behind all this? Maybe encouraging you to return to the jungle? Maybe Wade Patterson is an American operative, and the whole plan was to use you as bait again, except without your knowledge this time," Maya said, sounding suspicious.

"I've considered it," Kat said drily. "I don't know how long the military is supposed to work with a soldier experiencing night terrors and flashbacks. I figured it would have been longer than the time they worked with me. But the next thing I knew, they were medically discharging me."

Instinctually, Connor had a really bad feeling about this. He wondered if maybe the Army *was* using Kat to do their dirty work. If she hadn't been a jaguar-shifter like she was now, he would have gone to the papers with the story once he got her to safety. But as it was, they had to keep a low profile.

What would the Army think of her if they learned she had shifter abilities? They'd probably use her however they could in more covert operations. If they weren't able to have her killed off the first time, why not the next time or sometime after that?

"We'll get a hotel this evening that has Internet access," Connor said. "I want to see everything you have on this Wade Patterson." Connor was sure his expression was as dark as his mood when Kat cast an anxious look at him. She didn't know just how primal he could be when one of his own was threatened.

—⁂—

Connor and his sister and Kat had traveled for several hours when they got off the main highway to get gas, but when they tried to return to the highway, the road back had been closed off. At once, Kat felt ill at ease. Reluctantly, Connor pulled the rental car onto a smaller road and headed south. He and Maya were both quiet, and she assumed they didn't like the turn of events any more than she did.

Another detour took them down a dirt road through a jungle landscape, the vegetation encroaching on the road and making it feel as though they were driving through a tunnel of green, the trees and vines towering overhead and blocking out the hot sun.

Kat was feeling corralled as if they were cattle being herded to market. She realized she wasn't too far off the mark when they came around a bend in the road and found a truck barricading it.

Wearing camouflage fatigues and armed with automatic rifles, several men motioned for Connor to stop the car, making Kat's blood run cold. She didn't recognize any of them, but they all looked like Gonzales's men to her.

"Are they Gonzales's men?" Maya asked.

"I don't know," Kat said, her voice strained, her skin clammy. She didn't normally have panic attacks, but she was having one big time now.

"Could just be rebels or another bunch of drug runners. Hold on," Connor warned.

He twisted the car off onto an even narrower dirt road, slamming into a couple of branches and scratching the car. "They'll try to follow us, but we'll ditch the car for the time being and melt into the jungle."

He and Maya could vanish into the thick foliage as jaguars, sure. Their black rosettes and golden pelts blended in with the shadows of the forest. But Kat? The only way she was melting was into a puddle of nerves, and that wasn't going to help her hide at all.

Connor pulled the rental vehicle off the road and into the thick tropical vegetation. They all shoved at the doors to make enough of an opening to squeeze out of the car. "Go, Maya. Take Kat. I'll get our bags and the rifle," he said, his voice commanding, low, rushed.

"You can't get them all," Maya said, hurrying to the trunk.

He jerked the bags out, and Maya took hers and Kat grabbed her own. Then the three sprinted deeper into the jungle.

"What now?" Kat asked, wishing she was armed to the teeth.

Connor motioned to a great climbing tree covered in vines and broad leaves and bromeliads. They climbed high into the tree, secured their backpacks on different branches, and covered the bags with vegetation to ensure they couldn't be seen from the ground.

Connor's expression was dark as he furrowed his brow at Kat. He said to her, "I'm leaving the rifle with you for your protection. Maya and I will shift and scout around. Stay hidden in the foliage. Don't make a move unless you absolutely have to."

Kat didn't like being left alone in the jungle with the enemy surrounding them. She didn't like that Maya and Connor would face down armed men, either, but she knew that's what they intended to do. She wanted to assist them, but her jaguar self wouldn't be much help. Shooting an armed target who was out for blood was one thing. She had been trained to do that. Biting a man to death… she shuddered at the disagreeable image that brought to mind.

Kat took a deep breath to settle her nerves. She felt

like bait, sitting in the tree with the rifle ready as Maya and Connor removed their clothes, tucked them into their bags, and shifted. Both gave her a last look in farewell before they leaped for the forest floor.

Then they melted like a couple of jaguar wraiths, slipping unseen into the jungle.

And Kat was alone again in the jungle.

No, not alone. She heard the men moving toward the rental car in the distance and hoped they wouldn't shoot out its tires or disable it any other way. Even if Connor and Maya and Kat did get the upper hand with these men, how would they get to Bogotá if the men had disabled their rental car?

Chapter 24

AS A JAGUAR AND FULLY INTENDING TO TAKE THESE men down, Connor skirted well around where the men were searching for them. He counted six men total, all armed to the teeth and all approaching the rental vehicle with caution. One of the heavier men said in Spanish, "No one here. They've scurried into the jungle like little mice. Shall we chase the little mice down?"

As if he had to ask the question.

Two of the men laughed, while two others were trying the door handles. Unlocked. No sense in locking the vehicle and having the men break the windows trying to get in. But they would find nothing inside the car.

After a minute, the two men shook their heads.

"Let's play cat and mouse, then," the big man said.

Smiling to himself, Connor was game. Only he would be the cat and they the mice.

"You stay," the man said to one of his comrades. "Just in case they return before we locate them."

The man nodded and leaned against the car, his rifle cradled diagonally across his chest. The others began to move, spreading out and quickly losing sight of each other in the dense jungle.

Maya moved closer to Connor and inclined her head toward the guard at the car. She had to wait, let him think he had nothing to worry about, and ensure the others were well away from the car before she took him down.

Connor nuzzled her, giving her the go-ahead. He would trail after the others, taking down as many as he could one at a time once they were far enough apart from each other. Because no one had mentioned Kat's name, he thought either these men didn't work for Gonzales, or if they did, they were clueless about her being out here. Either would be good news.

※

Kat heard the men all around her, joking noisily as though they thought that if they made enough racket, they could scare the tourists into panicking. Kat tightened her hands on the rifle. She wasn't panicking. She was ready for them. One armed tourist.

The jungle vegetation was so thick that she couldn't even see anyone yet. But she heard a couple of the men moving closer, their boots crunching on debris on the ground, their legs brushing foliage aside.

Then she swore she saw something move a little distance from the tree she was hiding in. Like a dark shadow of a cat, but only for a flash of a second. Had it been Connor? Or Maya? She thought the shadow was too big to have been Maya.

A thud sounded a little way off. She barely breathed, her gaze riveted to where the sound had occurred. Freckles of perspiration dotted her skin as she stared at the vegetation, trying to see any movement.

Again, she heard someone moving toward the tree. One of the brigands appeared beneath her. A camouflage cap was squashed on his head, the rest of him in camouflage, too. He could be one of Gonzales's men.

She readied her rifle to shoot him, though she

wouldn't fire a shot unless it was absolutely imperative. He glanced up, looked around, but didn't see her. He was looking in the direction of their backpacks, but she hoped he couldn't spy them. Then he shouldered his rifle and grabbed a branch to begin hauling himself up.

Kat barely breathed. If only she had a silencer, she could shoot him before he got very far up the tree. But if she used the weapon without a silencer, the popping noise would alert everyone else to her location.

He still hadn't seen her, she didn't think. But something must have caught his attention and made him want to investigate further.

In the next instant, she felt a sudden overwhelming urge to remove her clothes. What the hell was wrong with her? Sure, if she stripped and the villain caught sight of her, he might be distracted momentarily, delaying his climb. But an exotic stripper she was not. And beyond holding his attention for a moment, what would she do after that?

She itched to tug her shirt over her head, the urge so great that she couldn't stop herself. Then she realized what was wrong with her. The craving to shift was the problem.

She set the rifle in the crook of the tree before she panicked and tossed it aside where it would fall to the ground and possibly fire off a round. Despite not wanting to shift in the worst way, she had no control over the urge and began pulling her shirt over her head. The movement alone could spell her doom. She knew damn well that if she sat very still, he might not catch sight of her, but if she started tearing off her clothes, he was sure to see her.

No…no…no…

She couldn't help herself. She couldn't stop the shift from occurring.

His head turned in her direction, and his black eyes widened and his mouth gaped wide.

He muttered something under his breath as she yanked off her bra. He didn't move any closer, just held on to the branch above him as he stood on another below that and stared at her in wonder. To her relief, he didn't call out for anyone to join him. No, he wanted her all to himself.

She was sitting bare-breasted on a tree branch, struggling to pull off a boot, when she lost hold of it and dropped it to the ground. *Shit*.

The man chuckled and spoke dirty to her in Spanish. She figured he thought she believed she could buy her way out of this nightmare by offering him sex. Fat chance of that, she wanted to tell him. She would just as soon as shove him off the tree branch he was standing on, hoping to break his damn neck. Instead, she'd show him her big menacing jaguar teeth and end his rampant leering that way.

She managed to get her other boot off without losing it. She tucked it with her other clothes against the massive tree trunk, glad she was getting better at this, then worked on her jeans while he watched as if she were a stripper there to entertain him.

"Juan!" a man yelled from down below, and she realized that because of being concerned about the man in the tree and struggling to get out of her clothes, she hadn't even heard the other man arrive.

Great. Now she had two of them to deal with.

"I'm busy," Juan said and began climbing higher,

as if he wanted to ensure he claimed her before his friend could.

"Did you find one of the women?" the man asked from the ground, and she wondered if he had found her size-six boot.

She couldn't see him from where he was standing at the base of the tree, but she was glad he wasn't climbing after her also—at least for the moment. Maybe she could shift before both of the men saw her naked.

She pulled off her panties and secured them with the rest of her clothes against the trunk of the tree and was ready to shift.

"Hey, Juan, what are you doing up there?"

"Going to have some fun."

"I'm coming up, too."

Kat frowned at the man climbing toward her, wondering why she wasn't shifting as she sat butt-naked on the tree branch high above Juan.

Now! Do it now! What were the magic words? How had she managed before?

She scowled at the man and at herself for her ineptitude. Maybe she hadn't been getting ready to shift. She would never get used to this business. Mortified that she wasn't going to change into a menacing-looking jaguar and was instead showing off her naked body to a drug dealer, she wasn't sure what to do next. Get dressed? Or keep waiting for the shift to happen and hope to hell it occurred before Juan reached her?

She could just imagine getting halfway dressed when the shift hit her. She would be a jaguar with one leg in her leopard panties. That would make her a real cool cat. *Not.*

Then the second man, who had managed to make it a little way up the tree, swore and gave a muffled cry.

Kat and Juan looked down, but Kat couldn't see anyone as high up in the tree as she was, as leafy as the branches were, and because of the location of the man when he cried out.

Sounding afraid of what had happened to his friend, Juan called out softly, "Ramirez?"

But the other man didn't say anything in response. Chill bumps pricked Kat's arms and legs as she peered down through the vegetation, trying to see what had happened to the man.

"Ramirez?" Juan said again, a little louder this time.

Still no answer.

Juan switched his attention back to Kat, apparently unable to decide whether he wanted more to reach the naked woman or to check out what had happened to his friend. He wasn't given any time to decide, though. A large male jaguar leaped onto the branch below Juan, then grabbed the branch the terrorist was on and joined him.

Both Kat's and Juan's jaws dropped when they saw the male cat. For an instant, the jaguar's golden eyes shifted from Juan to Kat. He lifted his head a bit as if he was greeting her, then he turned his attention back to Juan. With one quick swipe of his powerful paw, the jaguar sent the man flying to the ground before he could swing his rifle off his shoulder.

Juan never made a sound. Not when the big cat struck him or when he was falling or even when he hit the ground with a thud.

Kat was so shocked that she couldn't move. The jaguar

was more orange in color than golden like Maya and Connor, but he was just as big and menacing as Connor.

The jaguar looked up at her, his whiskers twitching, his nose sampling the air and *her*.

She was naked. And he wasn't just a big cat, she was certain. He was just like Connor had been when she first saw him as a jaguar and thought he was just a cat. This one had to be a man beneath the jaguar's spotted coat, too. He was seeing her as a man sees a woman, or as she supposed a male shifter saw a female, *naked*.

She was grateful that the cat had taken care of Juan and probably the man on the ground. Especially since her shifter genes were so unreliable that she hadn't been able to turn into a jaguar. But she wanted him to leave, to quit smelling her scent, to vanish before Connor returned and tore into him.

She heard Connor roar, and then Maya followed suit. They were okay. Kat gave a tentative sigh of relief.

The jaguar took another deep breath, then leaped from the tree, and Kat grabbed her bra. What would Connor do if he discovered the shifter had been with her in the tree? She wouldn't have to tell Connor. He would immediately smell the big cat, see the dead bodies, and, if she didn't hurry, find a naked Kat in the tree.

She was still trying to fasten her damnable bra without falling off the branch when Connor leaped onto one of the lower branches. She about had a heart attack, having not even realized he was in the vicinity. He did not look happy.

But since he was here and Maya had also roared, letting them know she was fine, Kat assumed the men were no longer a problem. Getting dressed and undressed on a tree branch was much more of a trial than she had thought possible, though.

Connor climbed branch after branch until he reached her, and then he shifted. "Hell, Kat. I leave you alone for a few minutes, and another damn male shifter comes after you." He helped her fasten her bra. "Are you all right?" he asked, cooling his temper and kissing her bare shoulder.

Frowning at Connor, she yanked her shirt from where she had stuck it in the crook of the tree branch. "Of course I'm not all right. I can't shift, damn it. Even when I think that I desperately need to get out of my clothes because I need to shift, I can't do it. Then when I'm sleeping, I manage just fine."

He kissed her cheek, then pulled her shirt over her head. "*That's* why you're naked."

She cast him the most disgruntled look she could give him. "Of course that's why I'm naked. What did you think?"

"That you'd shifted and killed a man, and *after* the male cat left, you'd shifted back."

Hell, now Connor knew that she hadn't shifted and had given the other male shifter an eyeful of one naked woman.

Attempting to change the subject, she asked, "Are they all gone?"

"Yeah." He helped her into her panties and jeans. "Hell, Kat. He was up here when you were naked?"

They were not going around and around about this. "I thought I was going to shift, Connor. And he *did* kill the men who were trying to get to me."

Connor grunted, then left her to finish dressing while he grabbed his bag and pulled his clothes out.

"Is Maya all right?" she asked.

"She took care of the guard at the car."

Thank God they were both okay.

Kat began climbing down the tree with one boot on, heading for the other one on the ground next to the base of the tree trunk.

In her jaguar form, Maya was down below, pacing. She quickly greeted Kat, rubbing her whole body against Kat's legs and nearly knocking her over. Then Maya jumped into the tree. Connor tossed Kat's bag to the ground and then his own. He hurried to climb down to join Kat while Maya shifted and got dressed.

"What the hell did he look like?" Connor asked Kat.

Kat was staring at the two dead men, trying to figure out how the jaguar had killed them. He hadn't left any bite marks. And no sign of blood was on either of the men.

"He took a swipe at them with his paw. With our powerful strength, we can break a prey's neck or stun it," Connor said, guessing at her puzzlement. He pulled Kat into his arms and embraced her tightly, kissing her forehead. "He's the same one who was following us before."

"How could he have followed us this time? We've traveled for miles by car."

"Apparently he has been, too."

Connor lifted his nose and sniffed. "He killed three of the six men who were after us."

"Three?"

"Another one in the jungle nearby."

That was the other thud she had heard earlier.

Hating to touch either of the men but thinking the one looked familiar, Kat shoved him over with the toe of her boot. She took in her breath a little too quickly. "One of Gonzales's men."

"Hell."

Maya's backpack flew past them and hit the ground with a thud, and then she climbed out of the tree, dressed and ready to go. "The other jaguar saved you," Maya said. "Maybe he can join our little party later."

She looked at Kat. At first, Kat thought Maya was just hopeful that she would agree and maybe put in a good word for the guy. But then she realized Maya had known Connor was helping her to dress and that Kat had been naked when the big cat came to rescue her. Did the whole blasted world have to know? That one of the bad guys had seen her was bad enough, but at least he was dead. But no. The jaguar who was just as much a man had to see her also.

Sure, she knew it was an inevitable part of shifting, but hell, she *hadn't* been shifting!

She sighed. She might as well let Maya know what a problem this was for her so she could be aware of it, too, for future reference.

"I thought I was going to shift when one of Gonzales's men began climbing into the tree. I planned to take care of him as a jaguar. But I don't know what happened. The urge to shift just sort of... *evaporated*."

Connor and Maya exchanged glances.

Oh yeah, Kat could see it now. She would be in the middle of the flight to Houston and have a horrible urge to change into the cat. In a panic, she would remove all her clothes and get ready to turn, and then? Nothing would happen. Except that she would be sitting in a cold airplane in the raw.

How was she ever going to manage?

Chapter 25

Six hours after they had left Santa Marta, Connor filled the car with gas at one of the service stations along the way. Kat knew he wanted to stop for the night. He had speculated long before this about staying in a small village to the east of the road to Bogotá. But when he asked the gas station owner about accommodations in the village, Connor was warned that tourists should not stay there. Too dangerous.

The hour was late; he and Kat and his sister needed to rest; and the village was the closest place with accommodations. Kat didn't like that it could be hazardous. But they were all tired, and driving any farther on the winding roads could be just as unsafe.

When they arrived at the village, they found quiet terra-cotta cottages for rent. The people were extremely friendly, piling out of homes to look the visitors over and glad to have them stay with them. The kids talked to Connor and Maya, asking them where they were from, and Connor put on a Texas drawl that enchanted them.

Then the oddest thing happened. Several policemen appeared and hovered around the area, friendly, protective, as if wanting to ensure that tourists were not robbed or kidnapped while they stayed here. Kat wondered what the police would do if Gonzales's men learned she was here. Would everyone look the other way?

Probably. But not because they wouldn't want to help. Gonzales and his men were just too dangerous.

Then she wondered about the mystery jaguar. Was he still following them? She glanced around but didn't see anyone sitting in a parked vehicle and watching them.

The man who had rented the cottages to them hesitated when referring to the ladies in the party. Was one married to Connor? At least, that's what she assumed he was trying to determine.

"My sister," Connor said, as if explaining why he was traveling with two women. "And my wife. We're newlyweds." He wrapped his arm around Kat's shoulder and gave her an intimate squeeze.

When had that happened?

Maya smiled at her brother, pleased with his declaration. Kat scowled at him. He could at least have told her beforehand that he planned to pretend he was married to her so she wouldn't have looked so shocked.

"Newlyweds?" Kat said as Connor led her into the cottage and shut the door.

Maya's place was right next door, the only way he would allow her to sleep alone. But it would have appeared odd if Connor had slept with his sister and bride in the same cottage.

He began stripping out of his clothes, and Kat raised her brows, folding her arms across her chest at the same time.

He smiled, a predatory gleam in his eyes as he stalked toward her. He threw his shirt on a chair. "You don't think I'm going to let you get away, do you, Kat?"

No, he couldn't be thinking of marrying her. "You have no intention of me getting away? You make it sound like I'm a prisoner."

"Bondage. Hmm."

She slapped his chest. "I've been tied up before. By the bad guys, all right? Under threat of death. The thought doesn't appeal to me."

His expression softened. "I'm sorry, Kat." He placed his hands on her shoulders and stroked her through her shirt, his gaze pleading for understanding. "I'm not used to the idea that you served in the military, fighting these bastards in an official capacity. I want to keep you safe from them and from anyone else who might learn what you are now. But I do intend to marry you."

She let out her breath in a heavy sigh but didn't relax.

"Come to bed. We have several more hours to drive tomorrow before we reach the city and can get another room until we have to take the midnight flight out."

She didn't move.

"Come on, Kat."

She had put off worrying about the flight for as long as she could. It was in the future, a long way off yet much too soon, to her way of thinking. The time was growing shorter with every passing hour. And she was afraid she'd ruin it for all of them. "What if I shift on the flight?" she asked, then bit her lip.

He pulled her into a bear hug. "You'll be fine."

She welcomed his warm embrace. Melted. Loved the way he made her feel secure when the situation was as bad as it could be.

"I'm sorry I didn't help more earlier," she said, wanting to at least get that off her chest.

He shook his head. "There's only one right or wrong way. We live, it was the right way. We die, it was the wrong way." He tilted her face up and looked into her eyes with heartfelt longing. "Kat, I'm sorry for being angry about the other jaguar. He saved you and that was a good thing. You couldn't have done anything else."

Kat hadn't had the urge to shift again, hadn't even shifted since she had sleepwalked. She was wondering if the shifter genes had vanished from her gene pool and she was back to normal again. That could be a good thing, couldn't it? Or maybe it was only wishful thinking.

"Because I haven't shifted in so many hours, I wonder if my blood has finally gotten rid of the alien jaguar-shifter blood."

Connor frowned at her as if wondering if such a thing could happen. Or maybe he didn't like that she referred to the shifter blood as being alien. But it *was* alien—as in she hadn't been born with it running through her veins.

Then he began to pull her shirt over her head. "Let's go to bed. We've had a long day of it, and the morning will come soon enough."

When he didn't say anything about her comment, she figured he didn't know the truth of what was going on with her shifter genetics any more than she did. But would he be disappointed if she wasn't a jaguar, if that was the case, or glad he no longer had to worry about taking care of a shifter who had no control over her abilities?

She could fly home without any difficulty. What a relief that would be.

Then a new thought occurred to her. She knew what they were. Could Connor and his sister let her live if she wasn't one of them but knew about them?

Great. She would be just as much a liability as before.

—w—

Connor didn't think that the jaguar-shifter genes would just disappear, that Kat's blood could destroy the invading genetics. But what if it did?

He'd changed his mind about her from when he had found her needing his help in the jungle again. Once Maya had turned Kat, Connor had wanted her for good, and he was ready to bite her himself to ensure she stayed with them.

She was so tense, and he wanted to help her get rid of the tension any way that he could. Rest should help. He pulled her to the large bed covered in a flowery comforter, the air conditioner on high.

Before long, he had her naked and in bed with his body spooning hers. She was so tired that she fell asleep before he did, but he couldn't help worrying whether she had lost her jaguar ties to them.

He pulled her tight against his body, breathing in her feminine feline scent. She had to still be a shifter. He took in a deep breath of the scent of her hair, nuzzled his face in the silky tresses, and ran his hands over her soft bare skin. He had been so weary of driving that he figured he would fall right to sleep, but having Kat in his embrace made all the difference in the world. Suddenly, he was wide-awake, and he wanted to bury himself deeply in her.

He would prove to her that she didn't need anyone else. That marrying him was the right thing to do. Mulling over the reaction she had to his mentioning that he meant to marry her, he supposed he hadn't asked her in a proper way. Had Roger asked her on bended knee? The ass.

If he hadn't been such a jerk and given Kat up, he could have been the one with her now.

Forget that. He would have sanctioned her further Army missions, putting her into a world of further danger.

Connor frowned. Not that she was safe for now. But that had everything to do with the mission she had gone on and nothing to do with him.

Then he thought about the other jaguar. He hadn't gone after Maya to protect her when the bastards had tried to take them hostage, damn him. He had tracked *Kat* down. Connor had to tell himself it was because Kat had been alone, armed with a rifle, but still so newly turned that she was at a strong disadvantage.

He had to remind himself that the other cat had protected her when Connor wasn't able to. He told himself that he should appreciate that the jaguar had saved her from the bastards. Yet, he still was having a difficult time dealing with it because he knew the jaguar was intrigued with Kat.

But he also worried that if the Army had been following Kat's progress, they might have seen something concerning the jaguars.

The more he knew about her and her past, the more mired in trouble they were all becoming.

Kat woke to Connor's mouth pressing kisses all over her naked breasts, his hand caressing her belly, his fingers drifting lower. Whether she was a jaguar-shifter still, she didn't know. But she sure smelled how hot he was for her, tripping her pheromones into overdrive.

His raspy beard brushed her sensitive skin as his soft warm tongue and heated breath caressed her nipples.

She squirmed, moaning as the tips of her breasts became sensitive and her nether region ached for his penetration. What a way to wake up in the morning. She wasn't a coffee drinker, and she normally didn't need any stimulus to get her going in the morning, but omigod, this was the only way to go.

"Quit teasing me," she managed to rasp with a husky breath. "Connor."

He chuckled darkly. "Someone woke up on the wrong side of the bed?"

She growled. "You started it."

He laughed and drove her insane with the way his mouth suckled at one breast, then the other. His fingers dipped inside her, then caressed her nub harder, faster, until she was arching against him, her hands in his hair stroking, clutching, trying to reach the peak, attempting to find release.

His heart was beating hard, nearly as hard as hers. Both were breathless as she became vaguely aware of the scent of their lovemaking filling the air. She was on fire, her skin flushed with heat, ready to explode when he inserted his finger deep within her swollen folds. She jerked with surprise and pleasure.

"Omigod, finish it," she said in a breathy pleading tone, the sweet pain of expectation nearly killing her.

He looked all smug, superior male in charge of making her come and making her beg for completion. Not really, but it felt that way.

"I love you," he whispered against her ear, licking and nibbling the lobe. Then he stroked her like she liked it, harder, faster, until she was trying to stifle the urge to cry out as it hit her.

A wash of pleasure and heat made her sink into near oblivion. Until he spread her legs, bent her knees, and with a deep push filled her with his rigid cock. Hot and hard and broad, he thrust his rigid erection between her slippery folds, his tongue in her mouth, caressing and poking, his hands on her breasts, massaging as if he couldn't get enough of her and wanted to touch and taste and breathe in her very essence.

"You're so hot," she breathed out, her hands on his buttocks, her heels pressed against the squeaky bed as Connor banged it against the wall.

She tried to think of only the delight she was taking in their joining and not worry about Maya next door and how she must feel.

"Kathleen," Connor groaned, lifting her legs over his shoulders and thrusting even deeper. "You taste so good," he mouthed against her neck, kissing and licking and nipping.

She couldn't speak, her body climbing higher to that sexual plane that sought release until he made a final thrust.

She could feel the hot, white explosion bathing her deep inside. She felt the ripples of contractions as she came again, sagged again under his delicious onslaught, and saw the self-assured satisfaction on Connor's face.

"You love me," he said and wrapped his arms around her in a loving but possessive embrace.

She couldn't help sighing, smiling, and yeah, loving the wild cat on top of her.

He rolled onto his back and cradled her against his slick, hot body, enveloping her again as if he was afraid she would try to get away. She loved this part of him, the caring, loving intimacy he shared after the act as if he truly enjoyed being with her, all of her, and not for just the sexual act.

Super serious, as serious as she could sound while she was naked and wrapped tightly in his embrace, she said, "About your marriage proposal…"

His smoky eyes gazed into hers, watching her expression as he licked her chin. "Yeah?"

"We've only had one date." She stroked his hair and kissed his chin.

He raised his brows and combed his fingers through her hair. "I took you on a jungle hike, a picnic in the woods, and a swim with the piranhas."

"And pink dolphins." She sighed, remembering how he had kissed her in the river and made her forget about anything that had been swimming with them in the water.

"Right." He caressed her back and smiled a little. "And I carried your bag on the hike."

"All right," she conceded.

"And found you a lovely air-conditioned cabana to stay in."

"Hmm," she said, running her fingers through his hair as she rested her chin on his chest and gazed at him. "You did."

"And then found you this lovely air-conditioned cottage to sleep in."

"Umm-hmm."

"Wasn't that the best wake-up you'd ever had?"

She grinned. "I'll admit that since I've been waking up with you, they've all been pretty nice and eventful. Although I doubt Maya will be very happy."

He laughed. "She'll expect it. And be happy for it. So what do you say we get married?"

She tugged gently at his hair. "What if I'm not a jaguar-shifter like you and Maya any longer?"

"You know too much about us," he said very seriously. "You're part of the family already, Kat. If you want to take time to decide about marriage, that's fine with me. But I do want to marry you."

She sighed.

He kissed her mouth. "Ready to get up? We need to grab a bite of breakfast and get on the road. How does taking a shower first sound to you?"

"I suppose you want to conserve water."

"No, I want to ravage you in the shower. You know, as jaguars, we *love* the water."

Smiling, she rolled off him, but just as swiftly as a jaguar could move, he was off the bed, scooping her up in his arms before she could agree or disagree. He swung around and headed for the bathroom.

With having her own shower masseur, how could she go wrong?

But still, she couldn't say yes to marriage, not yet. She had to know if she was truly one of them. If she wasn't, Connor shouldn't be tied down to her. He should have a shifter to love who was just like him.

She breathed in the smell of the water and wondered if the reason it smelled so… refreshing was because she still was a shifter… who couldn't shift.

The walls of the cottages were paper-thin, and since hers was butted up against Connor and Kat's and because jaguars had such good hearing, Maya heard everything, including Kat's indignation that Connor would call her his wife without first speaking with her about it and Connor's muddled attempt at asking Kat to marry him.

Maya was going to have to have a talk with him.

Then the lovemaking. Couldn't they have at least pulled the bed away from the wall?

And the shower running, and more lovemaking.

She stretched in bed and closed her eyes, still enjoying a lazy morning wake-up. Although she wished she had a mate to wake up to. She wondered again about the mystery jaguar. Was he staying somewhere nearby? Sleeping in a car? Or at one of the cottages?

She climbed out of bed and moseyed into the bathroom to take another shower, wishing again she had someone to share it with.

After showering, she had just finished getting dressed when Connor banged on her door. "What's wrong?" Maya whispered, letting him in, then shutting the door quickly behind him.

"They're here. Gonzales's men. And they're looking for blood."

Chapter 26

"I WANT YOU TO COME WITH ME, AND WE'LL STAY WITH Kat at our cottage. That way if we have to deal with Gonzales's men, we'll at least be together," Connor said in a rush, and Maya knew that he didn't want to leave Kat alone for even a moment.

He grabbed Maya's bag, but she quickly asked as she shoved on a pair of hiking boots, "Why didn't you bring Kat over here?" The move would have been the most logical, and if Connor was anything, he was the most commonsense one in the family.

"She has shifted."

Maya had thought he would look perturbed that Kat had no control over her shifting, that given the current situation, they could be having a lot more difficulty, and that Maya had been at fault, but he seemed guardedly pleased.

She cleared her throat and studied Connor's expression. She hadn't been wrong. He definitely had a sparkle to his eyes and a barely suppressed gleeful look. "And this is good, why?"

"She worried she might not be a shifter any longer."

Maya closed her gaping mouth. Omigod, she had never considered that Kat might all of a sudden lose her shifter status. That somehow her own blood would beat it back and dominate again.

All she could manage was a feeble, "Oh."

"If she did, I'd have to turn her."

Maya considered Connor's expression, dark with determination. He was serious!

"I'm not losing her, Maya, no matter what."

He didn't have to convince Maya of that! "I knew you felt something for her the first time you'd met her, trussed up by the bad guys. Took you long enough to admit it, though."

Ignoring her, Connor peeked through the curtains. "All clear."

"Where were they?" Maya whispered.

"Looking at our rental vehicle. The police spoke with them in a nice, cheerful way. I figure they knew who they worked for and were trying to smooth things over, but the police didn't tell them we were staying in these cottages."

He grabbed Maya's bag, and she cautiously opened the door. Then with one more look to make sure no one was about who might see them, she led the way to Kat's and Connor's cottage next door. He unlocked the door and they quickly moved inside, then he relocked the door.

In her jaguar form, her whole body screaming with unleashed primal power, Kat paced across the tile floor. She stopped to look at them, her expression feral. Maya had no doubt that if the men had broken into the cottage, Kat would have taken care of every one of them.

Maya beamed at her, then rushed across the floor, knelt, and gave her a big hug. Kat rested her head against Maya's shoulder and then rubbed in a cat's way of greeting, her tail whipping around with happiness.

Maya whispered against her ear, "Don't you agree to marry my brother until he asks you in the proper way."

Kat licked her cheek as if in total agreement.

Connor grunted to see the women ganging up on him, then peered around the curtain as discreetly as he could to see if anyone had followed their movements.

"Do you think they know that's our rental vehicle, or are they just checking because we happen to be tourists who might fit the descriptions of Kat and her male and female companions?" Maya asked.

"Either is a distinct possibility. They're not around now. At least in sight. But they could very well be staking out the car."

"Should we make a run for it?" Maya asked.

As a jaguar, that's what they would normally do. Leave, rather than confront someone with guns. When they were in the Amazon near their hut, it was a different story. Or like the last confrontation they'd had with Gonzales's men in the jungle where they didn't have any choice. If they faced men like these, the situation was truly a case of survival of the fittest.

But in civilization, they had to be more... civilized. Unless they had no choice. Already, Maya was considering stripping naked, then coaxing the men into the cottage, but only after Connor had shifted. Then locking the door, she would shift herself, and the jaguars would take care of the men.

But what a mess they would leave behind for the maid service to clean up. And everyone had been so nice to them here in the village that she didn't want to do that to them.

Connor raised his brows at Maya.

Maya considered Kat. "Guess we can't make a run for it, not until she shifts back. Although, what if we

left with her like she is? We'd confuse the hell out of
Gonzales's men. No Kat. Big cat instead."

Connor didn't say anything right away as he watched
Kat. She was looking back at him, and Maya swore she
was willing to do whatever would work. Connor folded
his arms. "We wait it out for a while. An hour. See what
happens. If Kat doesn't change back, we might just try
it. If she's agreeable. But the problem really is that it's
light out, we came here with my wife, and we leave with
a jaguar that we didn't have, and—"

"They don't know that," Maya reasoned. The more
she thought about her plan, the more she believed it
might work. "We arrived late. No one could see into the
vehicle. We might have had a jaguar sleeping in there.
Kat could have left you last night. If anyone asks, we
just tell them a story. Late last night, her brother came to
pick her up, and we're off to meet them somewhere else,
if it's any of their business. If we do tell them where
we're going, we'll give them a false heading.

"But with a jaguar walking with us to the car, I
suspect no one will want to get near us to even ask
any questions. They'll make up their own stories about
what happened."

"More jaguar god stories."

Maya snorted. "Jaguar goddess. Kat's the one who's
shifted, after all."

Kat rubbed at Maya's hand to get her attention. Maya
laughed. "I think we're all in agreement. Right, Kat?"

Kat nodded, then lay down on the floor.

"An hour," Connor said. "I sure hope she doesn't
shift right when we're trying to get her into the car."

For an hour, Maya and Kat rested on the bed while

Connor watched out the window. Maya had offered three times to be the lookout, but her brother was too wired.

Kat didn't seem to be turning back into her human form anytime soon. They had plenty of time to arrive in Bogotá, hours before their midnight flight to Houston. Which meant Kat had hours before she had to shift. The plan could work. And if she stayed as a cat for longer, maybe she wouldn't have the urge to shift on the five-hour flight home.

Kat's stomach rumbled. Maya patted her head. "I'm hungry, too. As soon as we can, we'll get some breakfast."

"Police are back," Connor said, but his tone of voice was warning. "Hell, they're looking this way."

Kat jumped off the bed.

Maya climbed off with her and rubbed her hand between Kat's ears.

"One's headed this way," Connor said.

Kat remained frozen next to the bed like a beautiful jaguar statue.

"What will we do, Connor?" Maya asked, her voice rushed.

"Kat, hide in the bathroom. If we have to, Maya, you can run the shower for her and pretend she's washing up."

"All right."

"But don't turn on the water unless the policeman acts as though he's coming inside the place."

"All right."

When Maya led the way, Kat balked about going to the bathroom. Maya wondered if it was because Kat was getting ready to shift like she had done before when she had stood in front of the steps to their hut, then suddenly shifted into her human form.

"If you're going to shift, we really need for you to go into the bathroom first," Maya said, half pleading.

Connor studied her. "Kat?"

She moved toward him.

"Are you all right?" He crossed the floor to her and crouched, giving her a warm embrace. She licked his cheek and looked back at the door. "You don't want to meet with the policeman, do you?" he asked incredulously.

Her sage-green eyes looked at him.

"I'm not sure this is the best thing to—" Pounding on the door made him stop speaking midsentence.

Maya motioned to Kat and urgently whispered, "Come."

But she swore Kat smiled at her, then nudged Connor's hand and leg, and walked to the door.

"All right," Connor said. "I'm not sure this will work, but here goes."

Maya held her breath. Should she shift also?

Kat took a deep breath and stood behind Connor as he opened the door. She liked Maya's idea of leaving while Kat was a cat. She didn't think she was going to change back to her human self anytime soon, and she was starving. They might as well get on their way, throw the bad guys off the track, and pick out a new place to stay in Bogotá in a few hours.

She was feeling more confident of her jaguar status. Not that she felt she had any control over it. But she felt strong and invincible. Lots more unbeatable than when she was in her human form without a gun. She did know some martial arts, but against men armed with automatic rifles, she wouldn't stand a chance.

The policeman stood on the porch while Connor remained in the doorway, blocking the policeman's view of her. Annoying her.

"A couple of men were looking this morning for a woman who fits the description of your wife. May I speak with her?" the policeman asked, his tone neutral, his spicy cologne wafting through the door.

She could smell a second man behind him.

Kat nudged at Connor's leg to get him to move so she could meet the nice policemen. Connor refused to budge—protective of her and Maya as usual. She was about ready to poke her nose between his legs, like a pet Labrador retriever used to do to her to get her attention some years ago.

She growled low and would roar next if Connor didn't move. She wanted to play! She thought she heard Maya softly chuckle from the direction of the bathroom.

"She left late last night," Connor said. "Her brother picked her up and took her to Santa Marta and the beaches up there. We're headed that way ourselves as soon as we pack our bags."

Good. Connor was giving them a location opposite of where they were bound.

The policeman said, "I understand you are newlyweds." Which said it all. Why would Kat's brother come to pick her up and drive her hours away when she and Connor were newly married? "Can I have a look around?"

Again, Kat nudged Connor's leg with her head. She would nip him in the butt next if he didn't move.

"Sure, officer," Connor said and stepped out of the way. The policeman and his buddy took a step toward the entrance, then abruptly stopped, eyes wide, mouths agape, the smell of fear cloaking them as their gazes riveted on the jaguar standing before them.

"She won't bite," Connor quickly assured them. "Just go on in and check around the place. My sister dropped by because we were getting ready to leave."

"Just got your shampoo," Maya said cheerfully, bringing out his shaving kit. "He always forgets it on trips, and we're always having to stop to get him a new bottle." She smiled brightly at the policemen, but they were still staring at Kat.

Kat imagined it would take a hell of a lot of incentive for them to look away from her, like someone began shooting at them or a bomb went off in a building down the street. For now, they didn't know what to do—back up, quickly say their good-byes, or try to slip by her and be manly men and check out the place like they had said they wanted to do.

"You don't mind if I get the cat in the vehicle, do you?" Connor asked.

Both policemen quickly moved out of the way, shaking their heads.

No. They didn't mind. Now, if only the bad guys would have that much respect for her. She glanced around the street where small crowds of two or three villagers stood watching the cottage. The Americans had provided plenty of entertainment when Gonzales's men had shown up and now with the policemen's interrogation of Connor. But as soon as Connor walked out of the cottage with Kat, all the chatter instantly died. All eyes grew as wide as tortillas, and every mouth hung agape.

No one ran off screaming into their homes like

she halfway expected them to. They stood still like a bunch of statues. Maybe they knew cats liked to chase moving objects.

Connor hurried to the car and opened the back door for Kat. But she didn't hurry to follow him. She wanted the policemen to know that if they tried to detain Connor or Maya, she would be there for them. And if Gonzales's men suddenly appeared, that they would have to take her on.

Maya carried her bag out to the vehicle. "Connor, I'll get her in the car. Can you get your bags? I couldn't manage all of them."

One was Kat's. She was glad Maya hadn't let it slip that Kat's bag was still here, if she was to have gone with her brother to Santa Marta.

Connor gave Kat a look like he was hoping she would climb into the car and let him take care of this. She just raised her brows a little but wouldn't move.

"All right," he said to her, as if he was saying it to Maya.

Maya threw her bag in the trunk and then scratched Kat's head between the ears.

Kat purred and rubbed her head against Maya's leg. She hadn't thought she would like such a thing, but it felt good. Maya seemed to understand Kat's need to stay with them until they were in the clear.

The policemen still didn't move from the porch. Connor entered the cottage and left it posthaste with the two bags in hand. "The place is all yours," Connor said to the policemen, not waiting for their response as he stalked toward the rental vehicle. He gave Kat a look that said, "The show is over. Get *into* the car."

She smiled but wouldn't budge. Not until he deposited

the bags in the trunk and closed it. Then she sauntered over to the open door to the backseat and jumped in. Maya shut the door and climbed into the front passenger seat.

Connor sat in the driver's seat, pulled his door shut with a hard slam, and let his breath out. "When you growled low, Kat, I thought you were ready to bite me."

Maya chuckled. "You know she was."

Kat curled up on the backseat and sighed. Yeah, she had been ready all right. Just a nip to get him to move out of her way.

Then she frowned. Connor had thrown her bag in the trunk. What if she shifted? All her clothes were in the bag.

"Find a drive-through so we can get breakfast bur- ritos, okay?" Maya said. "Kat and I are starving."

"Sure thing." Still holding on to the steering wheel, Connor stretched his arms.

"Did the policemen go inside the cottage?" Maya asked.

"Finally, as we were pulling away. I watched out the rearview mirror. They waited until we moved off, then finally went inside. Then they came out just as quickly when they didn't find any dead bodies or anything," Connor said.

Maya laughed.

After a few minutes, he stopped at a restaurant, no drive-through, and went inside to get them some food to eat on the road.

Kat stood and watched out the open windows, alert, wary.

Maya smiled. "You're drawing a crowd."

But Kat didn't care about that. She worried that they'd been followed. Then she worried about shifting and having no clothes to slip into. She poked her head over the front seat and nudged Maya's cheek.

Maya frowned. "What?"

Kat made a disgruntled sound. How could she tell her friend what she needed?

"Do you have to go to the bathroom?"

Kat shook her head.

"All right."

Before Maya could say another word, Kat nipped Maya's pale blue shirtsleeve and gave a gentle tug.

Maya opened her mouth, closed it, then turned to look at the restaurant. "The keys. You want your clothes out of the trunk so when you shift you can get dressed, but Connor's got the keys." She turned back to observe Kat quickly, her eyes big. "You're not going to shift, are you?"

Kat shook her head. What a disaster that would be. Shifting in broad daylight as people in the area stared at her. She couldn't even get on the floor to shift, if she decided she had to, because the room between the front seats and the backseat was too narrow. So she would be standing on the backseat, one second a jaguar, the next, one naked woman.

"Okay. As soon as Connor brings us our food, I'll have him get your bag. I'll fish out whatever you want to wear for when you need to shift."

That would work. On the road, she wouldn't have any spectators. Kat nodded, then began looking out the window again. She saw groups of kids pointing at her, their mouths curved up and huge brown eyes indicating their awe. Adults, too, were staring at her with mixed expressions of fear and excitement.

What if she jumped out the window? And ate one of them? But the day was already warm and they had to leave the car windows open while Connor bought the food. She sighed and glanced around again at the cars driving by. One caught her eye. It was dirty and dusty, black, an off-the-road kind of vehicle, big tires, dark-tinted windows, ominous.

A shiver slid up her spine and her fur stood on end.

Maya was observing her, probably worried Kat might all of a sudden shift, even though she had indicated she wouldn't. But after Kat had proven she couldn't control her shifting, Maya probably didn't trust her.

When the fur on the nape of her neck stood and her ears perked up, Maya looked to see what had caught Kat's attention.

Maya's lower lip parted. "He was following us before, wasn't he?" she asked.

Kat grunted in a yes reply.

"Great."

Connor headed out of the restaurant, two bags in hand. As much as the bags were bulging, she assumed he had bought enough for a small army.

As soon as he opened his car door, Maya reached for the bags. "Kat needs her backpack out of the trunk of the car."

His gaze swiveled to catch Kat's eye in the backseat.

"She doesn't feel the urge to shift yet, but she needs her clothes for when she does."

He relaxed and handed Maya the bags of food, then headed for the trunk.

Kat watched the black vehicle drive off slowly.

"He's going to follow us. Bet my savings," Maya warned.

Kat thought so, too.

Connor slammed the trunk, then shoved Kat's bag into the backseat and climbed into the driver's seat.

"We have a stalker," Maya said, setting out some of the burritos and letting Kat pick the ones she wanted. Then Maya opened the wrappers around the two that Kat had nudged with her nose.

As soon as Maya handed the first to Kat and she was able to grasp it with her teeth and began chewing it, the children watching her began to laugh. A jaguar who loved burritos. Yep.

Connor pulled onto the road and headed for their destination. "Where's the vehicle, Maya?"

"He drove off that way. Both Kat and I remember seeing him before."

"When you see him again, point him out to me. Okay?"

"Will do."

As they drove, Kat licked her chops, eyed the burritos Maya and Connor hadn't eaten, and then nudged Maya with her nose.

Maya looked back at her. "What's wrong, Kat?"

Kat sighed, hating this part of being a jaguar-shifter where she had such a time communicating with Maya and Connor. She poked her nose at two more burritos. Maya laughed. "That problem I can fix." She unwrapped the burritos and then fed them one at a time to Kat.

Connor shook his head. "They were supposed to last us through lunchtime."

Maya glanced at him and looked like she was ready to scold him, when he suddenly said, "We've got company."

Chapter 27

THE VEHICLE BEHIND THEM WAS QUICKLY CLOSING IN on them, like a jaguar canvassing its prey. Connor expected it to be the one that Kat and Maya had seen in the village, but when Maya looked in the side mirror, she shook her head. "That's not the one that was following us before."

Kat turned around and looked out the back window and growled softly.

Connor was beginning to wonder if Kat was stuck in her jaguar form now.

"I was only kidding about the burritos," he told Kat. "You can eat all that you want." He gave Maya a look of scolding back. He had been teasing, but then he had caught sight of the vehicle following them and speeding to catch up to them, and he couldn't think of anything else.

"What do we do?" Maya asked.

"They're getting ready to ram us. No, wait. One of them is leaning out of his vehicle's window and getting ready to shoot at our car."

"Then I'll shoot back."

"No. If you lean out of the car window, you'll be a target, Maya."

"We need to pull off the road and confront them. There," Maya said, pointing to a dirt road leading into the trees.

Showtime.

"Should I shift?"

"Get the gun ready."

They barely made the turn at the rate of speed Connor was driving, taking a couple of tree branches with them, and he sped up even faster.

"Are you sure you don't want me to shift?"

"It'll be hard for you to do so in the front seat."

"I'll climb into the back with Kat."

"Okay, leave the rifle on the front seat. You get in the back and shift. I'll park, let you out, and you take off into the jungle. I'll grab our bags and the gun, and split off from you."

"Then shift," Maya said, climbing over the seat back.

"Then shift. After I hide our gear." He didn't like any scenario he could come up with. What if Kat suddenly shifted? She'd be naked and without any resources. He changed his mind. "Kat, you'll come with me. I want you up in the tree with our gear, protecting it."

Maya gave him a knowing look.

He couldn't tell what Kat was thinking. He would just have to play it by ear.

He pulled the car off the dirt road and ran over a ton of ferns and shrubs, then jumped out to open the back car door to let the women out because Maya had already shifted. Maya had packed her clothes in Kat's bag, he supposed, as he saw none in the car.

Then he started gathering backpacks as Maya and Kat waited, their tails twitching. After shutting the trunk, he ran with the bags, searching for a perfect climbing tree. He soon spied one and figured the men following them wouldn't suspect that any of them would hide in a tree. Then he hauled up two of the bags, returning for his and the rifle after that, and then motioned to the tree because he intended to shift and leave Kat there.

A vehicle rumbled down the road, tires spinning on dirt, men's loud, boisterous voices hollering out the window, trying to scare their prey into panicking.

Then the vehicle stopped, and Connor knew that the men had reached the rental vehicle.

The engine cut, and doors opened and closed. The men were hollering for them to come out from wherever they were.

Connor glanced at Kat and motioned to the tree. She shook her head.

Maya nudged at her to come with her.

Connor didn't like it, but he knew Maya would show Kat the jaguar way while he stowed the rest of his gear and shifted. He fully intended to take down as many of the men as possible before Kat had to face any of them.

Wade Patterson shook his head as he pulled off onto the dirt road and followed the carload of Gonzales's men, keeping far enough back that they weren't even aware of him. Not when they had eyes only for catching up to Kathleen McKnight and her party.

He hadn't had this much excitement visiting Colombia in eons.

Here he had thought he would take Kat for his own mate if she was agreeable, but the other jaguar had beat him to it. Damn that he had missed his flight to Colombia, missed meeting her in Santa Marta, then lost her in the jungle completely.

He knew of the jaguars in the area, which was what

had gotten her to come there in the first place, but he hadn't realized they were shifters. Even if he had, the two that had been living there were obviously mated. So why did the female the male had been with allow him to have another?

He snorted. To him, it didn't matter that they were jaguar-shifters—the male jaguar half of their kind possibly needing to mate with several females. He wanted only one. So it really pissed him off that this Connor Anderson had started a damn harem. There weren't enough jaguar-shifters to go around. Wade was still of the opinion that he could get Kat away from the other man and give her exclusivity so she wouldn't have to share when the guy she had taken up with divided his affections with the other woman. Hell, Connor might decide to go for a third shifter female if he could locate one.

Wade was certain that when Kat realized how much better he could be for her, she would give the other guy up. Besides, Wade lived in Florida like she did. So they could compromise and settle in one place or the other. He was fine with her choosing. He just had to convince her to go with him and leave Connor.

He wondered who had turned her. But she didn't seem to mind that she was one of their kind now. That was one thing that had bothered him. That if he had turned her, she might have hated him for it. He hadn't planned to turn her right away. He wanted her to get to know him first and to ease her into learning something of the truth about him before he changed her. Although he wasn't sure how he would have done so without making a total muddle of it.

He'd thought he'd just see how well she did in the

jungle, maybe date her back in Florida for a while, then
return here to the Amazon when they were really a
couple. If it had worked out for him.

He'd never thought this Connor person would take
her for his own.

The shifting seemed to be the big problem for her
as she didn't seem to have a lot of control over it. He
assumed the man and woman intended to take her home
on a flight out of Bogotá, but he wondered how they
would manage.

He parked the rental car behind Gonzales's men's
car, got out, and slashed the tires. If any of them made
it out alive once they'd faced the jaguars, they weren't
going anywhere.

He wondered why they were after Kathleen. He had
tried to surreptitiously hear the scuttlebutt and had managed to learn that Gonzales himself wanted her. Alive,
not dead.

Everyone knew who he was—drug lord—and that
getting on his shit list was bad news.

But Wade hadn't been able to ascertain the reason for
Gonzales's interest in taking Kathleen hostage. Wade
returned to his vehicle, stripped out of his clothes, and
shifted. Then with his nose up and ears perked, he
breathed in the air and listened for the sound of where
any of them had gone. But particularly where Kathleen
had gone.

―∾―

The air was hot and muggy and still, the bugs and birds
as noisy as ever. Maya stood near Kat as they heard
the men moving around in the jungle. Kat was glad for

Maya's assistance. Even though she felt she could take down the men, Kat wanted to do it right without causing trouble for the jaguar kind. If she had to do it without any supervision, she would just take one bite and that would be the end of the man's plan to ever hurt anyone again.

The men were drawing closer, and Maya started moving away from the sound of them. Kat frowned. They had to take care of them. Connor couldn't do this on his own. Maya couldn't believe that Kat was only a liability and wouldn't be able to help.

Maya grunted at her. Kat gave her a disgruntled look back, then reluctantly followed her. Maya made a wide circle around the men, keeping them within earshot but out of sight, and Kat realized then what she was doing. Laying an ambush. She and Maya couldn't confront the men head-on. They were armed and dangerous. They had to sneak up on them. It didn't seem as heroic that way, but these men didn't play by any gentlemanly rules of warfare.

Then they saw the first of the men alone, vulnerable, as vulnerable as an armed murderous man could be. Maya ran up behind him, silent as a cloud drifting across the sky, a dark, angry spotted cloud.

But as soon as she leaped at her target, another man moved into Kat's vision. She didn't hesitate. The man raised his weapon to shoot Maya. Panicked and needing to save her jaguar sister, Kat jumped high, not expecting to leap quite that distance, and nearly went too far. She landed on his head with her full jaguar body weight, heard a crack, and thought it was his spine. He went down silently, except for a thud that only Maya and she could hear with their enhanced hearing.

Standing next to her own dead prey, Maya looked over at Kat, smiled in a jaguar's way, then joined her. She listened to the man's heart, but Kat had already done so. His head was turned at an odd angle, and she seemed to have broken his neck with the weight of her body. She didn't think that was a jaguar's way to kill its prey, but she was just learning after all.

She would have to practice jumping to learn how high and how far she could go to hit her intended target spot on.

They heard someone else rustling through the brush, and Kat knew the man or men would soon find the two dead men and raise the alarm. Maya quickly moved into the trees, making enough noise to draw the man's attention, even though the cats normally moved silently. Kat waited for the man to follow her, to see if he was friend or foe. He didn't call out, though.

Then she saw him trying to move quietly through the jungle, but he just wasn't able. Maya was still making noise but hidden in the brush. Kat leaped onto an overhead branch, thinking she might do a better job taking him down in a jaguar way if she pounced from a branch rather than leaping from the ground.

She jumped down on top of him and landed on his head like the other, but this man cried out before he was silenced. When he fell to the ground, she thought she had killed him in the same way as the first man. Maybe that would be her special technique, since she couldn't seem to master any other in quick order.

The man's cry brought others running, though. *Great!* How many were there?

Then the oddest thing happened. Men were shouting

to their fallen comrade, fallen *dead* comrade, tromping at a rapid pace to reach him, but they never arrived. Maya rejoined her, urging her to take cover. Kat hadn't quite gotten the notion that they ambushed and stalked rather than facing their foe in a frontal assault. That's how she had been trained in the Army. She would have to practice with Maya and Connor, like they probably did when they were cubs, tackling and taking each other down in an ambush.

She had a lot to learn. She jumped into a tree, and Maya leaped onto the same branch beside her. She licked Kat's face, saying in a jaguar-shifter's way that she had done all right.

They heard no one coming, and Kat felt antsy, wanting to look for Connor, to make sure he was all right. She kept telling herself that no gunshots had been fired, so the only way one of the men could have wounded Connor was if he'd drawn a knife. But she didn't think anyone would be foolish enough to chance fighting a jaguar with a puny knife.

Then Connor materialized out of the ferns, saw her and Maya in the tree, and grunted. It was time to get on their way. All the bad men were dead. What would Gonzales think about that? This time he would know for sure his men had come across Kat and died at the hands of her and her companions. But he would probably wonder how that had happened. No bullets fired. No knife wounds. Only two women and one man to fight off all his men. And all his men were dead.

They returned to the tree where their backpacks rested, and Connor climbed and shifted. He tossed down Maya and Kat's bags, then proceeded to get dressed.

Maya shifted also and dressed. Kat just stood there, panting as a jaguar, wishing she could shift, too, and get dressed.

She groaned, waiting for Connor and Maya to join her, and then they all ran back to their rental car. Kat smelled the scent of the male jaguar that had followed them before. She glanced at Connor. He didn't look happy.

When they were in the car and on the road, Maya pulled some clothes out of Kat's bag and tossed them to the backseat for Kat when she managed to turn back into a human. She might have gotten away with being a jaguar in a small village, but she didn't imagine she could do so in the city of Bogotá.

"How did Kat do?" Connor asked.

Maya smiled at her brother. "She's a great hunter. And you know what? She has a new technique we could learn from."

Kat stared at her in disbelief. Maya thought her "technique" was worth sharing?

"Oh?" He cast a look back over his shoulder at Kat, his eyes sparkling with amusement and pride.

"Yep. Works like a charm. Without fail. But I'll let her tell you about it later."

Three hours later, Kat finally had the urge to shift. What had taken her so long? At least she was glad she had been a help to Maya and Connor with Gonzales's thugs. But she was glad to be in her human form again, able to communicate, too. Maya had dozed off in the front passenger seat, and Connor was staring at the road, half-asleep himself, she thought.

"Connor," she said quietly, not wanting to startle him and cause an accident.

He glanced back at her, his expression one of relief.

"Yeah, I'm back." She pulled her hair back into a ponytail. "Are we almost there?" She thought they were because more urban sprawl existed now as they grew closer to the city.

"Half an hour. We'll get a room, and then it'll be another four hours before we check in for our midnight flight."

"I'm not interested in him," Kat said.

Connor nodded. "I know. But it doesn't mean that he doesn't want you."

"Did you see him? How do you know he doesn't want Maya and not me?"

"I saw him. If looks could kill, he would have eaten me alive. But instead, he acted as a part of our jaguar team and took out two of the men, while I brought down the other two. I might actually have liked him if it wasn't for the fact that he wants you."

"But what if he might be right for Maya?"

Connor's dark look made her think he knew what he was talking about. She sighed. "All right. But you have to know he means nothing to me."

But Connor still didn't look really sure of himself, and that surprised her, considering how much he always seemed in charge. Cats were fickle, she reminded herself. Maybe he thought she'd be like one of his parents, loving and then leaving him far behind.

─␣∾∾␣─

When they arrived in the city, they stayed at a classy hotel close to El Dorado International Airport. Connor paid for a suite with an adjoining room that Maya could have. That would give them all privacy and easy access in case they had any more trouble. They all ordered room service, ate fried cheese *arepas* and shish kebabs and then a dessert of *crema de arroz*, sweet rice with milk and coconut, in Maya's room. Then Connor and Kat left Maya to shower and rest up until their late-night flight.

But Connor had other plans for Kat. He took her down to the lobby, which was brilliantly lit with floral-shaped chandeliers, expansive eggshell tile floors, and white marble walls. Pine and bleach cleaners filled his nostrils as he walked Kat past a winding marble stair-case leading to a bar that overlooked an Olympic-sized pool, the aqua water inviting.

The place was ultra-elegant, but he preferred the jungle—the plants, the earthy and sweet floral fragrances, and the closed-in leafy cover—to this stark white openness with hard floors and pungent cleanser smells that left him feeling vulnerable and exposed.

Attempting to shake off the feeling that they were being watched, he led Kat to a bank of computers near the massive floor-to-ceiling windows overlooking the pool so they could use the hotel's pay-by-the-minute Internet service. Connor paid for the service, then motioned Kat to the chair while he pulled up another. "Let me see your emails from this Wade Patterson."

Sighing, Kat signed on to the Internet to show Connor her emails, and after an hour of researching and showing Connor all that she had said she knew about Wade, Kat received an email from him.

Startled, she stared at the subject line: *Sorry I Missed You!*

Connor swore beneath his breath. "Open it."

She felt uneasy as she did and read:

Dear Kathleen, I'm sorry I missed you in the city. I learned you had reservations at the resort near where the jaguar sightings had occurred, but they said you hadn't arrived. Please email me as soon as you get this message. I have to know that you are all right. Wade

Surprised to read the email, Kat looked at Connor. He frowned at her. "His message sounds as though he knows you're here, Kat. He hadn't emailed you, not once while you were in the jungle or traveling with us to reach Bogotá, but now that you're here, reading your emails for the first time, he writes to you? Coincidence or something else? He's followed us here."

A chill crawled up her spine. She looked around the lobby but didn't see anyone who looked like the man in the photos on Facebook. "Do you want me to respond? Ask him if he's a jaguar or works for Gonzales?" Kat asked.

Connor stood, placed his hands on her shoulders, and rubbed them, helping to massage the tension from them. "Ask him how you missed him in the city."

She emailed Wade, and the reply was immediate.

Kathleen, thank God you are all right. I was so worried about you. My flight was delayed a day, but by then you were already out of phone or email contact. Where are you now? Wade

She looked up at Connor. "What should I say?"

"Tell him you're engaged to be married and your fiancé wouldn't like you meeting someone on the sly in Colombia like this."

"I can't say that! He'll wonder why I said I'd meet him in the first place."

"You weren't engaged at the time."

She folded her arms. "I'm not engaged now, either. Don't you remember what Maya said? You have to do it right."

Connor grinned at her.

"Besides, if I said I was engaged, he'd wonder how that had happened when I've been out of touch with the world all this time."

Before she could type a response, Wade typed back:

Kathleen, I need to see you. I felt awful about missing you at the city. I want to get together with you before you leave. Wade

He sounded desperate.

"Tell him you're engaged, Kat," Connor said firmly.

She let out her breath in exasperation. "We are *not* engaged."

"Tell him you have a lover who won't permit you to see him, then."

She smiled at Connor and shook her head.

"Fine. Tell him good-bye then, so your lover can prove to you that what he says is the truth."

She chuckled. "Fine. I like challenges."

She typed in:

Sorry, Wade, but I've started seeing someone, and so we'll have to figure it was fate that we didn't meet. Good luck with all you do. Bye. Kathleen

She logged off her email and shut down the connection. "Okay, lover boy?" she asked, offering her hand.

"You're engaged to me," he said, taking her hand and moving her through the lobby. "We're getting married."

She chuckled. "You called me stubborn."

He looked down at her. "You are, about this marriage deal."

That's when she saw one of the men who had come to her rescue the year before in the Amazon. She recognized that hard, square jaw, those lean features and riveting blue eyes, and the scar from an earlier fight that cut in a straight line across his smooth, tanned cheek. Only he wasn't wearing camouflage this time. He was trying to blend in with jeans and a black T-shirt and a baseball cap, the bill shadowing his face.

What was an Army sergeant doing here? At this particular hotel? She didn't like coincidences. He glanced at her and quickly looked away. He was talking into a phone. Something wasn't right.

"I need to talk to someone," she said, pulling Connor in the direction of the sergeant.

"Who, Wade? You saw him?" Connor's voice was rough with agitation.

"No, someone in the Army. Someone who helped rescue me from the jungle."

"What is he doing here?"

"That's what I'd like to know."

Caught, the man couldn't very well escape without looking really obvious. He made a mock salute to Kat.

"What are you doing down here?" she asked, her voice sharp.

Chapter 28

THE SERGEANT LOOKED AT CONNOR AS IF HE WAS A man to fear. If Sergeant Stratton knew anything about Connor, he would be right.

"Sergeant?" Kat said again, trying to get him to answer her question. "Why are you here?" She knew his being in Bogotá at the same hotel where she was staying, when Gonzales's men had been chasing her for some time, wasn't just happenstance.

His gaze shifted from Connor to her.

"Answer the lady," Connor growled, taking a step forward.

The sergeant evidently wasn't supposed to have been caught in the open like this and hadn't been briefed on what to say if he was. He probably hadn't believed they'd leave the hotel room this soon to come down to the lobby.

Sergeant Stratton backed up against the wall. "He's a special operative, isn't he?"

Kat glanced at Connor and nearly smiled at the thought. Yeah, he was special, the most unique kind of operative she could ever have found.

"We heard you were down here," the sergeant finally said.

"Did Wade Patterson arrange this?" Kat asked, suspicious.

"Who?" He sounded genuinely surprised, like he didn't recognize the name and Wade truly wasn't involved.

"Forget it. How did you learn I was here?"

"Communication between Gonzales and his men. We've been monitoring him whenever we could. He said you'd arrived at the airport in Santa Marta, but before his men could pick you up, you had left." The sergeant squirmed a little. "Ma'am, the major won't like it if he learns I've talked to you."

"Major?"

"Singleterry, ma'am."

"Roger," she said under her breath. He had been having her watched, followed, and was using her as bait without her knowledge and without an Army paycheck to make the job worthwhile this time?

"Well," Sergeant Stratton licked his lips and said, "we lost you in the jungle. You just vanished. We didn't know where you'd gone. Gonzales's men couldn't find you. And…" He looked at Connor and then fixed his gaze on Kat. "Strange things happened."

"Strange things?" She was getting an uneasy feeling about this. What if someone in the Army had spotted them shifting at some point?

"Yeah. Villagers were talking about a jaguar god. Gonzales's men began communicating with Gonzales, saying that they'd found you in the jungle, but the men sent out there to pick you up vanished without a trace."

"Really," Kat said, figuring that was when Manuel and the first bunch of brigands had come after them in the jungle.

"But we couldn't get hold of the coordinates. Later, more communications from Gonzales's men said they had found you with a man and woman at another location. Gonzales's men were discovered in the same vicinity… all dead."

So the Army hadn't been there watching every move Kat and Connor and Maya had made. Relieved to an extent, she took a hesitant breath.

The sergeant chewed on his lip again but didn't look at Connor. "The men said whoever used the techniques to kill Gonzales's other men had to be a highly skilled spec ops man. Gonzales was pissed."

"Hmm," Kat said.

Sergeant Stratton cleared his throat. "More bodies were found a few hours ago after transmission abruptly ended between Gonzales's men and the team that had been sent in to retrieve you. We caught the part about them having lost you at a village but having found the man and woman you had been traveling with. They planned to take them hostage to learn where you'd gone." He swallowed hard. "They said the couple was traveling with a jaguar."

"The jaguar god, no doubt," Kat said, folding her arms.

"Yeah, well, when we finally found the location and arrived on the scene, we thought we'd discover men with bite marks if the man and woman had trained the jaguar to kill people."

"Get real. A trained jaguar killer?"

"Major Singleterry had talked to an animal behaviorist who said that wild cats could be trained to an extent, but they were unpredictable and could just as easily turn on their trainer."

Good, so that ruled out the killer jaguar, hopefully. "And you discovered I was here, how?"

"Gonzales's men have a tracking device on your rented car. So do we." He looked at Connor, this time as if to ask why he wouldn't have known that, since he was a special ops guy. "But we… ran into a bit of a detour and couldn't get to you in time before you had the last run-in."

"So when Gonzales arrives here to pick Kathleen up, you're going to take him down, right, Sergeant?" Connor asked, his voice dark, his expression darker.

"Yes… yes, sir."

"Good. Nice to know our tax dollars are at work. And next time, don't even *think* of using Kat as bait."

"Yes, sir. I mean, no, sir." The sergeant said, "About the jaguar…" He let his words trail off.

Kat gave him a shake of her head. "Amazing. What tales will people come up with next?"

Connor hauled Kat off toward the elevator before the sergeant could ask her another question. "Damn it to hell," Connor grumbled under his breath as he led Kat back up to their room.

"Gonzales will know which rooms we're staying in, won't he?" she asked, concerned all over again.

"Most likely, and you better believe we'll be saving our necks again all on our own," Connor said as they rode the elevator up.

"Maya," Kat said, fearing for her safety. She tugged Connor out of the elevator and down the hall toward their rooms.

They moved at a rush but as quietly as they could. When they reached Maya's door, the first room before their own, they listened.

They heard nothing, and Kat thought Maya might be napping before their long night flight. But still they waited. What if Gonzales's men were in the room? What if they were in Kat and Connor's room? Waiting to ambush them?

Connor took Kat's hand and walked her back to the

emergency stairs. What was he up to? Kat didn't want to leave Maya in the terrorists' hands for even a second, if that was the case. She knew from personal experience what that could mean.

Connor pulled out his cell phone and punched a button. "Maya?"

"Yeah, Connor. I saw you and Kat checking out the Internet. Did you learn anything important about that Wade Patterson?" Kat could hear his sister say as she spoke loudly over the phone, with splashing and the sound of kids shouting in play in the background.

Ignoring his sister's question, Connor said, "They've been tracking us. Gonzales's men. Are you in your room?"

"No. I'm downstairs checking out the pool. I was thinking of going for a swim, but… are they here already?"

"The U.S. Army is. Or at least a sergeant. I don't think he can protect us from the bad guys. Have you got your stuff?"

"You mean my important papers? Yeah, always with me."

"We're next to the stairwell by our rooms. They could be lying in wait in either of our rooms. Meet us in the lobby."

Kat rubbed her arms as Connor ended the call.

"My wallet, passport, credit card, driver's license, everything I need to travel is in my backpack in the room."

Connor ran his hand over her back and kissed her cheek. "It's all right, Kat. We didn't hear anyone in the rooms. You stay here, and I'll return to get your bag."

No way was she going to let him walk into a possible ambush without helping him in some way. "We stay together."

"Kat—"

"No, Connor. I got both you and Maya into this mess. We're going together."

She could tell Connor wasn't taking her anywhere near the rooms as he steadily looked at her, not moving an inch.

"We're civilians. Let the sergeant and whoever else is supposed to be here getting ready to take Gonzales down make sure that the rooms are clear. Come on," he said.

He grabbed her arm and was heading for the elevator... when it dinged. For a moment, he stood frozen and glanced at the stairs. She knew he was thinking maybe they should go down that way instead. The elevator door slid open.

"Gonzales," Kat said under her breath, seeing the man dressed in a suit, his dark brown beard shorn, his hair longer than she remembered it, his nearly black eyes taking her in... and then recognition dawned.

He didn't have any of his guerillas with him, thank God, and she moved with jaguar swiftness before he or Connor could even react. Part of it was her Army training, to take him while he was off guard before he could pull out a weapon and have the advantage. Part of it had to be due to her jaguar senses—smelling the threat, having to respond to it, and not backing down.

Gonzales reached under his suit coat, but it was already too late. Kat grabbed his arms, kicked her leg behind his, and shoved him hard. He fell on his back, spewing a slew of curses.

Connor was on top of him after that, disarming him, flipping him over, and pinning his arm high enough that if he tried to move at all, Connor wouldn't hesitate to break it.

Kat slipped Connor's phone out of his pocket, found Maya's name in the address book, and called her. "Find the sergeant in the lobby, Sergeant Stratton. Tell him we have the man he's been after, but we have the elevator blocked so he'll have to use the stairs. And hurry. Some of his thugs might be in our rooms waiting for him. And for us."

The sergeant took forever to reach them, but he had called in backup before he arrived.

Kat felt a unique camaraderie with the Army soldiers who swarmed up the stairs. And felt relief that her and Connor and Maya's part in this was over.

The U.S. soldiers were complemented by Colombian soldiers stationed near Bogotá who had been trained by the United States in pursuing and taking down men like Gonzales. Members of the Colombian National Police guerrilla unit, the Junglas, who are based in Bogotá, were also on hand.

The drug lord and some of his men who had been waiting in Maya and Connor and Kat's rooms were quickly taken away by the Colombian officials while Kat and Connor retrieved their bags and promptly moved to another hotel.

———∿∿∿———

Without further trouble and two hours before their midnight flight home, Kat and Connor and Maya sat waiting in the very high-tech and modern Bogotá airport after going through numerous checkpoints. As they watched passengers scurrying through the airport, Kat noted the high level of security and took a deep breath. Outside, tanks were lined up along the runway, since a military base was situated right there. She wondered what would happen if she shifted in the middle of all this scrutiny.

Disaster.

Each of them prayed that Kat didn't get the urge to shift. Kat was feeling great, though. She felt some satisfaction in having taken Gonzales down after he had murdered her team. Although Connor said she had nearly given him a heart attack when she rushed to take the drug warlord down and she wasn't ever to do anything that rash again. She had just given Connor a smile and a hug, and he'd nearly crushed the breath out of her.

She was relieved that Gonzales couldn't come after her any longer. But most of all, if they could make it home without her shifting, she was looking forward to being home, somewhere she could settle down with a man who would be her husband and his sister who would also be her own.

The call for boarding began, and with some trepidation, Kat strode to the back of the plane where their seats were located.

The problem with the seating in the back was that the location of the restrooms make it a heavy traffic area. Also, the seats didn't recline, and they were narrower. But still, there were no seats behind them, and the remaining seats in the last row were empty. So Connor and Kat took the window and aisle seats on the right side of the plane, and Maya had the aisle seat on the left side.

Because the plane took off at midnight and the flight was only five hours, the lights were turned down low, and pillows and blankets offered. Then everyone settled down to sleep. Hopefully no one would get up in the middle of the night to use the restroom, in the event that Kat shifted.

Of course, she would have to shift. It was inevitable.

—⁂—

Connor knew they wouldn't be safe until he had Kat in his Suburban at the Houston airport and they were well on their way home. But three hours into their flight, when he saw her pull her blanket onto her lap and heard her unzipping her pants underneath the soft brown fabric, he knew the worst was about to happen.

She didn't look panicked in the least, just resigned to making the most of it. And for that, he was proud of her. He looked up to see that the flight attendants were seated and no one was moving about in the cabin. Everyone was asleep.

Maya was soon alerted to Kat's difficulty as Kat pulled her blanket higher and wriggled out of her shirt and bra.

Connor and Maya watched Kat to see her progress and kept an eye on the walkway in case anybody began to move about the cabin. The thrum of the plane's engines seemed almost as noisy as the jungle as Kat sat next to the window, her blanket up to her neck. She wasn't shifting.

Was it like before? When she was in the tree and couldn't shift? That could be a good thing.

Snuggling under the blanket, she smiled at him and Maya, then closed her eyes. He pulled Kat down so she rested her head in his lap and made sure his blanket and hers covered her nakedness sufficiently. He even drifted off, but twenty minutes later, he felt her shift, felt the weight of her body and the size of her head increase, the change in the way she breathed, kind of a purring sound.

Maya was watching Kat, too, but they couldn't do anything about it. They had one hour and forty minutes left before they landed. The announcement would be made before that and passengers would begin to stir. Refreshments would be served. Tray tables replaced, seat belts refastened. And then the descent.

They had maybe one hour left before all that came to pass. After that, if Kat still hadn't shifted, they were in trouble.

—⁓—

Kat felt more comfortable sleeping on the seats, her head in Connor's lap, while she dreamed of marrying Connor in a superquick and simple way. She didn't need Connor to make a fancy proposal. She certainly didn't want any huge wedding when she didn't know anyone. Nor could she comfortably have a large wedding where she suddenly might shift while walking down the aisle in a gown fit for a princess.

She needed to say she would marry him, though.

She stretched out, realized she wasn't extending her human limbs, and her eyes popped open. Omigod, how did she shift again without knowing it?

She lifted her head and looked up at Connor. He leaned down and kissed her furry muzzle.

"I love you, you know?" he said, smiling.

She shook her head, not believing he didn't mind. Why hadn't she had any prior warning before shifting? Automatically, she tried to sit up.

"Stay down, honey," he whispered, and she realized

it would be easier for him to cover up what she was if she continued to lie on the seats.

She really had thought it would be like the time in the tree when she didn't shift. She wanted to pace, hoping she would shift before it was too late. Connor and Maya were keeping their cool, acting as though it was no big deal and that everything would work out as it was supposed to. But she couldn't help the anxiety racing through her blood.

The noise of the engines droned on as the cabin remained dark, the sky black outside the windows, the passengers sleeping, and no one walking down the aisle to use the restroom.

For the moment, she felt safe. Furry and bigger, rebellious in a small way, and even amused in an alarmed sort of way. She knew that if anyone found her like this, she and Maya and Connor would be in real trouble.

She began telling herself that it was time to shift *now*. Then she heard someone moving along the aisle, headed for the bathroom. Connor immediately covered her head with Maya's blanket.

Now she was hot. She listened for the door to the restroom to open, shut, the toilet to flush, the door to open, shut, and the passenger to move back down the aisle. When she figured he had moved far enough away—she could tell by his hefty cologne that the passenger was a male—Connor pulled the blanket off her. She was panting.

As a naked human, the blankets had been perfect. But in her jaguar coat, she definitely didn't need them.

Another passenger headed down the aisle, and Kat gave a muffled groan. A creaky serving cart made its way to the back of the plane. So not good. Announcements that refreshments were being served and that the plane would soon be descending made Kat's heart pound with increased concern. As another passenger drew near, Connor covered Kat's head again.

Okay, shift! Even if she did manage to shift, then what? She would be trying to get dressed while people were making their way to the bathroom for their morning pit stop.

"Anything to drink?" the flight attendant asked.

"Orange juice," Connor said. "Two."

Now why would he do that? It would mean bringing down the seat-back tray, and she would have even more difficulty trying to shift and change.

But when the cart was in the aisle, the flight attendant told a passenger, "If you'll wait until we're done serving snacks, you can move about the cabin then."

Good. The cart was moving back up the plane's aisle away from them, and the passengers would be blocked from…

Another passenger headed for the restroom. Oh, yeah, except for all the seats that had already been served and were now on *this* side of the cart.

Kat thought she would die from heat exhaustion. Cats didn't sweat, so the only option for her was to pant and wish she could go for a swim to cool off.

Next came the announcement for the pickup of trash, setting trays in their upright position, pulling seat backs forward from the reclining position, and refastening seat belts. At least everyone was seated and not coming to the back anymore. But the worst was that she felt the plane descending.

Connor had again removed the blanket from her

head, but she was still feeling terribly hot when the plane landed with a thud. Her heart hit the pavement, too, as she realized she wasn't going to make it in time to shift and dress.

She tried to sit up, the natural instinct to see what was going on. But Connor encouraged her to keep her head down.

The plane was still taxiing toward the airport.

Shift. Shift.

The plane came to a halt. Oh, God, everyone was going to look over their seat backs and see her.

But no one was in the seats directly in front of theirs, and as soon as the Fasten Seat Belt light went off, people were busy standing and getting their bags from the overhead bins. The place was chaos, and no one could see her in the farthest seat back. Maya was standing with her bag and Kat's, blocking the aisle in front of the last row of seats.

"We're okay, Kat," Connor said, rubbing her head and speaking in a reassuring manner.

Easy for him to say. He was human!

Chapter 29

THE PLANE'S PASSENGER DOOR OPENED IN HOT, MUGGY Houston. The floor of the plane rumbled while the door to the baggage compartment banged open and the baggage handlers began off-loading the luggage. They created such a racket that they reminded Kat of the advertisement showing gorillas handling the luggage.

Passengers began to deplane. That gave her heart another lurch.

At first, the air was oppressive with all those bodies packed together and all those people standing up, some hunched under overhead bins, waiting their turn to step into the aisle. But as they began to deplane, the air seemed more breathable. And that wasn't good. It meant that before long only Maya, Connor, and one highly frustrated jaguar would be left on the plane with the crew.

She looked up at Maya who smiled warmly at her. "Did I tell you that you've enriched our lives immensely?"

With a twinkle in her eye, Maya appeared serious! Yet, Kat couldn't believe she or Connor would feel that way. She suddenly felt a burst of heat overwhelm her, right before she was shivering under the blankets in her naked human form.

Connor scrambled to get her clothes as Kat panicked at trying to locate them also. She was human! She had her panties and bra on and her shirt half-buttoned when

Maya cleared her throat and Connor rose, ready to block any crew member from seeing Kat.

"Can't find her shoe," he said to someone.

"Found it!" Kat said gleefully, grabbing for Connor's hand as she scrambled out of her seat, now dressed, and pulled him down the aisle.

She was ready to bolt out of the plane, pulling Connor along, but she managed to keep calm. Once they were in the concourse, she was moving again at a quickened pace. She didn't think she would shift again, but she wasn't chancing it.

When they were outside in the dark, their bags in hand, they headed for the long-term parking lot. Kat couldn't have been happier.

"I'll marry you," she said, looking up at Connor.

He chuckled, wrapped his arms around her, and swung her around, then set her down. "I'm glad, Kat. You don't know how much so."

"Yeah," she said as Maya smiled at her. "How could I not? Who else would have stood by me so many times when I needed you? And yes, Maya made me this way, which is causing trouble galore, but I know eventually I'll have it under control. At least I hope so. I've never been known to enrich anyone's life. And you've both done that for me, too."

"You really should have made him beg for the marriage," Maya said, her golden eyes sparkling, the lights in the parking lot giving them a fluorescent green cast.

"I couldn't make him suffer any longer."

Connor wrapped his arm around her waist. "We were getting married, one way or another," he said with no humor at all, just very matter-of-factly.

Kat ignored the jaguar god's dictate, loving him just the same. "You knew I could change before it was too late, right? I admired the way you were both so cool about it."

Maya and Connor shared looks.

"Oh," Kat said, realizing at once that they hadn't known how it would play out any more than she had. "Well, just the same, you both were terrific with making sure I didn't panic."

"We hadn't any choice, Kat. Do you think Wade Patterson from Florida was the shifter we saw?" Maya asked.

"You're not getting in touch with him," Connor ground out.

Maya huffed. "I'm *not* part of your harem." She patted Kat on the shoulder. "Kat and I are going to design a new website for our business, and we're going to show a side interest—tropical plants that we have in our greenhouse and the jaguars that visit the jungles where the plants usually thrive. You know, like some nurseries have cats living in the gardens? We'll feature a jaguar, though the jaguar won't be around to scare off the customers."

Connor gave both Maya and Kat a look that said he didn't approve.

Maya shrugged. "It's just marketing, Connor."

"Yeah, just marketing," Kat said, smiling broadly at Maya.

The jaguar pictures would be just of Maya, a subtle way to let the jaguar-shifter world know she was available, the best way to market for a jaguar mate, they both had concluded.

When they arrived at Maya and Connor's house and gardens, Kat was in awe. Forests bounded the property, a small private lake was nearby, and the hot, humid greenhouse was filled with tropical plants that made her feel she was back in the Amazon, minus the howling monkeys, chattering parrots, and noisy bugs.

"We have sounds from the Amazon played in here while we work," Maya said, as if she knew just what Kat had been thinking. "Customers love it when they shop for their garden rooms, too."

"It's lovely," Kat said, taking in a deep breath of the rich humus-filled earth and floral fragrances.

Maya escorted her through the gardens—herb, evergreen, and deciduous—as well as the water garden, the floral garden, and the shrub garden. But Connor had quickly bowed out, carrying their bags into the house.

Kat wondered what he was up to when she smelled steaks grilling on an outside grill. Maya smiled. "He's still in courtship phase. Usually, when we get home from the jungle, we get cleaned up, make sure anything that needs watering is taken care of, and cook something easy like frozen pizza. But it's early morning and he wants to do something special for you, so he's making steak and eggs."

"Steaks," Kat said, her stomach already rumbling.

"After all the strange food you had to endure, I'm sure he wanted to prepare something you'd like."

Loving him for remembering how much she had wanted steak when she got back to the United States, she was thrilled.

Connor soon called for them to join him, and after eating a juicy grilled steak with cheese-and-chives-flavored eggs, hashed brown potatoes, and watermelon for dessert, Kat joined Connor for a tour of the house while Maya returned to the gardens to putter around.

"What do you think, Kat? Does this feel like it could be your home?" Connor asked. He barely let her see the rest of the house, including her favorite room, the special greenhouse sitting room where they could have meals if they wanted, and Maya's master bedroom suite, before he took her to his own suite.

She studied the room, which was decorated in deep forest green and had a sitting area and an office off the main room. She almost expected to see a jungle-print bedspread and curtains. But everything was just solid forest green. Soothing and peaceful on a hot sunny day. Pictures of the jungle decorated the walls.

Despite his annoyance with his parents for abandoning them, she saw to her surprise that he had a picture of his parents and Maya and himself, the two of them about ten years old, framed in bamboo and sitting on his dresser. Connor definitely looked like a younger version of his dad now, strong of character, same blond hair and tanned features and muscled form, same penetrating golden jaguar eyes. Maya looked a lot like her mother, with long blond curls piled on top of her head, the same amber eyes that looked as though the woman was seeing straight into Kat's soul, and a smile that met her eyes.

Kat couldn't believe anyone could give up her children like that and wanted Connor to know she was the kind of woman who would stick with him for the long run.

"Yeah," she said, snuggling up to him, "this feels like home."

He wrapped his arms around her, his mouth close to her upturned lips. "I worried about you after we left the Amazon last year. I couldn't quit thinking about you or looking for you."

Kat wrapped her arms around Connor's neck. "I was overjoyed finally to see you and be able to thank you personally for saving my life."

"You are thanks enough." Connor kissed her slowly, tenderly, as if he had loved her forever.

And she succumbed, kissing him, loving the way his strong fingers stroked her back and his hard body pressed against hers, his mouth taking possession.

Her body tingled with need and desire. Her skin was hot, and she melted against him, glad when the air conditioner kicked on and poured cool air into the room.

She started to unbutton his shirt, but he didn't seem to be in any hurry to undress. She was!

He smiled against her mouth as she jerked his sleeves down his arms. "Not in a hurry, are we?" he said with a smile to his words.

"We made it home without my getting caught in a jaguar's spotted coat. If nothing else, that's a reason to celebrate."

He chuckled, slipped his hands underneath her shirt, and cupped her bra-covered breasts. "While I slept in my hammock in the jungle on our way to the city, I dreamed of being here with you in my bedroom, with a comfortable bed to sleep on and the air conditioner on high and you safe from the rest of the world. I dreamt what it would be like to make love to you and not be in a rush while I savored every moment."

"Some other time," she said, fumbling to unfasten his belt.

He laughed. His large hands were gentle as he coaxed her bra down, her shirt still in place, then ran his thumbs over her nipples in a sensuous heated caress. When she couldn't make any progress on his belt, she began to unfasten her shirt buttons instead.

That prompted him to let go of her breasts and jerk his belt free. He was naked before she knew it, primed for making love to her.

She loved how aroused he became with her. She didn't need fancy undergarments to spur him on. Just a lick on his lips and rubbing her body against his turned him on faster than she could believe.

He was fully erect as he pressed his nude body against her while he unfastened her bra and kissed her mouth at the same time, as if he couldn't quit kissing and touching her before he had her in his bed.

She was burning up, needing him to quench the fire building inside of her, to fulfill the ragged ache she felt for him.

The maelstrom continued as he pulled her jeans and panties down partway and slipped his fingers into her tight sheath. "You're so wet for me," he whispered against her mouth, his voice straining with need.

He sounded as glad that he could turn her on with a whisper of a kiss as she was that her touching him lit his fire.

Without hesitating a moment further, he pulled off the rest of her clothes until she was as naked as he was.

His fingers stroked her between her legs while his mouth slanted over hers and kissed her with such passion that she felt she would be swept into a vortex of no return.

Her soft moans and frantic stroking over his naked back and arms and buttocks ramped up the pleasure, which prompted him to lift her onto his hips, spreading her before him, and then back onto his bed.

He pulled her tight against him, his erection sliding in, deep, thrusting, and rubbing her, the friction sending her over the edge.

She cried out with complete surrender and dug her heels against him, cherishing the way his cock thrust deeper. He pushed harder, seeking his own release and finding it moments later, fierce primal satisfaction filling his expression.

"Next time, we take it slower," he promised, rolling over and capturing her, then pulling her against his body.

"Next time," she murmured against his chest, sliding her hand over his nipple.

"Yeah, after we take a nap."

Early the next morning, after a day and night spent in bed making love to Kat, Connor poured a second cup of coffee while Kat had joined Maya in the greenhouse. That was when Connor saw a black sedan pull up the drive. Something made him think that the new arrival wasn't a customer looking for plants to use in landscaping or interior decorating.

He sipped some of his coffee while he watched through the kitchen window as the man got out of his car, shut the door, locked it, and then headed for the

front door of the house. He was in excellent shape, wearing neatly pressed khakis, a pin-striped, button-down-
collared shirt, and a pair of expensive-looking leather
loafers—dressy, but casual. His hair was cropped short,
and Connor guessed he was a military man. He strode
toward the porch with purpose in his long stride, like he
was ready to storm the castle, his face stern, his whole
manner starched.

Connor placed his empty coffee cup on the counter
and headed for the front door, ready to nip this in the bud
and ensure that Kat didn't have to deal with the man.

Connor yanked open the door, startling the man,
whose raised fist had never contacted the wood.

"Who the hell are you?" Connor asked, knowing
damn well he had to be one of the men involved in Kat's
Army mission of trying to take down Gonzales.

"Major Roger Singleterry." He reached out his
hand to shake Connor's, but Connor didn't offer his
hand in return.

Acknowledging the slight, Roger gave him a small
smile, but it quickly faded. He stiffened and shoved his
hands in his pockets. "I understand Kathleen's staying
with you and... your sister... for a little while."

The inference was that his sister was a girlfriend, too?
Threesomes do it better?

"Kat's busy," Connor said, folding his arms across
his chest. He wasn't about to let this jerk see her or intimidate her or anything else. Besides, she was working
with Maya in the greenhouse, so he wasn't really out-
and-out lying. Work always needed to be done, and she
would be busy.

This time the man's brows arched. "Really. Well,

I need to talk with her." His icy matter-of-fact tone bugged the hell out of Connor. "Is there a better time to call?"

"No."

Again, the raised brows. Roger was probably used to giving orders in the military, and Connor assumed Roger didn't like having a civilian obstacle block him from seeing anything further of Kat.

Connor thought to ask if he could give her a message, just to get the officer to leave, but he didn't even want to offer that much.

"It's important," Roger insisted, not budging from the front porch.

"You and your people can go to hell."

Roger narrowed his eyes. "You want a battle on your hands? You don't want to go there, Anderson. I've got the resources—"

"Maybe you do, but you've got shit where I'm concerned. Kat's worth more than any damn mountain of resources available to you. You leave her alone. She's made a home with us and doesn't need anything further from your kind."

Roger's jaw dropped. Connor eyed him with new suspicion. What had the man thought? That she was just staying with Connor and Maya for a few days? And then she would be back to being the Army's pawn? No way in hell.

"I'm not going until I speak with Kat," Roger insisted.

Connor heard movement behind him before he saw her, smelled her delightful scent, and knew it was Kat. She had probably heard the car pull up, but when the "customer" hadn't entered the greenhouse or the outdoor gardens looking for plants, she must have gotten curious.

She slipped in beside Connor, wrapped her arm around his waist, and snuggled close. He quickly encircled her shoulders with his arm. She lifted her face to smile at him, and he took her smile as an invitation to a kiss. So he obliged her, long and hard and thoroughly. Just to prove he wasn't letting anyone hurt her again.

Looking a little flushed and breathing a little heavier, she finally took her gaze off Connor and turned to face Roger. "What are you doing here, Roger?"

Connor finally realized this Roger was Kat's former fiancé. Connor should have decked the son of a bitch before she arrived on the scene.

But when he looked at the man who had given her up because she was no longer suitable as a wife and Army careerist, he noticed just how red-faced and angry the man had become. Connor smiled, glad he had kissed Kat and proved just what she meant to him.

"I need to talk to you... alone," he said, trying for dark and persuasive.

Kat raised her chin a notch in her usual stubborn fashion. "Say what you have to say. I don't have any secrets from Connor."

"It's classified."

"I'm no longer in the Army, so sharing sensitive information with me could hurt your career, Roger. I'm really not interested in anything you have to say. So if you have nothing else to speak with me about, I've got work to do."

He looked down at her dirty fingers stained green, then met her gaze again and waved his hand at the gardens. "*This* is what you choose to do instead of protecting Americans from the drug trade?"

She laughed without humor. "You have *got* to be kidding. I'm out of the service, medically discharged, remember?"

"It…" He glanced at Connor, then said to Kat, "This isn't for a civilian's consumption."

"*I'm* a civilian, if you don't recall," she said, her voice hard.

"They want you back."

She laughed again. "No. I'm happy saving plants from voracious bugs and strangling weeds. You go save the world from the drug lords."

"Kat… let me explain what happened between us."

"No, I know exactly what happened between us. As long as I was useful to your career, I was perfect to be your wife. But once I had been captured and—"

"It was all a ploy. Don't you see, darling?"

Connor snorted.

Roger gave him a scathing look, then said to Kat, "None of it was real. It was part of your continued covert operations."

"Even ditching me?"

Looking chagrined, he shook his head. "You ditched me, threw your engagement ring at me, and told me to go to hell." He suddenly seemed to remember that Connor was listening to the conversation, saw him smiling, and gave him a dirty look.

"You used me and so did the Army. At least you could have been there for me. But you wouldn't even speak with me when I left the hospital! You were too busy. Always. I knew then it was over for us."

"That was part of the plan. If the doctor could

convince you to relive the experience, and Wade Patterson gave you a plan to do it—"

Kat's jaw dropped. "Wade was part of your operation?"

"No, he just conveniently convinced you to go to the jungle in search of the tourist who had saved your life, and it couldn't have been more to our advantage. I backed out of the equation so you had to fight to get through this on your own, knowing you'd do it. You'd overcome the trauma and help us to take the bastard down. And you did do it. Although we're still not sure how. But what did you think? We'd just let you go without watching your back?"

She snapped her gaping mouth closed, narrowed her eyes, and shook her head. "You weren't watching my back! Connor was. And as far as you are concerned, Roger, you're so full of it. I don't care what you say. It would never be the same between us.

"So what part of *no* don't you understand? I'm done. Through with the military. Through with you and glad I learned the truth about you before it was too late. I'm happy to be with Connor and his sister."

"You can't want *him*," Roger said derisively. "Hell, he's nothing more than a glorified gardener. What the hell do you see in him?"

Kat whispered conspiratorially, "But haven't you heard he's special ops? He has killer moves you've never even contemplated." Her gaze took in all of Connor, and then she smiled wickedly at him.

"We're getting married, if you didn't know." She stroked Connor's stomach through his cotton shirt. "What's his is mine and what's mine is his."

His face hard, Roger said, "You'll be begging to

come back to me when you get tired of digging in the dirt, Kat. But don't wait too long."

He turned on his heel and stormed toward his car.

That's when Connor saw Maya watching from the gardens. He waved at her, then said for her benefit and Roger's, "Kat will join you in a bit. We've got something to do in the house first."

One military man wasn't going to win against a jaguar who had claimed his mate.

Roger's car scattered gravel as he sped out of there.

"You could have waited to tell me you wanted to have sex with me again," Kat said, smiling up at Connor.

He grinned down at her. "No, I couldn't. I had to let him know just where you and I stood with each other. And tonight when the moon is full, I'm taking you to swim in our lake."

———⁓⁓⁓———

That night, Connor had intended to go alone with Kat to the lake, but Maya wouldn't be left out. And damn if Kat didn't side with her. He did appreciate that Kat didn't want Maya's feelings hurt.

Maya did at least wander off to another part of the lake to swim. Connor and Kat slipped into the warm silky water and embraced. "I thought I was going to have to fight Roger off if he didn't go willingly."

Kat smiled up at him. "You wouldn't have needed to. You were the bigger man, and he knew it." She kissed Connor's lips. "Thanks for letting Maya come along."

He grunted.

"She needs a mate now."

"We're not using Facebook networking-type sites to

locate one," Connor reiterated for the hundredth time. "I'll go along with a picture of a jaguar in the greenhouse amongst the tropical plants to show an exotic touch for now, as long as it's done right."

She pulled away from him and swam into the deeper waters.

He swam after her. "I mean it, Kat." He knew when he used those words that he had already lost the battle. Before he could grab her foot to play with her in the water, she screeched.

"What is it?" Maya hollered from much farther away.

But Connor dove after the culprit, ready to rescue Kat from the alligator snapping turtle. Damn thing better not have injured Kat the way the one had cut up Maya so many years ago.

Kat was already headed into shore when Connor grabbed the huge turtle and hauled it to the beach after her.

She was sitting on the grassy area and examining the bite to her big toe, the beak-like injury bleeding.

Maya raced along the shore to join them, then folded her arms and gave Connor an annoyed look. "Ha! He rescues *you* from the turtle, but he saved himself when the one attacked me."

Kat made a face, grimacing with pain. "He's exonerated, back to hero status, as far as I'm concerned." Then she frowned. "What are you going to do with it?"

"Turtle soup," both Maya and Connor said at once.

Kat looked dismayed, but Connor said, "Really, we'll take him to a river nearby where he can live in peace, away from our lake."

"Are you sure it's safe to carry that thing?" Kat asked,

still looking bothered about the injury and the turtle that had done the biting.

"Yeah," Maya said, "they can actually swing their necks around to reach their tails, but with Connor holding it by the shell behind the neck and before the tail, it should be fairly safe. Their jaws are so powerful that the darn things can amputate fingers."

But not as powerful as a jaguar's. The big cats often bit right through the turtle's shell in the Amazon when they were hungry.

Kat smiled. "Good. While Connor's taking the turtle to the river, you and I can set up our jaguar site on the Internet."

Maya grinned and nodded, giving Connor a sly sideways glance.

Connor knew then being a jaguar god with a harem of jaguar goddesses was bound to keep him in trouble.

"Don't publish anything to go live until I've seen it," Connor warned them, then headed for the river not far from the lake and hoped the turtle stayed there. He had to show Kat and Maya that he had some control over his life and theirs.

The women both laughed as Maya helped Kat back to the house while Connor carried the huge turtle to the river and a second chance at life.

Just like he had with Kat in it now. He sighed. So maybe they could put out some feelers to locate a jaguar-shifter that might suit Maya.

But for now, he had to provide his own injured jaguar-shifter with some tender loving care.

"My hero… again," Kat said, chuckling as he rejoined them, and he lifted her into his arms.

But he knew from the conspiratorial looks between his sister and Kat that his *harem* had him right where they wanted him.

Even so, he wouldn't give up Kat or his sister for the world.

Epilogue

AFTER THREE MONTHS OF PERSUADING, KAT AND MAYA finally talked Connor into allowing photos to go up on their nursery website showing Maya in her jaguar coat peering through tropical plants in their greenhouse. They had also given some links to informational sites about jaguars in the Amazon. And now it was live.

But that was only the beginning as far as Kat was concerned.

Next, she wanted to help Maya set up a Facebook page that showed her interests—loving the Amazon and the beauty of the jaguar. They had to be careful, though, when they set it up. They were still working on exactly which photos and interests when Connor came in from digging holes in the garden for new trees.

He had already rinsed off under the garden shower when he strode inside, his golden chest glistening with water droplets. His expression wary, he immediately looked from Kat to the computer monitor and frowned.

But she had news to wipe away his scowl after he saw the Facebook page they were working on.

Kat rose from her seat, took Connor's hand before he could say a word about the page, and ran her free hand over his hot chest. "I haven't shifted once this month without it being my choice." She smiled sweetly up at him.

"The page," he said, motioning to it, not about to be deterred.

She ignored his concern about the Facebook page. "And that's good news—about the shifting." She pulled his hand to her belly and kept it there. "Because we're going to have a baby."

His mouth gaped, his darkened expression brightening, and he quickly looked at Maya as if she had known the truth when he didn't.

Maya smiled up at him, looking pleased as could be. "I'm going to be an auntie."

Connor grabbed Kat and held her tightly as he swung her around. She knew from the happiness in his face, his eyes even watering, that he was thrilled with the news.

"I'm going to be a father," he said, kissing Kat on her lips and cheeks and neck as he set her back down on the floor.

"And the best one there is," Kat agreed.

No foster care for their child, but one adoring aunt and a mother and a father who were all rather on the unusual side. Vacations wouldn't be to the usual family resorts either, but rather to the Amazon jungle where Kat's life truly had begun.

"Kat, have I told you how beautiful you are?" Connor asked.

"Almost as many times as I've told you how beautiful you are." Kat touched a bit of dirt on his shoulder and said in a purring kitty-cat way, "You missed a spot or two. I'll help you clean up." Then she hauled him off to their master bedroom suite, leaving Maya with the freedom to work on her Facebook page alone.

Maya smiled. It was past time to find herself a mate.

Acknowledgments

Thanks to Deb Werksman, who always believes in my work whether it's about wolf-shifters or big cat-shifters; who knows what might be next! And to my critique partners, Carol, Vonda, Tammy, Judy, Randy, Betty, and Pam, who help me with ideas and phrases that aid me in getting the story down right. And to my son, Blaine Spear, his wife, Malinie, and my daughter, Jennifer Spear Fasano and her husband, Michael, who are proud of what I do. But most of all, I have to thank my fans who encourage me through all the conflict-filled minutes while I write (not my conflict, my characters') and in the end cheer me on to write another book!

A SEAL in Wolf's Clothing

by Terry Spear

Her instincts tell her he's dangerous...

While her overprotective brother's away, Meara Greymere's planning to play—and it wouldn't hurt to find herself a mate in the process. The last thing she needs is one of his SEAL buddies spoiling her fun, even if the guy is the hottest one she's ever seen...

His powers of persuasion are impossible to resist...

Finn Emerson is a battle-hardened Navy SEAL and alpha wolf. He's a little overqualified for baby-sitting, but feisty Meara is attracting trouble like a magnet...

As the only responsible alpha male in the vicinity, Finn is going to have to protect this intriguing woman from a horde of questionable men, and definitely from himself...

Praise for Terry Spear:

"High-powered romance that satisfies on every level." —*Long and Short Reviews*

"Hot doesn't even begin to describe it." —*Love Romance Passion*

For more Terry Spear, visit:

www.sourcebooks.com

Dreaming of the Wolf

by Terry Spear

He'll protect her
or die trying…

Alicia Greiston is a no-nonsense bounty hunter determined to bring a ring of mobsters to justice. Her dogged pursuit of the crime family has forced her to avoid relationships —any man would only become a target for retribution. Luckily, Jake Silver is more than a man, and his instincts are telling him to stop at nothing to protect her.

However, the mob isn't entirely human either, and soon Alicia must flee for her life. When Alicia and Jake's passion begins to spill over into their dreams, Jake learns he will have to do more than defend her—he'll have to show his mate the way of the wolf.

Praise for **Dreaming of the Wolf***:*

"Riveting and entertaining…makes one want to devour all of the rest of Terry Spear's books." —*Fresh Fiction*

"Sensual, passionate, and very well written…another winner of a story." —*The Long and the Short of It*

For more Terry Spear, visit:

www.sourcebooks.com

About the Author

A *USA Today* bestselling and award-winning author of urban fantasy and medieval historical romantic suspense, Terry Spear also writes true stories for adult and young adult audiences. She's a retired lieutenant colonel in the U.S. Army Reserves and has an MBA from Monmouth University. She also creates award-winning teddy bears, Wilde & Woolly Bears, to include personalized bears designed to commemorate authors' books. When she's not writing, gardening, or making bears, she's teaching online writing courses. Originally from California, she's lived in eight states and now resides in the heart of Texas. She is the author of the Heart of the Wolf series and is now working on the Heart of the Jaguar series. She has also written *Winning the Highlander's Heart, The Accidental Highland Hero, Deadly Liaisons*, and a popular fae young adult series starting with *The Dark Fae*.